Praise for *The Lemon Orchard*

"Rice here takes her signature themes of family and loss into the difficult and enigmatic landscape of illegal immigration to powerful effect. . . . Lovely and compelling, with quiet yet brave social commentary that enhances the book's impact."　　　　　　　　　　—*Kirkus Reviews*

"Entrancing."　　　　　　　　　　—*People* (***)

"Trust Rice, known for fiction that explores the power of family, to find the humanity in illegal immigration, a topic too often relegated to rhetoric and statistics. . . . An unexpected plot turn will leave readers begging for a sequel."　　　　　　　　　　—*Booklist*

"Rice's fans will appreciate the evocative setting and unconventional romance, as well as the harrowing . . . depictions of border crossing and the fascinating parallels drawn be   research interests (she studies the Irish who arrived in Amer   day Mexican immigrants."　　　　　　　　　　*ekly*

Praise

"Poetic and stirring . . . beautifully combines [Rice's] love of nature and the power of family."　　　　　　　—*Publishers Weekly* (starred review)

"Bestselling author Rice's thirtieth book is an outstanding read that both chills and warms the soul . . . Highly recommended."　　　　　　　　　　—*Library Journal* (starred review)

"Never rushing her story or revelations, Rice reaches the satisfying conclusion that while wounds run deep, love runs deeper."　　　　　—*Booklist*

"A classic Rice page-turner."　　　　　　　　　　—*Good Housekeeping*

"In *Little Night*, Rice plumbs the depths of the damage that physical and mental abuse cause the recipients and allows us into the heads of those who suffer these situations. In spite of the serious nature of the subject matter, the story is filled with happy moments and an undying hope for future happiness."　　　　　　　　　　—Bookreporter.com

Praise for *The Silver Boat*

"Rice's portrayal of the imperfect McCarthy women and their emotional struggles will strike a chord in every mother, daughter, or sister."

—*Marie Claire*

"Popular Rice, in her mellifluous style, captures the essence of family and sisterhood as each character deals with love and loss." —*Booklist*

"Rice's writing effortlessly conveys the way family can bind as well as buoy us. . . . Another winner from one of America's most beloved authors."

—*BookPage*

"Atmospheric and deeply moving . . . a spellbinder." —*Irish Voice*

Praise for the novels of Luanne Rice

"Exciting, emotional, terrific. What more could you want?"

—*The New York Times Book Review*

"A light, sure touch." —*Time*

"An appealing writer much loved by her fans." —*The Daily News*

"Rice has an elegant style, a sharp eye, and a real warmth. In her hands families, and their values . . . seem worth cherishing."

—*San Francisco Chronicle*

"Rice writes unabashedly for women, imbuing her tales with romance and rock-strong relationships." —*Chicago Sun-Times*

"Ms. Rice shares Anne Tyler's ability to portray offbeat, fey characters winningly." —*The Atlanta Journal-Constitution*

PENGUIN BOOKS

THE LEMON ORCHARD

Luanne Rice is the author of thirty-one novels, twenty-two of which have been *New York Times* bestsellers. Five of her novels have become movies or miniseries, and two of her short pieces were featured in Off-Broadway productions. There are more than twenty-two million copies of her books in print in twenty-four territories around the world. A native of Connecticut, she divides her time between New York City and Southern California.

the lemon orchard

Luanne Rice

PENGUIN BOOKS

For Armando

PENGUIN BOOKS
Published by the Penguin Group
Penguin Group (USA) LLC
375 Hudson Street
New York, New York 10014

USA | Canada | UK | Ireland | Australia | New Zealand | India | South Africa | China
penguin.com
A Penguin Random House Company

First published in the United States of America by Viking Penguin,
a member of Penguin Group (USA) Inc., 2013
Published in Penguin Books 2014

A PAMELA DORMAN / PENGUIN BOOK

THE LIBRARY OF CONGRESS HAS CATALOGED THE HARDCOVER EDITION AS FOLLOWS:
Rice, Luanne.
The lemon orchard / Luanne Rice.
pages ; cm.
ISBN 978-0-670-02527-5 (hc.)
ISBN 978-0-14-312556-3 (pbk.)
1. Bereavement—Fiction. 2. Separation (Psychology)—Fiction. 3. California,
Southern—Fiction. I. Title.
PS3568.I289L46 2013b   813'.54—dc23   2013009690

Printed in the United States of America
1 3 5 7 9 10 8 6 4 2

Book design by Amy Hill · Set in Sabon LT Std
Photograph on title page copyright © 2012 by Paul Giamou / iStock

acknowledgments

Much love and gratitude to Armando, Armando Sr., Delfina, Brandon, Antonio, Eliza, and Melanie.

Much gratitude to my agent, Andrea Cirillo, and everyone at the Jane Rotrosen Agency: Jane Berkey, Don Cleary, Meg Ruley, Annelise Robey, Christina Hogrebe, Peggy Gordijn, Christina Prestia, Carlie Webber, Danielle Sickles, Rebecca Scherer, Donald W. Cleary, Brooke Fox, Ellen Tischler, Liz Van Buren.

I am thankful to everyone at Pamela Dorman Books/Viking and Penguin, especially Pam Dorman; Kiki Koroshetz; Clare Ferraro; Kathryn Court; Julie Miesionczek; Dick Heffernan, Norman Lidofsky and their sales teams; Lindsay Prevette; Carolyn Coleburn; Nancy Sheppard; Andrew Duncan; Patrick Nolan; John Fagan; Maureen Donnelly; Hal Fessenden; Leigh Butler; Roseanne Serra; and Jeannette Williams.

Thank you to Deborah Dwyer for copyediting this and so many of my novels.

Veronique de Turenne is a graceful writer and wonderful friend whose blog, *Here in (the) Malibu*, introduced me to Malibu's history, nature, and secret places.

I am thankful to Asha Randall for countless kindnesses and for introducing me to Adamson House.

Many thanks to Bernard Wolfsdorf for his expertise in immigration law and his generosity in discussing it with me.

Much gratitude to Jim Weikart, Tim Donnelly, Jay Tsao, Ted O'Gorman, Injae Choe, Lauren Gardner, Elvira de Leon, Delsy Hermosa, Oscar Castillo, Nick Chambers, Jackie Bass, and Becky Murray.

I feel very inspired by Luis Alberto Urrea's brilliant *The Devil's Highway*. Reading it changed the way I see the world—I know it will turn out to be one of the most influential books of my life. Luis opened my eyes to life along the border and I'm so grateful.

Love and thanks to Maureen, Olivier, and Mia Onorato; Molly, Alex, and Will Feinstein; Robert and Audrey Loggia; and William Twigg Crawford.

I'm grateful to my family of immigrants on both sides: for their hope, beliefs, struggles, and love.

prologue

FEBRUARY 2007

This is how I picture it: Eleven o'clock that cold and sunny morning, she is behind the wheel, hands in the two-and-ten position because she's a good girl and that's the way her father, sitting beside her holding the large black coffee he'd bought at Kendall's, likes her to drive, and she's taking care because she doesn't want him to spill it and scald himself. The station wagon is twelve years old, and it smells of dog, and if she looked in the rearview mirror, she could see where we used to buckle her car seat.

Bonnie Blue, our seven-year-old and the latest in a long line of blue-merle border collies, rides with me because she's still rambunctious and likes to nuzzle the driver's ear from the back seat, and Peter and I worry she might distract Jenny. Bonnie and I are two miles behind, with one last stop to make, to pick up the chocolate cake at Hoffman's Bakery, where Viola and Norma have decorated it with goalposts and a fifty-yard line and know to spread raspberry preserves between the layers because that is Jenny's favorite.

My daughter: Jenny Hughes. She is wearing the bulky Nordic sweater, endearingly lopsided, she knit for Timmy from yarn that still contained bits of burrs and brambles from the sheep's wool, and it's so Jenny to be wearing it, just two days after he gave it back to her as part of the breakup, along with her telescope and dog-eared copy of H. A. Rey's *The Stars*.

The February day is frigid but bright, and although there's plenty of snow left from last week's storm, the roads are clear of ice. Jenny is thinking of the party. She and I don't care about watching sports but Peter played football at Brown, and every year we go all out for the Super Bowl. Jenny loves to cook, and together we'll make chili, Buffalo wings, and guacamole. Last year Timmy came over, and the two of them huddled on the couch whispering and laughing, surrounded by Peter and our friends; I don't think I watched a full minute of the game, I was so taken by the sight of my daughter in love.

Jenny was sixteen in November, her license is new, and she brings her sense of responsibility to driving the way she does everything else. Straight As last semester, a talent for the violin, a blue ribbon in last summer's horse show, caring for our animals, such good-heartedness, and a head-down pure-hearted determination to go to Brown University like her parents, and I wonder if her choice is a way of trying to hold us together, to remind Peter and me of where we met, and I know she feels bad for leaving the house angry this morning, calling me a hypocrite for inviting people over and entertaining relatives just when Peter is planning to move out. My aunt and uncle from California are staying with us; they are in Connecticut because he's a professor, guest lecturing at Yale, where I am an adjunct professor of cultural anthropology. Jenny is afraid that they have picked up on the tension and are judging Peter.

So there she is, driving home from the barn along the Shore Road, past the marsh brown and glistening, the creeks frozen over, pure white in the sunlight, her father beside her sipping coffee, telling her how well she rode that morning, how she kept her elbows in and heels down and took Gisele over the jumps.

Peter and Jenny adore each other and have since her birth. At night, as an infant, when she'd wake up crying and refuse to sleep, she'd quiet only when he would cradle and walk her, singing her made-up songs as he carried her back and forth across her room overlooking the meadow, that single stately elm framed in the window, ghostly in moonlight.

And even those years when Jenny was ten and eleven, and I finally went back to school for my master's, taking classes in New Haven, studying and writing about the anthropology of movement, my books and papers spread out on the dining room table every night, Peter would come home from the office and he and Jenny would take dinner into the den and eat in front of the TV, laughing, Jenny shrieking; they both loved comedies and cartoons, especially French ones—Asterix and Tintin were huge in our house.

She drives toward home and the meadow, gleaming with crusted snow, the road straight and clear, no traffic in either direction, pavement sanded and clear of ice, tree branches interlocking overhead and throwing morning shadows, and her elm—she thinks of it as hers—comes into view. Shore Road takes a sharp left, a boomerang bend, just where our driveway veers off to the right.

Ancient stone walls built by Connecticut's settlers, arrived from England in the 1600s—evidence, as if we need more, of migration and movement, and how the history of the world is made up of people leaving one place for another, looking for more food, religious freedom, a better life—line the way; when she was little she loved to walk to and from the bus stop on top of the walls, and sometimes we'd hide messages for each other in a lichen-bound crevice that we called our mailbox. She remembers our secret hiding place, the shivery pleasure of finding a note, and she is wearing Timmy's sweater, the smell of him inseparable from the feeling of being in love, and in that instant she steps on the gas.

The sunlight bounces off the snow, off bright mica and quartz threaded through the granite walls, blinding her for just a second. The road is clear, she knows the way, she is such a good driver, her father is with her, he taught her to drive himself, she would never hurt him, never hurt herself, she loves her family, she loves her life, so there is no explanation.

Ten minutes later Bonnie and I meander along, finished with our errands. We still have a few hours before friends will show up to watch the game, and I'm eager for time with Jenny—her father had the morning, and I'll have the early afternoon to nurse our child and her broken heart, to just be with her because I'm smart enough to know that words don't help, there's no explaining that everything will get better, that she'll heal, that time will pass and the day will come when it doesn't hurt so much.

Black Hall is a small town, and when you hear sirens your stomach drops because you're pretty sure whatever it is will affect someone you know. Driving along Shore Road, I slow down to let the fire truck pass. Bonnie, in the back seat, paces back and forth. I tell her to calm down, everything's okay, we'll be home in a minute. I flip on the signal light, to veer off the main road and head toward our driveway, and see the burst of flashing lights.

Some thoughts are too unbearable to allow. I see the town constable gesture for traffic to turn around, go back the other way, and I roll down the window to tell him I live here, and still, I won't let myself think that this accident belongs to us. But Bonnie is barking, and she knows, and when the constable recognizes me and approaches the car with that look in his eyes that no human being wants to see, my heart stops because my heart knows.

I open the car door, he tries to block me but nothing in this world could hold me back, I am right behind Bonnie running to the front of the long line of police cars, fire engines, and ambulances. I hear someone say, *She didn't even hit the brakes, she had to be going fifty,* and someone else saying, *Shut up, that's her mother.* The sun glistens off the snowfield and Long Island Sound, but it doesn't blind me, I see everything, and my mind takes a picture of all that is there and all that isn't.

The memory will stay with me always, even when, in the future, I travel three thousand miles away. Distance is no match for this: the car crumpled against the wall, billows of black smoke, rescue workers with no one to rescue parting to let me through, spider-webs of blood on the faces of my daughter and husband as they lie on the snow-covered ground, Bonnie between them not howling but keening soft and low, and the beloved elm tree, branches bare against the blue sky, that must have been the last sight that Jenny and Peter saw on earth.

chapter one

Roberto

Before dawn, the air smelled of lemons. Roberto slept in the small cabin in the grove in the Santa Monica Mountains, salt wind off the Pacific Ocean sweetening the scent of bitter fruit and filling his dreams with memories of home. He was back in Mexico before he'd come to the United States in search of goodness for his family, in another *huerto de limones,* the lemon orchard buzzing with bees and the voices of workers talking, Rosa playing with her doll Maria. Maria had sheer angel wings and Roberto's grandmother had whispered to Rosa that she had magic powers and could fly.

Rosa wore her favorite dress, white with pink flowers, sewn by his grandmother. Roberto stood high on the ladder, taller in the dream than any real one would reach. From here he could see over the treetops, his gaze sweeping the valley toward Popocatépetl and Iztaccíhuatl, the two snow-covered volcanic peaks to the west. His grandmother had told him the legend, that the mountains were lovers, the boy shielding the girl, and tall on his ladder Roberto felt stronger than anyone, and he heard his daughter talking to her doll.

In dream magic, his basket spilling over with lemons, he slid down the tree and lifted Rosa into his arms. She was five, with laughing brown eyes and cascades of dark curls, and she slung her skinny arm around his neck and pressed her face into his shoulder. In the dream he was wise and knew there was no better life, no greater goodness, than what they already had. He held her and promised nothing bad would ever happen to her, and if he could have slept forever those words would be true. Sleep prolonged the vision, his eyes shut tight against the dawn light, and the scent of *limones* enhanced the hallucination that Rosa was with him still and always.

When he woke up, he didn't waste time trying to hold on to the feelings. They tore away from him violently and were gone. His day started fast. He lived twenty-five miles east, in Boyle Heights, but sometimes stayed in the orchard during fire season and when there was extra work to be done. He led a crew of three, with extra men hired from the Malibu Community Labor Exchange or the parking lot at the Woodland Hills Home Depot when necessary. They came to the property at 8 a.m.

The Riley family lived in a big Spanish colonial–style house, with arched windows and a red tile roof, just up the ridgeline from Roberto's cabin. They had occupied this land in western Malibu's Santa Monica Mountains since the mid-1900s. While other families had torn up old, less profitable orchards and planted vineyards, the Rileys remained true to their family tradition of raising citrus. Roberto respected their loyalty to their ancestors and the land.

The grove took up forty acres, one hundred twenty-year-old trees per acre, planted in straight lines on the south-facing hillside, in the same furrows where older trees had once stood. Twenty years ago the Santa Ana winds had sparked fires that burned the whole orchard, sparing Casa Riley but engulfing neighboring properties on both sides. Close to the house and large tiled swimming pool were rock outcroppings and three-hundred-year-old live oaks— their trunks eight feet in diameter—still scorched black from that fire. Fire was mystical, and although it had swept through Malibu in subsequent years, the Rileys' property had been spared.

Right now the breeze blew cool off the Pacific, but Roberto knew it could shift at any time. Summer had ended, and now the desert winds would start: the Santa Anas, roaring through the mountain passes, heating up as they sank from higher elevations down to the coast, and any flash, even from a power tool, could ignite the canyon. It had been dry for two months straight. He walked to the barn, where the control panel was located, and turned on the sprinklers.

The water sprayed up, catching rainbows as the sun crested the eastern mountains. It hissed, soft and constant, and Roberto couldn't help thinking of the sound as money draining away. Water was delivered to the orchard via canal, and was expensive. The Rileys had told him many times that the important thing was the health of the trees and lemons, and to protect the land from fire.

He had something even more important to do before his co-workers arrived: make the coastal path more secure. He grabbed a sledgehammer and cut through the grove to the cliff edge. The summer-dry hillsides sloped past the sparkling pool, down in a widening V to the Pacific Ocean. Occasionally hikers crossed Riley land to connect with the Backbone Trail and other hikes in the mountain range. Years back someone had installed stanchions and a chain: a rudimentary fence to remind people the drop was steep, five hundred feet down to the canyon floor.

He tested the posts and found some loosened. Mudslides and

temblors made the land unstable. He wished she would stay off this trail entirely, walk the dog through the orchard, where he could better keep an eye on them, or at least use the paths on the inland side of the property. But she seemed to love the ocean. He'd seen her pass this way both mornings since she'd arrived, stopping to stare out to sea while the dog rustled through the chaparral and coastal sage.

He tapped the first post to set his aim, then swung the sledge-hammer overhead, metal connecting with metal with a loud *gong*. He felt the shock of the impact in the bones of his wrists and shoulders. Moving down the row of stanchions, he drove each one a few inches deeper into the ground until they were solidly embedded. The wind was blowing toward the house. He hoped the sound wouldn't bother her, but he figured it wouldn't. She rose early, like him.

The Rileys had left to go to Ireland for several months, leaving their niece to house-sit. She had arrived three days ago, having driven cross-country alone with a dog that had white, brown, and blue-gray markings, with one brown and one blue eye.

The woman was small, pale, with silver hair and blue eyes. She looked nothing like the women Roberto had seen in California. Everyone here seemed glamorous, almost perfect, with skin golden from the sun and hair colored lush brown or bright blond, nails done and makeup on—he'd never once seen Mrs. Riley without lipstick. But the niece was different.

She had introduced herself the same morning she arrived. He'd been in the barn, increasing the sprinkler controls to ten gallons an hour per tree, and she'd walked right in and shaken his hand without any regard for the fact his hand was greasy and his face streaked with dirt.

"You must be Roberto," she'd said, shaking his hand. "I'm Julia Hughes, Graciela and John's niece. And this is Bonnie."

"Hi, Julia," he'd said, embarrassed and wiping his hands on his pants, too late. "You made it here safely. Long trip?"

"Yes, thank you. Luckily, Bonnie is a good traveler."

They locked eyes, and Roberto couldn't have said why the hair on the back of his neck stood on end. He bent down to pet Bonnie to escape the feeling, running his hands over her silky blue-gray coat. She had a smiling, friendly dog face, but with those spooky eyes, his grandmother would call her a *perra bruja:* a witch dog. Julia's blue eyes troubled him even more; when he looked back at her, he felt jolted, as if he'd looked in a mirror.

"I'll let you get back to work," she said, as if sensing his uneasiness.

"Thank you," he said. "Please let me know if you need anything."

She had walked away, Bonnie leading her onto the cliff path. He had seen her return again since that first meeting. In this world he couldn't save everyone, but he could do his best to make the trail safe for her.

Working his way along the posts, he realized that he would have to reinforce some—those too loose to grab the earth—with concrete. A kick with the toe of his boot sent pebbles and clay tumbling down the canyon. He grabbed an armful of brush from the hillside and blocked the trail; he'd leave it that way—even adding some yellow hazard tape—until he could fix the danger zones.

Heading back to the barn, he heard trucks arriving and voices talking. The crew had arrived to irrigate and prune the orchard, but Roberto could think only of danger zones. They were everywhere. Some were compact and marked with warning signs, a few feet of cliff along a hiking trail, fixable with the right tools and a bucket of concrete. Others spread for miles, from horizon to horizon, across land crossed by thousands. The luckiest made it with their lives.

The youngest ones who hadn't survived were angels now. They haunted the pilgrimage route, the dry creek beds and narrow canyons, filling the air with their ghostly wails. Some had been taken by La Llorona, the weeping woman who stole others' children to replace her own. Rejected by heaven for losing her children in the Santa Fe River, she wandered the borderlands and captured any young ones she found alone at night.

"Hola, como estas?" Serapio asked, parking his truck in the shade.

"Bien, y tú?" Roberto answered.

"Bien. We're digging drainage again today?" Serapio asked.

"Yes," Roberto said. "You and the guys pick up where we left off yesterday. I'll be there soon."

Serapio nodded without question. Roberto could have asked the crew for help, finished reinforcing the trail that much sooner. But the job fell to him, and he knew it. Once in a while he felt inspired—was that the right word? Perhaps not—it was more like the relief of punishment being lifted, the chance to work and redeem himself and his sins. He wasn't even a believer anymore. His mother had died in childbirth and his grandmother had raised him Catholic. He still carried her hand-carved black wood rosary in his pocket, but it was more for sentiment and love of her than any religious reason.

Still, when he got this feeling—straight from his gut, not his brain—he obeyed it. He grabbed a bag of concrete mix, filled the first bucket with water, slung twenty yards' worth of yellow hazard tape over his shoulder. Bees buzzed in dark pink bougainvillea growing up the side of the barn, and as he hiked back to the cliff edge, he felt the breeze rushing through sage and coastal scrub up from the sea. It cooled his skin, gave him goose bumps even in the morning heat.

The Pacific Ocean went on forever, as blue but not a fraction as deep as the sky. The wind cracked the surface into small white waves that built and surged and crashed at the foot of the cliff. The pounding was relentless. The noise kept him awake on nights when he stayed in the orchard, and made him lonely for his farm town at the foot of the mountains. He had never seen any ocean before arriving in Los Angeles. If the fall from the cliff didn't kill him, he would drown—he couldn't swim.

After mixing the concrete, he filled the holes he'd dug and placed the posts upright. They were solid steel and, once properly anchored, would make the chain strong and effective. Short of standing right here by the edge, this was the best he could do to keep her safe from the dangerous land. The sun rose higher and the sweat that formed on his brow ran into his eyes and made them sting, but he didn't wipe it away—he didn't want to stop swinging the sledgehammer, feeling the jolt to his bones so strong it kept him from thinking of loss or danger, or anything at all.

chapter two

Julia

This is Malibu but nothing like the Malibu you hear about when you live on the East Coast. Back there it's all movie stars and scandals and tan blond girls in late-model Porsches who make people wonder, "Are they up-and-coming actors on shows that haven't aired yet and if so did they buy the car themselves, or are they just so pretty they're being kept by an older man rich and lonely enough to trade expensive presents for attention and affection?"

She knew a little about such things. She'd been coming here since she was a child—although this was her first time in five years—and she heard gossip from Lion, whom she'd be seeing for dinner that night.

As much as she loved him and always had, she wasn't in the mood, would have preferred to stay home. She liked the way this landscape enclosed her, made her feel protected in a strange way, because really, what could be more dangerous than Malibu, with its earthquakes, mudslides, and wildfires?

Maybe that outward danger comforted her somehow and reinforced her sense of how impermanent it all was. Just look at the Chumash people, how they had thrived on this coast for ten thousand years, as hunter-gatherers and superb boatbuilders and basket makers. Being an anthropologist, she could vividly imagine their life here, and how timeless it must have seemed—until 1542, when Juan Rodriguez Cabrillo had sailed in and claimed California for Spain.

Anthropology, it turns out, had been her perfect field of study: learning about the cosmology of civilizations uprooted from one place and settled in another. She felt the loss of Jenny so acutely, the specifics of their days together, the constellations marking moments in their lives, their own lost culture. Who they had been, Jenny and Julia, mother and daughter, would last forever; but who Jenny, and what their relationship, would have become, ended with the accident.

In her profession Julia dealt with the real, the evidentiary, the tracks left behind by people. Even as an undergrad she'd loved hiding in her carrel at the Rock—the main library at Brown—and using long-lost and recently found artifacts to assemble, in her imagination, the way people had lived. It had always been her passion, to keep the dead alive through learning how they had behaved, where they had trekked in search of food, water, love.

She had been an emotional girl, and that never changed. At Vance School, in first grade, she'd attended class with the kids who lived at the Children's Home—a big brick building at the top of a hill. They were there for various reasons: their parents had died, or had hurt them, or for some reason couldn't take care of them. Julia could see the home from her bedroom window.

There was one boy, Billy, who sat next to her in school. He had freckles and a cowlick. When they went on a field trip to the fire station, he was her partner, and they held hands. It was fall, and walking down the Connecticut street, they kicked through fallen red and yellow leaves. Billy didn't talk to anyone except their teacher. They spent the whole walk in silence, but he kept squeezing her hand, as if in Morse code.

The insides of his wrists were dirty, and he had a hole in the sleeve of his sweater, and something about that raveled yarn and his not talking told her a story about his whole life.

In fourth grade Julia saw a filmstrip about Margaret Mead working with children in Samoa. But by the time she got to high school, it was Margaret's mentor, Ruth Benedict, who captured Julia's imagination and made her want to be an anthropologist.

Ruth studied tribes in the Southwest and was the first woman to really make strides in the field. She wrote about the relationships between culture, language, and personality. She was interested in human behavior and the way it is shaped by traditions. Julia wanted to learn all she could about people's behavior, including her own family's.

How Jenny had behaved: a hurricane of love. She took after her mother when it came to emotion. It wasn't unusual for Julia to return from her office and a late-afternoon trip to the grocery store, enter the kitchen, and have Jenny barrel over, leap right onto her, arms locked around her neck, saying "Why were you gone so long?"

"I came straight home from work."

"Don't you remember? We were going to have a picnic and watch the moonrise." Or the sunset, or the bluefish in a feeding frenzy, or the monarch butterflies staging for their long migration south to Mexico, or the tree swallows in their funnel cloud formation each night at twilight.

That September night it had been the moonrise. Jenny had

prepared sandwiches, delicious concoctions of smoked bluefish and whatever was left in the garden. Peter was home—Julia remembered that now—but he hadn't wanted to join them. He was working on a case, or had a Red Sox game to watch. They'd never meant to leave him out, but he'd never seemed eager to join in, either. He and Julia seemed to be living two separate lives, and that, more than anything, was contributing to their impending separation.

Julia and Jenny hurried down the twisty, wooded path, stunted oaks and pines overhanging the sandy trail. They got to the beach just as the sun was setting. They sat on the smooth gray log—long stripped of bark, after years of storms and wind and blowing sand—and faced east.

They tried to do this every month on the night of the full moon, but it wasn't always possible. But that night, they saw the apricot moon crest over an eastern headland, then spread its orange light across Long Island Sound in a path that seemed to run straight toward them.

"Oh, Jenny," Julia said. "I'm so glad you thought of this."

"Mom, you invented moon picnics."

"I did?" she asked. But she knew it was true. She had always loved nature and the magic it brought to human love. As a kid, she'd been like Jenny: in love with everything. She didn't believe in love unfolding, but being born in a big bang, like the universe.

Jenny's enthusiasm was like Julia's, and the contrast with Peter couldn't be sharper. The older he got, the more measured and cautious he became, and the harder it was for Julia to find ways to feel they had anything but years and a daughter in common. It had taken Julia a long time to admit that she was desperately unhappy in what most people would consider a very good marriage. Staring at that full moon, holding her daughter's hand, tears had rolled down her cheeks because she'd begun not just thinking about but actually taking steps to divorce Peter.

Divorce, as it turned out, hadn't been necessary.

The Santa Monica Mountains ran east-west, north of the Los Angeles basin, all the way to the Pacific Ocean, and the house was nestled in a canyon overlooking endless, sparkling blue. In the days since Julia and Bonnie had arrived from Connecticut, Bonnie had already claimed her role as queen of the property. She was getting old, and it touched Julia to see her happy again.

Collies were sensitive to their masters' moods. Julia knew she was Bonnie's master, like it or not. Julia was happiest hiding, being low on any kind of hierarchal totem pole, but when it came to dogs, the relationship was built-in. It had been five years, just Bonnie and Julia, and they belonged to each other. She'd made peace with the fact that Bonnie looked to her for everything—she had long since accepted the reality that until this trip, their lives were limited to the bedroom, the kitchen, and the as-infrequent-as-possible trips to the grocery store.

Bonnie rested next to her on the bed, watching with sad eyes when Julia thought of Jenny and tried to keep breathing. Five years after the fact, it felt like no time had passed. Breath was still a razor blade in and out, in and out. Why did Julia get to breathe when Jenny didn't? A childish thought, but she would never stop hating that fact and wishing she could trade places with her daughter. Let Jenny be here with Bonnie, let her be in college, let her be house-sitting in this mysterious canyon that smelled of flowers and lemons and sea air.

She hated seeing people. She had nothing against anyone person-ally, but she'd become something different, other, since Jenny's death. Jenny had loved Bonnie, used to pet her, snuggle her, throw the tennis ball and grab the slobbery thing and throw it again, run through the field to the dead tree and over the bluff to the beach, swim in Long Island Sound together, come home and hose off the sand and salt and tendrils of seaweed. So in a way, because Jenny had hugged Bonnie, when Julia stroked Bonnie she knew that somehow she was touching a part of her daughter.

Looking out the window, down the long slope of lawn and garden to the orchard, she saw Roberto smacking those posts into the cliff and felt weird fury boiling up. Why was he fixing up the path? Obviously he had seen her walking Bonnie along there yesterday, and fuck and shit, she swore he'd read her mind—that fleeting moment when she thought about how easy it would be to just stand on the brink and let go and fly down into the sea.

All of a sudden, even though she avoided seeing people, she knew she was going to walk out to see him. Why was it, having met him so briefly, she didn't classify him as "people"?

He was the latest in a long line of orchard managers, all of them migrants, and she'd known most of them, joked around with them, gotten to know their families and—as a child—let them lift her into the branches to pick lemons. They had come from Mexico seeking a better life.

From her earliest memories, her uncle John had told her that the Mexicans and the Irish—her Irish family in particular—were related in ways deeper than blood. Both groups immigrated to the United States in great numbers seeking the same things: relief from starvation and poverty, a place to raise their families and create lives that would give their children increased opportunities.

He had told her about John Riley, their ancestor who'd come from Ireland to join the U.S. Army during the Mexican-American War. Seeing injustice, he switched sides to form the Saint Patrick's

Battalion and fight for Mexico. The Americans eventually caught him, branded his cheek with a "D" for "deserter." And Mexico lost the war.

Her uncle John had encouraged her to study anthropology. On a visit here when she was seventeen, he had given her René Grousset's classic *The Empire of the Steppes,* published in 1939. She'd become fascinated with the Bulgar tribes in southern Russia, and how the eastward and westward migrations of the steppe nomads affected developing societies in Europe, China, Central Asia, and India. Every place in the world owed its identity to the people who had moved there from somewhere else.

She'd followed her dream and majored in cultural anthropology at Brown. Instead of going straight to grad school, she'd held off. She and Peter couldn't afford two tuitions at once, so he'd gotten his law degree first.

Then Jenny was born. Julia never stopped reading and being curious about tribal movement and diasporas; when Jenny entered fourth grade and began asking questions about their family background, Julia tracked down a copy of the film about Margaret Mead and showed it to Jenny. It inspired Jenny to do a school project about Julia's ancestors migrating from Ireland and her father's from England.

Julia understood that the connection with Roberto had to do with the flash she'd seen in his eyes when she asked if he had children and he seemed unsure of whether to answer yes or no. He'd finally said, "Yes, a daughter," but he looked away from Julia's eyes the way a person does when he's lying. She did that. She could never speak straight to anyone about Jenny.

The house was soothing. Her uncle was an academic, her aunt an actress. Graciela's mother was Mexican, her father a native Angeleno who had run a small studio just over the mountains in

North Hollywood. John and Graciela met at a beachfront bar a few miles away—John was developing the Mexican Studies program at UCLA; Graciela had been cast in a Western and was filming at Paramount Ranch.

They had both grown up in greater Los Angeles and in spite of their differences were instantly fascinated with each other. John proposed before primary photography on the film had finished; they got married in the lemon orchard, and moved into the house—Casa Riley—with his parents, living with them until they died.

This branch of the Riley family loved Spanish colonial architecture, and their house showed it. The walls were thick stucco, the arched windows too small to let in the full grandeur of the view, and the red tile floors set off the white plaster and dark wood columns and window frames. Julia's father, William, had grown up in this house, but he'd attended Harvard, settled on the East Coast, and never really looked back. He ignored the Mexican parts of their story and focused on the Irish, living and writing in Connemara whenever he could.

Uncle John cherished local history, and over the years he and Graciela had collected many pieces from the legendary and long-lamented Malibu Potteries—the factory had existed on the beach five miles down the coast for only six years, from 1926 to 1932, before being destroyed by fire—brightly glazed tiles in the bathrooms and kitchen, bookends shaped like mischievous monks, a multicolored tiled fountain in the courtyard with a king's head that spit a steady stream of water. Collecting such old and beautiful things had given her aunt and uncle a hobby together that made up for not having children. Yes, Graciela had actually said that.

Bonnie was now in the courtyard, lapping water from the fountain.

"Come on, girl," Julia said. "Let's go for a walk."

In spite of the arthritis in her hips, Bonnie loped from the courtyard, heading left on what had become their regular route. Julia followed her; it wasn't too difficult because she had slowed down so.

They walked down the lawn, the cultivated paradise: white roses blooming along the pathways, bordered by sweet alyssum and dark blue lobelia. Coral geraniums filled round pots made of seashells: thousands of channeled whelks per pot, patterned in unending circles. Dark pink bougainvillea cascaded over the fence by the barn, and bright green hummingbirds hovered at the deep-red flowers, darting around Julia's head as she walked past.

She heard the clang, clang of Roberto's sledgehammer. She hesitated for a minute, wondering whether she should go in the opposite direction, not bother him, let him continue with his work. She stood in the shade of a wind-sculpted pine, watched him putting everything he had into the hammer strikes. He wore a white T-shirt and baggy blue jeans, a heavy silver key chain looping into one pocket, and scuffed boots. Just before she would have walked the other way, he looked toward her.

It took him a moment to smile, but when he did, she saw how beautiful he was. He had worry in his face, and it killed her a little to see relief fill his eyes, as if she had provided him with sudden solace. His brown-black hair was close-cropped, and he had a neatly trimmed moustache and a fine two or three days' growth of beard. His face and arms were light brown, his muscles long and lean.

He had some lines around his eyes and mouth, but she realized that he was younger than she'd first thought. He might have been in his thirties, but no more. She walked toward him.

"Hola, Julia," he said.

"Hola, Roberto. How are you?"

"Bien, bien. How are you? Hi, Bonnie . . ."

She watched as Bonnie bumped against his legs and he bent to pet her, running his hands through her fur.

"Thank you for fixing the guard rails," she said. "Jenny and I used to . . ." She stopped herself.

"Of course," he said. "I want it to be safe for you. No one else walks here very much."

"Sorry for taking you away from the orchard, though," she said. "I'm sure you have lots to do there."

"That's okay. Serapio and the others are on the job. I'll get there soon enough." He stood erect, holding the sledgehammer instead of leaning on it, but then he laid it down and wiped his brow with the back of his hand as if deciding to take an official break.

"Are you thirsty? Do you want me to get you some water?" she asked, then felt like an idiot because she should have just brought it as she had once done for Tonio and Ricardo, his predecessors.

"No, I'm fine," he said.

"So, you're running the orchard now," she said.

"Yes," he said.

"You obviously do a great job," she said. The sun had risen over the mountain and the lemons glowed with white light. Canyon dust coated the glossy green leaves, making them look like tarnished silver.

"Thank you. I'm lucky your uncle hired me. This is good steady work."

She nodded, struck by the choice of words: "good steady work."

"And you live on the property?"

"No," he said. "I stay here sometimes, but I live somewhere else."

"Like where?" she asked, a little surprised—Tonio and his family had lived in the cottage; it had been a perk of the job.

He looked startled, and for a minute she wanted to take back the question, wondering if somehow it was rude or forward.

"In East L.A.," he said.

"Oh," she said. She didn't know Los Angeles well, but everyone knew the stereotype of East L.A. and its tough reputation—gangs and drug dealers. She thought of his daughter, if he really had one, and wondered who was taking care of her. He didn't wear a wedding ring.

"I was thinking about our talk yesterday. Your daughter . . ."

"Rosa," he said.

"Does she live with you?"

"No," he said. "She lives in Mexico."

"Oh." Maybe that explained why he'd seemed so evasive. "Do you see her often?"

"I can't," he said.

That seemed incredible to her, made her second-guess her own first impressions of him. The idea that he could have a child in this world and not see her as often as he could instantly changed her opinion of him. "Why not?"

"It's not that easy," he said.

"You must miss her terribly."

"Yes," he said.

"Don't you get along with her mother?"

"That's not why I don't see Rosa."

She already knew. It was hardly a secret—in many ways it was the story of L.A., or at least of the workers who kept it running. "You don't have papers," she said. "You can't cross the border."

His gaze was proud and steady; his silence let her know she was right. Her uncle had always hired illegal workers; although the circumstances were different, as an immigrant himself he honored the desire to find a better life. She loved her uncle's compassion but right now she judged Roberto for valuing his job and life in the States over his daughter. Still, when she looked into his eyes, she saw despair so dark it scared her.

"Why don't you see Rosa?" she asked.

"Something bad happened," he said.

"When?"

"Five years ago," he said.

The coincidence punched her in the chest. She backed up just slightly, stepping off the dry dirt path.

"Who is Jenny?" he asked. The sound of her name scraped Julia's skin, like a peeling sunburn. Roberto said it again: "Who is Jenny?"

"My daughter," she said. She turned away from him. Bonnie lay in the shade, but seeing Julia move, she rose creakily and headed off down the path. Julia followed her around the bend, without another word to Roberto.

Lion

Lion Cushing lived on a steep driveway, twisting and turning straight up a mountainside off Old Topanga Canyon Road, and had been there so long some people called him the Dean of Topanga. They came to him for tales of Jimi Hendrix partying at Moon Fire Temple, rumors of Charles Manson living in his barn before his days with the Family, rampant legends of UFOs using the canyon for navigation, takeoff, and landing in clouds of green haze, tales of who was doing whom in the Malibu Colony, and decades of gossip and memories from Lion's Hollywood days. Those good old days.

At one time they had come for weed. Back in the day, Lion had had the best on the Westside, and everyone knew it. It made him rather sad, standing on his stone terrace amid a great and ancient stand of eucalyptus trees, to realize that so much of his life was in the past. Back then pot was part of something bigger—a life even Lion couldn't believe he'd led. Now a joint was just a joint.

How quickly life had sped by. He had had one of the best managers in the business, who'd kept him from squandering his money, so even though he was ancient and mainly retired, he could still live an appallingly decadent life. He'd somehow kept his looks—good genes was the only explanation—by the standards of most seventy-five-year-old men, but that was a far cry the days when *Variety* had described him as having been "chiseled from the same granite as the mountains in his home state." New Hampshire. That was a lifetime ago.

The gong rang, a relic from a Tang dynasty Buddhist temple. The sound pleased him, not just because it meant he had company, but also because it reminded him of filming *Two for the East* on the Yangtze River, with his co-star Graciela Crawford Riley. He went to the door and there stood Graciela's niece Julia.

"Welcome, my darling," he said, kissing her on both cheeks before wrapping her in a hug. "You made it up the mountain without incident!"

"Well worth it to see you," she said.

"I've got a crumbing castle and a private road the county would like to close and condemn, but having a beautiful dinner companion lie to save my feelings makes life worth living another day."

"Oh, Lion . . ." She smiled.

"And not just any beautiful companion—you."

He'd known her since she was a little girl; Graciela used to bring her up here to ride his horses. Grief had washed over her, given her the soft aspect of a watercolor, aged her—not beyond her years, but he missed the bright spark in her eyes, the ready-for-anything enthusiasm she'd had for life before Jenny's death. He missed the quick rush of emotion that had been her trademark, whether she knew it or not.

He led her inside, through the baronial living room, and onto the terrace. The house sat on the top of Topanga's highest peak, and he took deep pleasure in seeing her drink in the wraparound view—the Pacific, Catalina and the Channel Islands, the Palos Verdes Peninsula embracing the southern end of Santa Monica Bay, four mountain ranges, the lights of downtown Los Angeles. The sight seemed to relax her, and that pleased him even more.

"Join me in a martini?" he asked.

"Not lemonade?" she teased.

"You remember," he said, laughing. As a little girl, she would arrive with Gracie and, when unavoidable, John, bearing lemons she'd picked from the orchard. While the grown-ups drank gin, she would have fresh-squeezed lemonade.

"Of course," she said.

"Well, did you bring me a basketful?"

"Not tonight," she said, and he watched her smile drift away so completely it jarred him.

He mixed drinks in a silver shaker, poured them into fine-stemmed crystal glasses. They sat on the terrace watching the light change from blue to tangerine, the sky's unearthly glow coating the ocean and hillsides with amber, folding shadows into the canyons and valleys.

"Tell me everything," he said.

"You always say that," she said.

"Because I want to know! Every single thing."

"Well, I'm here," she said. "That's the big news."

"Indeed it is," Lion said. This was her first time in California since the accident. He had seen her back East—for the funerals, and when he'd done *Agamemnon* at Hartford Stage. She hadn't attended the show, but each day the theater had been dark during the six-week run, he had driven down to Black Hall to stay with her and force her into pretending to be alive at least for the duration of his visits.

"And how is Casa Riley?" he asked.

"Dreamy as I remembered," she said. "Bonnie is loving it, too."

"Bonnie! Why didn't you bring her tonight?"

"She seemed content to stay home. She's getting old, Lion."

"Aren't we all, darling? I'm the oldest man in Hollywood."

"You never get old," she said. "When I was little, I thought you were my friend more than theirs."

"Thank you, love, but one can be both immature and antiquated," Lion said.

They chuckled, sipping their martinis. Lion studied her over the misted rim of his glass. She was every bit as lovely as Graciela had been at her age—but where Gracie had black hair and her mother's Latina dark fire, Julia's beauty was pale, Irish, understated: freckled skin, gray-blue eyes, high cheekbones, small mouth. While Gracie had the need of every actress Lion had ever known to be noticed and adored, Julia had always seemed quiet, more introspective, with a secret smile that never begged for attention.

"What do you hear from your aunt?" he asked as offhandedly as possible.

"They're having a great time," Julia said. "The house is good, John's work tracing his namesake is going well."

"How thrilling," he said.

"You don't *sound* thrilled," she said, and there was that secret smile. He gazed at her without expression; he'd always wondered how much she knew or had guessed about his feelings for Gracie.

"They'll be gone for so long," he said. "One gets lonely without one's best friends. How will I amuse myself with the Rileys abandoning me for Ireland?"

"You're never bored," she said. "I know you go out every night; I'm lucky to have you all to myself tonight. Everyone is in love with you."

"Well, that's true," he said. "But I'd rather spend the evening by the fire playing canasta with your aunt than at some red-carpet thing on the arm of whomever."

"Whomever," Julia said, scoffing. "I saw you in *People* with that girl from the Shady Lake movies."

"Ah, yes. Bee Sting, I call her. Those lips everyone wants now. As far as I'm concerned, they broke the mold with your aunt—and you. Simple elegance is far sexier than pillow lips. Womanhood is a lost art."

Julia shook her head, laughing and—finally—beaming with a real smile. Good, Lion had succeeded at something tonight. She slouched down in her chair, comfortable at last. Her gaze swung round to the twinkling lights of downtown. Poor Los Angeles didn't have a real skyline; all its buildings clustered in one small area, more like a sky lump.

Ana Guzman, his housekeeper, had cooked and left sitting on low heat *mole poblano*—one of the specialties passed down from her mother—and the delicious odor of ancho chilis, cloves, tomatilloes, cumin, all together with turkey and deep Mexican chocolate, wafted temptingly through the open doors. Lion loved the smell. But one glance at Julia, still looking east, showed that trouble was back between her brows.

"The lights of downtown offend you, my love?" he asked.

"No, they're beautiful," she said.

"Graciela calls them our galaxy. Our own collection of nighttime stars."

"That's romantic," Julia said softly, and Lion's heart skipped. After all these years he still wanted to talk about his beloved, have people recognize their connection. But Graciela had always been so discreet—while other actresses wanted gossip to push their careers, even in the old days, no matter what the studios said—and had wrapped them in a secret.

"Do you know Roberto?" she asked.

"Rossellini? He was a little ahead of my time, but I did know Ingrid. In spite of her love for him, and the cost to her career, he couldn't keep it in his pants."

"No, Roberto at Graciela and John's. He runs the orchard."

"Oh," Lion said, taken aback. "I thought Tonio did that."

"Tonio left. Now it's Roberto."

"Why would you ask?"

"I just wondered if you knew his story."

Who knows the stories of help? Lion wondered. You cared about them, they became part of the family, but their tales of poverty and coming to the States in search of a better life where they wound up getting paid thirty dollars a day, if that, were uniformly too much to bear—he had learned early, especially living in L.A., that one couldn't save the world, it was a heartbreak even to try.

"No, I don't," Lion said.

"Why would he live in East L.A. when the cottage on the property is so nice? It seems such a long way for him to drive back and forth each day."

That explained it: her long, worried gaze across the great expanse of hills and valleys to the light grid of greater Los Angeles. She was staring toward East L.A., and for what? Lion saw no smile on her lips or in her eyes—so it wasn't that she had a crush on the orchard manager. Perhaps he had offended her somehow.

"Would you like me to have a word with him?" Lion asked.

"No, why?"

"You seem bothered. As if he'd upset you."

Lion waited. She merely sipped her martini and didn't reply; the expression on her face led him to believe Roberto had upset her indeed. But she wasn't asking for help. His darling Julia was a thinker, just like all the intellectuals on the Riley side. She was probably pondering the anthropological implications of something or other as they related to orchard workers.

They finished their drinks and went inside. Ana had left everything perfectly ready for them: the table set, stove on low, the *mole* barely simmering, corn tortillas in the steamer. Julia exclaimed over how great it smelled, helping Lion serve the dinner. She was here, they were talking and laughing and eating, but every so often she'd glance east, at a wall that had no windows, as if she were trying to look through plaster and see all the way to the barrios of East L.A.

Julia

The road down from Lion's mountaintop house was even more treacherous after dark, hairpin twists and turns and some stretches unpaved. Topanga Canyon smelled like sage, and the air, heavy with moisture from the ocean, felt like black velvet. By the time Julia got home, she was sweaty and shaking.

The property welcomed her. Low lights lined the driveway, and the Casa's front porch was lit warmly. Globes of moist air surrounded the lanterns, casting a tantalizing glow—all the more so because she couldn't remember leaving them on. The night felt hot, her skin clammy. She parked in the circular drive, fumbled in her bag for the keys, and let herself into the house.

"Hi, girl," she said to Bonnie, who was waiting in the front hall, creaking to her feet to greet Julia. "Want to go for a walk?"

But as she was looking for the flashlight, she heard the fountain trickling and thought of how good water would feel on her skin. After quickly changing into her blue one-piece suit, she flipped the switch by the kitchen door and watched the underwater lights illuminate the big swimming pool. She and Bonnie walked down the orchard path, smooth stones crunching underfoot.

Her aunt and uncle had taught her to crave night swims as a child, and she'd passed that love on to Jenny. They would walk five hundred yards down to the beach and dive into the Long Island Sound, with nothing more than moon and starlight to show them the way.

The weather didn't matter. They would swim on stormy nights as happily as warm, calm ones. Now she hurried down the orchard path toward the cliff trail and wondered how she could make her way down to the Pacific. She heard the surf pounding, saw white lines of big waves in the black water, and had a sudden craving for the ocean.

Both she and Jenny had loved rough water, swimming after storms. It took everything she had to make Jenny stay inside till the worst was over—and when it was, they'd run down to the beach, lean into the strong wind, feel the power of the tremendous waves in the usually tranquil Sound.

The summer before Jenny died, Hurricane Noreen came barreling up the East Coast. They'd watched it on TV, seeing houses on the Outer Banks battered by surf that crashed over their rooftops, knocking down chimneys and sweeping several houses out to sea. People in Black Hall and weather forecasters were saying this might be the storm to rival the Great Hurricane of 1938, the last one to really devastate the Connecticut shoreline.

Jenny and Timmy went to Black Hall Hardware to stock up on supplies. They bought extra candles, flashlights, water jugs, and two-by-fours to secure the shutters over the windows. Peter was in Denver, taking depositions, but he called to make sure the boat was hauled and the terrace furniture stowed in the garage.

Timmy's parents needed his help at home, up Route 156, near the Connecticut River. Julia had watched the two kids clinging to each other, as if the hurricane might rip them apart forever. They were together constantly, and when that was impossible, texting and phoning. There was almost bound to be a power outage, and Julia could already imagine Jenny's panic. But she was secretly glad to have her daughter to herself.

Together she and Jenny shuttered the windows, and nailed in the two-by-fours to reinforce the wrought-iron closures on the house's most vulnerable east- and south-facing sides. Julia let Jenny climb the ladder and bang in the nails. Together they climbed out on the gently sloping roof over the seaward sunroom and cleaned out the gutter, to keep the rainwater flowing.

Bonnie felt the change in barometric pressure before they did, and began barking and running down to the beach and back. The temperature rose and felt damp and tropical. The air was still, the sky blue with high thin clouds. When the wind barely started picking up, it turned the leaves on the maple and oak trees upside down, and the sky became the color of a yellowing bruise.

Julia and Jenny changed into their bathing suits and ran through the yard and down the long sandy oak-lined path, Bonnie flying ahead of them. This stretch of beach was wild, part of a nature sanctuary. It was backed by marshland, with fine green grasses rippling in long patterns.

Hard against the marsh grass were huge tree trunks, wood silvered by countless storms. Julia could name each hurricane or blizzard during which each tree had washed up.

She wondered whether Noreen would uproot oaks and pines, wreck docks and cottages, and deposit the detritus along the shoreline. And Jenny was right—storms sometimes shifted the sand and earth, revealing artifacts from the Indian period, and here on this very beach was revealed a nineteenth-century 350-ton warship that had fought the British in the War of 1812 and been wrecked here during a hurricane.

For now the elements were just starting to rise, the normal-sized waves swelling to giant rollers that broke on the bar and came seething into shore with a layer of white foam.

Julia and Jenny dropped their towels and dove in. The air was so warm, but so was the water, as if the tropical storm were already here but hadn't yet fully shown itself.

One year a message in a bottle had washed up. Jenny had opened it immediately.

Hello, my name is Willa, I am 12. The storm is coming.
My family lives on Chincoteague, Virginia. If you find this,
please write me.

Jenny had written back, and for a few years she and Willa had been pen pals, but the friendship had trailed off. Since then, during every serious storm, Jenny had sent her own messages in bottles, and had heard back twice—once from a girl in Bass Harbor, Maine, and once from a World War II veteran in Devon, England.

Julia and Jenny swam for a long time, then dried off and headed back to the house. Julia had stocked up at the A&P and Ritter's farm stand with provisions that would last if the power went out. They had the outdoor grill for cooking, and an antique oak ice chest that had come with the old house. Just in case, Julia had bought two blocks of ice from the fish market to hold the food.

Bluefish were running, so Julia had picked some up. She and Jenny made a classic summer dinner: grilled fish, red potato salad made with vinaigrette and grain mustard, butter-and-sugar corn on the cob, and fresh peach ice cream from Paradise Ice Cream for dessert. They ate outside, on the porch, with candles in hurricane lamps. The wind began to shake the trees, and they could hear the surf smashing over the sandbar.

"I want to get married in a hurricane," Jenny said.

"With a tent in the yard that can blow away?" Julia said.

"Yes! And Timmy and I will wear wetsuits instead of a suit and a gown, and we'll all go swimming at the peak of the storm. Maybe we'll say our vows in the water."

"That's romantic."

"You're the best mom."

"I want everything to stay just like this," Jenny said.

Julia nodded because she knew exactly what she meant.

"I'll go away to college in a couple of years," Jenny said. "We won't be together."

"What? You think I'm not moving to college with you?" Julia asked.

Jenny laughed and snuffled. "Don't joke."

"I'm not."

"If I get into Brown, Providence isn't so far. An hour and a half."

Julia nodded. Jenny had thought this through. They were still holding hands on the table, and Jenny wouldn't let go. Julia had thought Jenny's biggest worry was what would happen with Timmy. He probably didn't have a chance at Brown, but they'd been talking about his applying to other schools in Rhode Island.

"Mom, what if I decided not to go?"

"To Brown? First of all, it's so hard to get into—I think you have a great chance, but I don't want you to get your hopes up. Also, just because Dad and I went there doesn't mean you have to. There are lots of other great choices."

"No, I mean not go to college at all."

"Why would you say that?"

Jenny shrugged. "I don't know. What if I just stayed home and worked?"

"I'd say you're giving up a really good chance at life and finding out who you are. Sorry if I sound corny and motherly, but that is my job."

"I love what we have," Jenny said. "I love being home. What if I was away and something happened to you?"

"I'm healthy. I'm going to live a long time and be a great old lady. You don't have to worry for decades and decades."

"Promise?"

"Cross my heart."

"But still . . ."

"Jenny, I know how you feel. You're making me remember exactly what it was like. I loved my parents, too. I remember some nights, lying in bed, knowing they were safe in the next room, closing my eyes tight and just wishing so hard that we could just stay like that, the way we were right then, forever."

"That's exactly how I feel."

Jenny moved her hands over the candles as if casting a spell.

"Let us be this way forever," she chanted.

"Let it be so," Julia said. "The spirits have spoken."

Jenny laughed. She seemed to shake off her dark mood, and jumped up from the table. They cleaned up the dishes, and Jenny disappeared into her room to call Timmy. The storm picked up, and wind howled off the water. The first rain started to fall, pelting the shuttered windows. The lights flickered, but stayed on.

"It's here!" Jenny said, running into the kitchen.

"Let's call Dad before the lines go down," Julia suggested. They dialed his cell, and it went straight to voicemail. Jenny left a message telling him he was missing a great time. Julia decided to try his room at the Brown Palace Hotel. The operator rang his room, and he picked up.

"We just wanted to say hi before the hurricane knocks the power out," she said.

"How's it look so far?"

"It's blowing hard."

Jenny ran to check the anemometer. "Steady forty, gusting to sixty-five so far! Can I talk to him?"

"How are the depositions going?" Julia asked.

"Good, but very busy. I'm sorry I'm not there with you," he said, but Julia felt sad because she knew he was saying it because he thought he should, not because he really meant it.

"Thanks," she said. "Hope it goes well tomorrow. Here's Jenny."

"Hey, Dad! It's howling here. Mom and I are about to go swimming again." As she spoke, Jenny watched Julia for a reaction. "Yeah, it's dark, and the waves are huge. We'll be careful." Jenny smiled. "Okay, have a good night, Dad. Too bad you're not here. I really miss you."

She hung up the phone and turned to Julia, waiting.

"Yeah," Julia said. "Let's do it."

This was just the storm's front edge—it would get much worse later. They put on dry bathing suits, but Jenny paused before running out the door. She scribbled a note, found an empty wine bottle.

"Mom, you write something, too," she said.

Julia read what Jenny had written:

Hello from Black Hall, Connecticut, USA! My mother and I are about to go swimming in Long Island Sound in Hurricane Noreen. We hope this note reaches you wherever you may be . . . hurricane currents travel far and wide. Write us back here: Julia and Jenny Hughes, P.O. Box 198, Black Hall CT 06371

Julia wrote:

Tonight we are mermaids, and the sea is ours. We're a force to be reckoned with. Mothers and daughters forever!

They sealed the note in the green wine bottle, stuck the cork in as tight as it would go, and headed down the path with flashlights, Bonnie beside them, barking at the wind.

When they reached the sand, they felt the hurricane plowing into them. Holding hands, they stood knee-deep in the surf; the tide was going out, so they walked a few more yards before dunking in. Jenny held the bottle. The waves were steady, big and beautiful, with white tops that glistened even in the darkness. Julia saw Jenny let the bottle go. It bobbed on the surface, the tide and currents sweeping it to who knew where.

They swam and dove and played in the waves. Being a beach girl had no expiration date; Julia loved the storm energy as much as Jenny did. They hadn't even brought towels. Heading home, they felt the rain wash the salt from their hair and bodies.

By the time they reached the house, the power was out. They lit candles and sat on the porch, listening to the storm build and build.

Julia held on to that hurricane memory. While Bonnie wandered through the lemon trees, Julia headed for the pool and dove in. The water cooled her skin, calmed her heart. Seeing Lion had undone her in ways she'd never expected. Visiting his house alone had made her feel like a child again, as if she'd never had Jenny. And seeing him get old, so obviously in love and longing for Graciela, had made her sad. More than anything, she still felt troubled by the talk she'd had with Roberto earlier. Five years without Jenny, and for him five without Rosa. She swam hard, doing laps, burning off the emotion. It was a saltwater pool, and closing her eyes, she could almost imagine that she was swimming in the ocean.

Coming up for breath, she treaded water, glancing around for Bonnie. Not seeing her, she whistled. The air felt soft on her skin.

She smelled lemons and pine, and listened for the sound of her collie nosing through underbrush. Instead she heard human footsteps. They stopped just outside the circle of light, and she felt someone watching her.

"Hello?" she said.

"I didn't want to disturb you." She recognized Roberto's voice before he appeared, Bonnie at his side.

"You're not," she said, although she felt self-conscious in the bright pool. It was late, at least 11 p.m., and she knew he rose early. "Did the lights wake you up?"

"No," he said. "I was waiting . . ." He hesitated. "I wasn't sleeping. I heard Bonnie outside my cabin."

"Sorry about that."

"Don't worry for me," he said. "But for Bonnie. The coyotes are out at night. I'm afraid one of them could take her down."

"Thanks for getting her," she said.

"No problem. Want me to put her in the house so you can finish your swim?"

"That's okay," she said. "I was finished anyway."

He'd walked closer to the pool, and the sparkling light reflected into his burnished face. His hair looked black and, although short, untamable. She swam to the steps, pulled the towel around her shoulders.

"Did you turn on the porch lights?" she asked.

"Yes," he said. "I saw you drive out, and thought you might be back after dark."

She nodded. She was primed to feel intruded on—she'd been so independent all these years, hiding out from the world, never expecting someone to keep the light on for her. But his tone was soft, and she felt very glad to see him. She wondered whether he felt their earlier conversation was as unfinished as she did.

"I thought you might have gone home to sleep tonight," she said. "The wind stopped blowing."

"It's true," he said. They were surrounded by silence—the trees were still, the branches and leaves unmoving. Even the waves at the foot of the cliff seemed hushed.

"So why didn't you go home?" she asked.

"I guess I wanted to stay on the property until you get used to it. It can feel very empty here alone at night." He smiled. "Besides, Bonnie needed looking after."

"I won't let her out alone at night again, I promise," she said. "Are coyotes the only predators?"

"At night there are many," he said. "*Búhos* . . . owls, but Bonnie's too big for them. But mountain lions, bobcats, *cascabeles* . . ."

"Cascabeles?"

"Tch, tch, tch," he said, shaking his index finger. "*Serpientes* . . ."

"Rattlesnakes. We saw them in the desert."

"The desert?" he asked.

She shrugged. "Field study for my master's degree."

"Well," he said, "they hunt on hot nights."

"Thanks. We'll be careful," she said, starting toward the house. He walked her to the door. His shoulder was close to hers, and she felt heat coming off his skin. "You should take a swim on your way back to the cabin," she said. "The water felt really good."

"Thank you, but . . . ," he began. They had reached the front door; she waited for him to finish his sentence, but he stopped himself and didn't seem inclined to continue. Her mind had been racing ever since their talk by the cliff, but swimming had calmed her down.

"Roberto, did you stay here tonight because you wanted to talk?" she asked.

He didn't reply, so she sat on the top step and he had no choice but to sit beside her.

"Yes, maybe," he said once Bonnie had turned in narrowing circles and settled at their feet.

"Today, on the cliff path," she said. "Jenny and Rosa."

"Sí," he said. "Our daughters. I asked, I thought . . . it is too hard for you to talk."

"I thought the same about you," she said.

"Rosa is lost," he said.

"Lost" could mean so many things. Parents said their children were lost: to drugs, to the streets, to the wrong friends. "You can help her, can't you?" Julia asked. "You're her father. She needs you."

"I think she doesn't need a father like me," he said.

"Of course she does!"

He shook his head, looked away. His face was in shadow, but she could see it etched with worry and shame.

"You don't understand," he said. "*I'm* the one who lost her."

"What do you mean?"

"You mentioned the desert. Which one did you mean?"

"The Sonoran."

"You know it?"

"Not really. I was there with a professor studying migration patterns . . . never mind. Why, Roberto? What happened?"

"We crossed from Mexico into Arizona," he said. "Through the desert. I let go of her hand, just for a minute I thought. She was hot and tired, and I told her to wait by the boulder, in the shade of the big rock, and I went ahead. We were supposed to meet a driver who'd take us to a safe house, and I wanted to find the road."

She listened, feeling chills.

"I got picked up," he said. "By the Border Patrol."

"But didn't you tell them about her? Wouldn't they have gone back to get her?"

"At first no one believed me—thought I was lying to distract them, maybe escape, I don't know. Finally, when they took me to the detention center, I got an agent to listen. He was the boss, Señor Jack Leary, and went to where I said," he said. "But she wasn't there."

"Oh, Roberto, no," Julia said.

"After I got processed and deported, I crossed back on my own. No 'coyote,' no one to guide me, I found my way to the same spot, the same boulder. But Rosa was gone."

"No!" Julia said. "Where?"

"I have no idea. It's five years, and I know she's gone, but I dream of her looking for me, circling that rock and waiting for me to come back."

"When I first asked, you said she was in Mexico."

"Sometimes I hope she is," he said. "That she survived, and she's with a good family."

"What about home in Mexico? What about her mother?"

"Her mother and I were young when Rosa was born. She left us both. Rosa doesn't know her. My grandmother was mother to her."

"Wouldn't Rosa have told someone where she was from?"

"She was only six during the crossing. I taught her the name of our town, she knew it, but my grandmother, no one in my family, has ever heard anything."

"Oh God, six years old."

"And Jenny?" He pronounced her name "Yenny."

"Sixteen."

He took her hand then, waiting, and she felt ready to tell him.

"She died in a car crash five years ago. With her father."

He held her hand tightly, waiting.

"She was driving. It happened on our road, at the end of our driveway. She was a good driver, but she missed the turn. The police think she did it on purpose."

Roberto put his arms around her. She leaned against his body and smelled his sweat and let him hold her. No one had in a long time—she couldn't stand being close to anyone—but she felt words moving between them, stories of their daughters passing from her heart to his and back.

They were so silent she could hear moths in the night-blooming jasmine vines that grew up the house columns. Distant waves crashed on the rocks below the cliff, relentless and discordant. Julia couldn't help doing the math, adding the years, and when she closed her eyes and leaned her head on Roberto's shoulder, she could feel twenty-one-year old Jenny and eleven-year old Rosa sitting on the steps beside them.

Roberto stayed for a long time. Julia didn't want to move. The longer they sat there, the more she could feel their daughters, just like in her old dream of Luna and Maria and the man with the scar seared into his face. She glanced up at Roberto, traced his cheek with her fingers. It felt smooth, no evidence of a burn.

"I used to have this dream," she said. "From the time I was young. Two little girls in Mexico, always in danger, and a man nearby to protect them."

"There's no one to protect . . . ," he began.

"But in the dream he was so real. So good. I'd feel scared for the girls . . . maybe I was one of them. But I knew he'd protect them. Us."

"You dreamed of Mexico?" he asked. "Why?"

"It means something to me, to our family. Hasn't John ever told you?"

"Señor Riley?" he asked. "No."

She hesitated, debating whether to tell him her family legend—it even connected to John's reasons for being in Ireland now—but stopped herself. The protector was just a figment of her dreams. He hadn't helped Jenny, and he couldn't help Rosa. Bringing him up to Roberto would just make her sound as crazy as she sometimes felt.

A coyote called from the hills and another answered. Bonnie growled, struggled to her feet, and Roberto caught her by the collar.

"I'd better get her inside," Julia said.

"Yes," Roberto said. "Keep her safe."

"Thank you," Julia said, opening the door.

He nodded, watched until they were inside and she'd bolted the door. She watched him through the window, making his way back toward the cabin, and she waited until he'd disappeared into the shadows before turning off the porch lights.

chapter three

Julia

The weeks went by slowly. Julia felt lazy and quiet, as if the molecules of her body were knitting together, healing the parts of her that had stayed so raw at home in Connecticut. As September rolled into October, she slept a lot, everywhere but in her bed: in a wicker chaise on the oceanfront terrace, on a blanket on Leo Carillo Beach.

After their talk, she and Roberto kept their distance. She had guarded herself for so long she felt strange and exposed—not only had she told him about Jenny, she'd listened to his story about Rosa. It haunted her—not only the horror of losing her, but the fact that nothing was resolved. He'd had no body to bury, no certain knowledge of her death.

Julia had spent a summer in the desert, south of where Roberto lost Rosa. She'd focused on that part of the world because of Uncle John, her time spent in California, her early familiarity with families who had made their way north from Central America. Meeting Roberto brought that desert time, nearly all of it spent with Jenny, back to her.

Julia had had five years of insomnia, but this time was different. Usually she relived that last morning: breakfast with Peter and Jenny, plans for riding lessons and Super Bowl errands, the ease of it all, the astonishing ordinariness of that last day. And the truth, impossible to bear even after all this time, after the proof of it, that there had been no signs that it was the end, that life as they'd all known it was over. Jenny had smiled. Julia remembered that every sleepless night: Jenny's pretty, tired smile at the breakfast table.

Peter believed—or acted as if he did—that first love was no big deal, Jenny would get through it, outgrow her feelings for Timmy, learn a lesson and be stronger for it. Julia had wanted him to be supportive of Jenny—stay up talking as long as she needed, take her side against Timmy. Jenny's heart was breaking, and she had never needed her father's love more. Peter raced off to work every day, armed for battle with his briefcase, but at home he had seemed to lose track of what they needed. Not just Julia and Jenny, but the three of them, all together, as a family.

Peter wanted to think Jenny was fine, that horseback riding would take her mind off the breakup. When Julia had gazed at her daughter across the table that morning, she'd expected to see dark crescents under her eyes, worry and anxiety and a wish the phone would ring, a constant vigilance, hoping and waiting for Timmy to come back. Instead she saw Jenny smiling, with something like relief.

All those sleepless nights when Julia had remembered Jenny's smile, she'd asked herself: if Jenny could look that way at breakfast, even for a few seconds, with laughter behind her eyes, and real humor, how was it possible for her to feel such despair just two hours later that she'd push down on the gas so hard she'd hit the wall going fifty or more?

These last weeks in Malibu had given her moments of distraction from those thoughts. Roberto's story about his daughter touched a soft, painful spot in Julia's heart. It kept her awake, thinking about Rosa and where she could be. She thought of that moment, sitting with Roberto, when she'd felt Jenny right there with her.

How close she had seemed, how real. It was almost as if the story of this little girl, separated from her father, had made Jenny materialize. Nothing in life had soothed Julia all these years, until then. She wished there was some way to help him find some comfort, too.

That morning she got up at dawn. She fed Bonnie and stood in the cozy kitchen waiting for the coffee to finish brewing. Staring out the window, she couldn't even see the fountain ten yards away: the fog was so heavy it swaddled the house and every tree in the orchard, made every object invisible to everything else.

Her aunt and uncle's kitchen was old-fashioned in the extreme, dating back to when her uncle and father had been boys. The wooden furniture was rustic, with a few pieces painted turquoise and bright yellow to match small square floral tiles set among the larger terracotta ones.

The stove and refrigerator were vintage Maytag, eggshell enamel with rounded corners. Open shelves above the tiled sink were stacked with red, blue, and green pottery plates and bowls. Ornately tooled, tarnished silver trays were displayed on a hutch containing cookware and drawers of silver flatware.

Julia stood in front of the corner bookcase. Floor to ceiling, it contained cookbooks and plastic three-ring binders. While Bonnie finished her breakfast, Julia stood with her coffee mug staring at the books. They covered decades, if not a whole century—some

looked glossy and brand-new, others had titles worn away by time
and salt air—and many were in foreign languages.

Julia knew, from previous visits, that the entire kitchen library
concerned lemons. There were texts on the design and maintenance
of lemon orchards. She found art books with drawings and paintings of lemons by Matisse, Picasso, Cézanne, Cassatt, Sargent,
Velásquez, and Goya.

There was a whole shelf devoted to women surrealist painters,
mostly Mexican, who had painted lemons: Frida Kahlo, Louise
Bourgeois, Leonora Carrington, Dorothea Tanning, and Remedios
Varo. There were histories, novels, and, especially, cookbooks with
"lemon" in assorted languages in the title: *limón, citron, limão,
citrom, λεμόνι, limone, cytryna,* and more.

Julia first gravitated to technical books regarding structure and
design of citrus groves, and Chumash Indian sites uncovered during
construction—abalone shells covered with red ochre ceremonial
paint, petroglyphs carved into a rock ledge, a steatite boiling stone.

She reached for a well-worn cookbook. Its cloth cover had been
green with gold leaf lettering, but age had turned it all brown. She
turned the pages, saw her grandmother's fine handwriting on the
flyleaf and in the margins.

Standing there, she felt the desire to make something simple that
would taste delicious—Jenny had loved baking. Julia's skin tingled,
as if Jenny were right there with her, helping her come up with a
plan to help Roberto and Rosa. She glanced outside, looking for
him, but the fog was still too thick to see.

"Come on, Bon," she said. "Let's go out."

Bonnie seemed to smile—she always looked that way, happy,
her tongue hanging out. Julia clipped on the leash, slipped a canvas
bag over her shoulder. The air was damp, but not cold like New
England fog: beneath the slight chill, she felt the land's warmth

pulling the water droplets straight off the ocean. The sun hadn't risen over the mountains, but the day's light permeated the marine layer and turned it silver.

She and Bonnie walked through the orchard, circling toward the barn and Roberto's cabin along the old rutted, unpaved service road. Walking in the ghostly mist, she felt Jenny's presence. A rabbit scampered across their path, and Bonnie let out a sharp bark.

The ranch trucks were parked in the turnaround, but she didn't see Roberto's old black Toyota Tundra. For a moment her heart sank, but then she heard the barn door creak open. She turned, smiling, expecting to see him.

"Hola, miss," Serapio said.

"Good morning," Julia said. "How are you?"

"I am fine," he said.

"Is Roberto here?" she asked.

"No," he said. "He worked many days in a row. With the fog and no wind, he take today to go home."

"Oh, okay," she said, disappointed.

"Is there something I can help with?"

"No thanks," she said. Starting to walk away, she paused. Baking muffins would prolong the sense of Jenny being with her, and she'd do anything to hold on to that.

"I'd like to borrow one of the lemon pickers," she said.

Serapio disappeared into the barn, returned a moment later with a long extendable pole that had a clipper and small basket at the top end. "When the rest of the crew comes, we can pick as many lemons as you want," he said.

"That's all right," Julia said. "I used to be pretty good at it when I was young. Let's see how I do now."

Serapio laughed, as if he could see no point in a grown woman wanting to pick lemons when she had an entire crew at her disposal.

She walked through sheets of gray cloud, the gnarled and twisted trees lining the path, their bitter fruit hanging low on the boughs. She dropped the leash to pluck the first lemon.

Another rabbit darted into the brush, but Bonnie pretended not to see. Her arthritis was too bad, and even without the excuse of the leash tugging at her throat, she didn't want to bother giving chase to an animal she had no hope of catching.

Roberto

Roberto Rodriguez lived in the back apartment of his father's house, on North Boyle Avenue. He didn't have a particular day off, but when the winds weren't blowing he put Serapio in charge and returned home to see his family. Family was everything to Roberto, the reason he had come to the United States in the first place. It seemed confusing, considering how much he missed the grandmother who had raised him—and Rosa—and all his *tíos* and *primos* in the village where he'd grown up, but he was here for them. The money he sent home helped them to survive. His grandma had cancer, and his *tía* took her to the hospital for treatment every week.

He stripped off his dusty clothes, took a shower. The walls were thin, and even with the water running he could hear the *La Reina del Sur* on television in his father's house. He dried off, pulled on fresh jeans and a white T-shirt. By habit he splashed on Polo cologne and walked outside to enter through the front door.

"Hola, Esperanza," he said to his father's wife, and leaned down to give her a kiss.

"Su papá está durmiendo," she said, giving him a hug, then returning to her knitting and the TV show.

Roberto nodded. He sat on the couch opposite Esperanza and settled down to wait. Even now, at thirty-five years old, the idea of

seeing his father warmed him. Roberto was his own man, no ques-
tion, and there was only one opinion he cared about in this world.
His father had left Mexico when Roberto was five, to come to the
States in search of a better life.

His father's snores, coming from the bedroom—the only other
room in the apartment besides the kitchen—comforted him. The
room was dark; the day was getting hot, and Esperanza had closed
the curtains to keep out the sun. The yellow walls were hung with
old photos—of Roberto's father as a young man, of Esperanza and
her mother, of Roberto's grandmother, of Roberto himself, and of
Rosa. A statue of Our Lady of Guadalupe stood in the corner surrounded by candles, but Esperanza lit them only on Sundays and
holidays.

The darkness and the sounds of his father's snoring, Esperanza's
knitting needles clicking, and the voices on TV lulled Roberto. He
felt tired from too many days without a break, and he stared at
Rosa's photo. It had been taken at school, first grade, just before
they'd begun their journey north. His grandmother had saved it and
sent it to Roberto once he'd reached L.A.

The airless room and the droning noise made his eyes heavy. He
remembered the first time his father left. He felt as if the world had
ended. Without his father there to help him and kiss him good
night, he thought he had disappeared—not just his father, but
Roberto himself. He would walk to school, but he couldn't learn,
or more that he didn't want to, and anything that seeped into his
mind happened accidentally. All he could think of was the empty
hole where he and his father used to be.

He worked hard in the fields, before and after school. His hands
were covered with calluses, and his feet hurt because his boots were
too small and they couldn't afford bigger ones. In spite of the money
his father sent home, the family never had quite enough to eat.

Roberto grew tall, and he was very thin. At eleven he was ashamed of his height. The fact the kids called him Flaco—skinny—didn't help.

Every other year his father would return. On those occasions Roberto came back to life. He could feel the excitement in the house building. His grandmother would have gotten word somehow, and the smells of good food cooking would fill the house. She didn't even have to tell Roberto; he knew by the way the worry lines around her eyes and mouth softened. His *tías*—sisters of his father—would show up with food, and everyone would wait.

No one waited better than Roberto. He would go to the edge of town, where the only road from Puebla came in, and he would sit on a rock and watch for dust in the distance, a sign that a car or bus was approaching. His heart would skip beats, more and more, till he could barely breathe. Then he would see his father's face in the window of his uncle's car or the big blue bus, and he'd jump up and follow it all the way to his grandma's house, dying to be the first one to greet his father as he stepped onto the yard.

"Papá," he called his father. It was confusing, because when his father was away, he also called his grandfather "Papá." It was almost like having two fathers—one who was there, and the real one who was only there sometimes. The real one was Roberto's king. His father would hug and kiss everyone, give small presents he had brought back from L.A., maybe something extra special like a dress for his grandmother, and then they would all have dinner.

There would be candles and music, best of all some kind of meat, not just beans and rice. His grandfather liked to drink, so there would be *cerveza*, and after many beers his grandfather would get mean and start saying things like "Why don't you send more money? Are you spending it on women? You leave your son here and we have to raise him, the least you can do is send us enough money."

His grandmother would try to soothe him but nothing worked. The *cerveza* had power over him and eventually the old man would nod off at the table and the family would carry him off to bed. After everyone cleaned up, the aunts would go home. His grandmother would say good night and go to her room, and Roberto and his father would sit on the couch.

Always, there was his father's strong arm around him, and his voice telling Roberto about the better life, and asking him about school, and work in the orchard and cornfields, and what was happening in the family. And he would tell Roberto other things, too.

"You have strength inside," his father would say. "No one can make you do anything."

"No one?" Roberto asked one time. There were many things people tried to make him do. His oldest cousin, Hernandez, was lazy, and when they were in the fields he told Roberto to do extra work while he lay in the sun or went climbing in the hills to look for hidden gold. Carlos, a boy at school, had weed and agave and was always saying he'd tell everyone Roberto was a *flaco* pussy if he didn't smoke and drink with him. These pressures were hard to resist.

"Not one person in this world," his father said. He seemed to sense the stresses Roberto was under but didn't ask for names or stories. "You have power, son. And you are the only one. Even I cannot tell you what to do."

Roberto wanted to say that wasn't true. His father could tell him anything and he would do it. His father was darker than Roberto, and stocky. He had thick black hair and a moustache, and sometimes a beard. His eyes were black, while Roberto's were brown, but there was no mistaking the fact they were father and son.

When his father was home, he worked in the field and orchard like before. Roberto wanted to skip school to be with him, but his father made him go. He never told his father about Señor Tedoro, the teacher who would rip up his papers and make fun of him in front of the class because he never got his homework right. Roberto knew it was because he worked so many hours it didn't leave enough time for study—and besides, he had no one to help him with school-work.

Other kids had mothers. Even if their fathers had gone to the United States, their mothers stayed home and cared for them. Roberto couldn't even remember his mother's smile, or the touch of her hand, or the sound of her voice—she had died when he was born. His grandmother had never finished sixth grade; his grandfather couldn't even write his own name, but made an "X" to sign papers.

So they would sit there on the couch, his father telling Roberto lessons about life, with one arm around his shoulder. Then, as Roberto grew sleepy, his father would pat his chest the way he had when he was a baby, and made the sound *ssh, ssh, ssh.* Over and over again: *ssh, ssh, ssh,* until Roberto couldn't tell the difference between his father's voice and the sound of blood coursing through his own veins, and he would fall asleep.

When he was twelve, and Geraldo, an older boy at school, started shoving him around, his father told him he needed to learn to fight. On that trip home, his father taught him to do push-ups, a hundred at a time, to run fast, and to climb trees. He told him the most important thing was to keep his eyes on his opponent, never look away. Move in fast, strike hard, use his speed. Never fake, never think it's a game—if you fight, you fight to win. After a few matches, Geraldo and his friends left Roberto alone.

Roberto didn't like to fight, but he would if he had to. His father had taught him there were many things in life a person would rather not do. But you had to survive, and one of the ways to do that was to maintain your honor.

Now, in the living room with *La Reina del Sur* filling the TV screen, Roberto looked up at Rosa's picture and wondered, as he did every time he looked at it, why he hadn't taken the biggest lesson from his father: leave his child in Mexico and go to America to work. Send home money, and visit when he could. Crossing the border had become much more dangerous during the years since his father had first left, and getting a green card, as his father had, was now almost impossible.

But Roberto hadn't been able to bear the idea of being apart from Rosa. And as beautiful as the reunions with his father had been, the long stretches of months and years in between had been unbearable. Each year his father had come home to the village wearing Polo cologne, and one time when he'd left to go back to L.A., he'd forgotten the bottle in the bathroom. Every night Roberto would open the bottle and stand there with his nose in it, just to bring back the sense of his father.

He had wanted Rosa to have more than just a few visits, a remembered scent to help her hold on to her father. He wanted her to have *him*, for them to be together. In his family, for some cursed reason, all the women in his family, except for his grandmother, left.

Adriana had run off to Mexico City, too young and wild to give up her life to be a mother to Rosa and a wife to Roberto. And Roberto's mother had died. When his grandmother was most angry at Rosa's mother for leaving, she blamed it on a curse put on the family by a bruja who lived in the hills high above the village.

Nearly every day, Roberto thought he should give up life here in the States and go home. When they were kids, he and his cousins went to school and worked hard in the fields, but when they had a moment of spare time they would run into the hills and look for more gold. Sitting in his father's dark living room, Roberto dreamed

of being there now, with Rosa, finding the gold and building a good
house and taking care of everyone.

"Hey, hijo," his father said, coming into the living room. He
wore an undershirt and baggy jeans, and his face was wrinkled
from the pillow. He never hugged Roberto anymore, hadn't since
he became a man. But being called "son" felt good, and Roberto
stood to greet him.

"Bien, bien, y tú, Papá?" Roberto asked.

"Good. You're not at work?"

"I'm going back soon," Roberto said. "Just came home to eat
and get some things."

"Eat with us," Esperanza said, putting down her knitting and
going into the kitchen.

Roberto waited for his father to sit, then followed suit. His
father's eyes were still heavy from sleep; he blinked as he used the
clicker to change the channel and find something else to watch on
TV. He stopped on a program about tigers on Discovery en Espa-
ñol. They watched the male lying in jungle shadows, his stripes
making him invisible to the gazelle. Roberto glanced at his father.
He would wait for the commercial before speaking.

He looked up at Rosa's picture. Seeing it here on the wall with
the rest of the family comforted him. He saw the sparkle of her
smile, her sheer exuberance bursting out of the frame, and it made
him believe she was out there somewhere, just waiting for him to
find her.

What was easier, knowing or not knowing, finality or crazy
hope? He thought of Julia, of what she knew about Jenny, and he
realized he wouldn't trade places with her.

Weeks later he remembered their talk. They had sat on the front
step until fog rolled in from the ocean and stars went behind the
mountain. She was *gringa, Americana,* and Roberto's English

wasn't perfect. But they had both lost daughters, and they under-stood each other. What she had for Jenny, he had for Rosa.

He pictured her blue eyes. He had never been close to anyone with eyes that color, and he thought they were strange and perfect. He wondered what color Jenny's eyes had been.

He wondered if Julia had looked into his brown eyes, or glanced down at their arms, entwined around each other, and noticed how pale her skin had looked next to his. He had lived in this country for five years, and he had worked for the Rileys part of that time, but most of his time had been spent with other Mexicans, living here in Boyle Heights, working for Americans but not hanging out with them and definitely not holding them and feeling as if their hearts were speaking, as if his knew every single thing in hers. They hadn't kissed; it wasn't like that. After a long time they'd said good night. He'd watched until she was safe inside and waited for the porch light to go out before he'd walked back to his cabin.

They had kept away from each other since. For him, it was because his feelings were too strong. For her, it might have been that she felt embarrassed for opening her heart to the man who worked in her uncle's orchard.

The commercial came on, loud music and a woman saying Pop-eye's chicken was the best. His father yawned. Roberto wanted to ask his father something. His mind was racing, but when he imag-ined putting the thoughts into words, he could hear his father giv-ing him advice. *Don't make a mistake, don't jeopardize your good job, don't imagine that she could ever feel anything real for you.*

"What is it, son?" his father asked.

"There is a lady staying at Casa Riley," he said.

"While the Rileys are in Irlanda?"

"Sí. Their niece."

"What is she like?"

"She's very nice."

"Remember she probably talks to her aunt and uncle. So make sure everything in the orchard is better than ever."

"I will."

"It is a very good job," his father said, as he always did, reminding Roberto how important it was to work—not just for him, but for the family back home. He wasn't criticizing, just reminding.

"The best," Roberto said.

"Is the niece good-looking?"

"Beautiful," Roberto said.

"And rich," his father said. "Be careful and behave yourself."

Roberto nodded. He knew his father was trying to protect him and his job. He would never understand what had happened between them, and Roberto wouldn't even try to explain.

After a while Esperanza called them into the kitchen for lunch, chicken and rice.

They ate without saying much. At one point Roberto glanced at his father and saw him watching him. It made Roberto feel uncomfortable; his father was trying to figure out what was going on. Then they both went back to their food, while in the other room the voice on TV talked about how one single tiger killed seven gazelles in a matter of minutes.

chapter four

Julia

Another week passed. It was fall, and the orchard needed a lot of tending. Julia saw Roberto working with his crew—eliminating fire hazards, cutting back brush on the hillsides, pruning low branches in the orchard, raking dry leaves and fallen bougainvillea blossoms.

The men—Roberto, Serapio, and anywhere from two to five others—worked hard each morning, then stopped for lunch in the shade of the barn at noon. Roberto was always the first to stand, brush himself off, and walk back into the orchard. He directed the guys, but did the same hard work himself. When Julia walked Bonnie, she waved and called hello, and Roberto always waved back. But he was busy, and she didn't want to bother him.

Besides, her plan was evolving. She approached it the way she had her thesis: gather information from as many sources as possible, make an outline, and seek support. In this case, her support came from Jenny. Jenny had sometimes given her a hard time about going back to school, dragging her to the middle of nowhere for fieldwork one summer, but inside she had been proud, and she'd let Julia know.

Now, sitting at her uncle's desk, Julia pored over maps of the Sonoran Desert, remembering the hot months she and Jenny had spent there with Dr. Christopher Barton and his team. Julia could almost feel Jenny perched on the desk, urging her to find Chris online. He was still on staff at Yale, but spent most of his time in the field and was currently working on a project in Honduras. Julia emailed him, but she knew how carefully he guarded his work, how reclusive he could be, and knew not to expect a reply any day soon.

The third week of October, Julia saw Serapio in charge of the men, so she knew Roberto had left the property. He returned early two days later, his dusty black truck pulling up to the barn, headlights soft in the predawn fog. As she watched from the kitchen window, her heart was racing. She hadn't said a word to him about what she'd been doing, but today she felt ready.

Once she heard the sprinklers start and saw him walking through the grove, she stepped outside and waved. Bonnie met him halfway down the path, her tail wagging.

"Good morning," she said.

"Good morning. You and Bonnie are up early," he said. It was still mostly dark, the day's first light penetrating the fog.

"We like early mornings," she said. "It must have been good to be home last night."

"Sí," he said.

"Are you married?" she asked.

"No," he said. "I live in my father's house. Well, in my own apartment."

She smiled, surprisingly happy. "Do you have time for coffee?"

"Sí, gracias," he said. "But . . ." He glanced at his boots, well worn and flaked with dirt and grass.

"Oh, don't worry," she said. "Bonnie and I track in the whole outdoors."

He hesitated on the threshold for a moment; she wondered if it felt strange to him. Then he came through the door. She gestured at the kitchen table, and he took a seat as she poured coffee into blue mugs. She drank hers black, but put out cream and sugar for him.

"You've seemed so busy," she said.

"Yes, this time of year there's a lot to do."

He looked around the kitchen, seeming to take in the pictures, beams, books, and copper pans in a more leisurely way than before.

"Don't you come in here often?" she asked.

"No," he said. "Señor Riley and I usually talk in the orchard. There's no reason for me to be in the house."

"I see," she said.

He spooned three sugars into his coffee, added cream, sipped. "Delicious," he said, beaming. He had beautiful white teeth, but was missing one toward the back on the right side.

"This was very nice of you," he said. "You didn't have to invite me."

"I wanted to."

"You're my boss while the Rileys are gone," he said. "You don't have to do this." Maybe he saw her expression change, her face fall, because he spoke quickly: "But I'm glad you did. Gracias, Julia."

She looked down, aware of how tenuous her plan felt. So far it had all been in her head—a way of keeping Jenny close. Madwomen behaved this way, talking to their dead children, holding them near.

"Julia, what's wrong?" he asked.

"There's something I wanted to speak to you about," she said.

"Okay," he said.

She met his gaze. Was this rude, intrusive? She'd lost perspective.

"Roberto, would you tell me everything you can about Rosa and your crossing?"

He squinted—pain and confusion in his eyes. "I told you," he said.

"I know," she said. "But I want to know more."

"I thought . . . ," he began.

"Thought what?"

"That I had upset you with what I already said. That you must have decided what kind of man I am, who would lose his daughter in the desert."

"It wasn't your fault," she said.

"How do you know?" he asked angrily.

Julia stayed silent. She thought of Jenny and Rosa, their two lost girls, and of the study she had begun, slowly and methodically and inspired by Jenny, to search for Rosa.

"I just know," she said.

"You want to hear what really happened?" he asked. "Okay. But it's—it's the worst thing."

"Roberto, I've already lived through the worst thing."

He nodded, touched her hand as if remembering Jenny.

And then he started telling the story.

Roberto
MAY 2007

Roberto and Rosa had traveled by bus from Puebla to Mexico City to Hermosillo and finally to Altar, just south of the U.S. border from Nogales. The buses were hot and crowded and Rosa was carsick. She held her doll, Maria. Roberto's grandmother had made it for her, sewn on angel wings, and said Maria had magical powers to protect her and her father.

While Rosa held Maria, Roberto held Rosa on his lap, hand on her forehead, telling her stories about when he was little and he and his cousins would go searching for treasure in the hills.

"And you found it," she said, because this was a favorite story.

"Well, there were a few gold coins," he said. "We imagined that the stones were gold, too. Once we did find an old statue, small and round, an old man. My grandfather said he was a thousand years old."

"Why didn't you take me looking?"

"Always working, *preciosa*, and not enough time," he said, holding her tighter. Working nearly round the clock for nothing, barely enough to feed himself and his daughter, or support his grandmother's medical care.

"Will it be different where we're going?" she asked.

"El Norte," he said.

He could only dream how different it would be. He'd grown up working in the fields from dawn until eight, when he went to school, then after school until dark, never enough time for homework. He was smart, and so was Rosa, but he didn't want her to endure the same shame, never being prepared for class, falling asleep on her desk because she was so exhausted from work.

His family and everyone in their small pueblo tended a rich man's orchard and cornfields. As a child, Roberto and his cousins planted the seeds—his grandfather was already training Rosa to do the same thing. When they got older, they used the plow, learned to harvest, prepared shipments for market. Staring at Rosa, he knew he'd do anything to keep her from working that hard, dropping out of school at sixteen, the way he had.

The bus chugged along, spewing carbon monoxide through the cabin. People had windows open but there was no getting away from the smells of sweat, beer, chickens, and dirty feet.

"Papá, I feel sick," she said.

"Where's the picture?" he asked, to distract her.

"In my pocket," she said weakly.

He reached in, and pulled it out to show her: there they were, Roberto and Rosa and his grandma, standing under a lemon tree. She touched the photo and smiled.

"That's us," he said. "And Abuela. Smell the lemons, Rosa? How beautiful and fresh? Remember how you help me pick them, what a good girl . . ."

"Sí, Papá," she said. "But I miss Abuela."

"The picture will help us remember her," Roberto said. "And when you look at it, you'll know how much she loves us and how much I love you."

"Gracias, Papá, te amo."

"Te amo, Rosa."

"But I still feel sick."

He slid the photo back into her pocket. "Then let's think about where we're going. Everything will be better. Easy to get work, good jobs, and I come home to you every night, I pick you up at school."

"Not helping," she said, turning pale green. Roberto held his hands near her mouth, ready to catch if she threw up. "Tell the good part, not the work part."

"Okay," Roberto said. He closed his eyes, and the image felt like a dream—he'd never seen it himself, only heard about it from his father. "We're going to live next to a public square, the most special and magical square in all of Los Angeles. But instead of angels or fairies, there are . . ."

"Mariachis!" Rosa said. "In their black suits and hats, white braids on their shoulders, brass buttons, and all their instruments. They're always there." She smiled and closed her eyes as if remembering the many times Roberto had told her about his father's neighborhood. She'd loved hearing about mariachis as if they were archangels instead of normal workingmen. "Why are they always there, Papá?"

"Waiting to be hired. Restaurants and people having parties need mariachis, so the men wait in one spot until someone drives by and picks them up."

"Will they play music for us?"

"Grandpa says we'll be able to hear it from the porch every day, every night."

"I want to hear them," Rosa said, bouncing on his knee. "And see Grandpa again. Does he know we're coming?" She had looked forward to Roberto's father's infrequent visits to Mexico nearly as much as Roberto had.

"Oh, yes. He helped make the arrangements. We have a good coyote, Rosa. Grandpa made sure of it."

She nodded, resting her head on Roberto's chest. The bus bumped and swayed, but she'd stopped fighting the movement, and let herself be rocked to sleep. She didn't question the concept of "coyote." Even though the fields and hills around their town were full of the animals, who howled at night and stole into barns to kill chickens, she'd known since she could talk that "coyote" meant a guide, a person who would help them cross the Mexican-U.S. border with as little chance as possible of getting caught by the Border Patrol or ICE—U.S. Immigration and Customs Enforcement.

The bus rumbled into the next town. It was dark and Rosa didn't wake up, even though church bells were tolling seemingly overhead, when he carried her into the next bus—smaller than the last and filled with more people. It was a fight to get seats.

Roberto clutched Rosa and their small bag and tried to rest. The ride went on all night. They sat near the back, where he could smell the exhaust and feel the engine's heat. Still, he knew he had to sleep. The next days would be long and hard, and he needed to stay strong to take Rosa across the border.

Thinking of her kept him from feeling too scared. He had never crossed before. His father and aunt and several cousins had; some, like his father, more than once. He had always kept his father's stories in his mind, like fairy tales, but now they were all coming true, and Roberto and Rosa were about to live them. Tomorrow, when they got to Altar, his cousin Miguel would meet them and help them through the next step.

He reached into Rosa's pocket to pull out the photo she carried of them. Mexico, home, the place they knew and loved. His throat tightened and he tried not to cry. This journey had to be the right thing. He couldn't stand Rosa growing up hungry the way he had. He slid the picture back into her pocket, and just before dawn broke, he slept.

Altar was their last stop in Mexico. Roberto and Rosa woke up the minute they heard the bus's squeaky brakes, felt the vehicle come to a stop. They filed off with all the other people, standing in the town square, blinking into the morning light. They might as well have had a sign saying *Pollos*—the nickname for border crossers—pinned to their shirts; the coyotes were circling. Roberto scanned the crowd for Miguel.

"Atlanta, Chicago, Nueva York, I get you there."

"San Diego, Los Angeles, San Francisco, I am the best."

Rosa clutched his neck. They had stopped in several town squares along the way north, to drink water and change buses, but this felt different. He could feel Rosa picking up on this new energy, frantic with predators and prey. He spotted the Centro Comunitario de Atención al Migrante y Necesitado, a free shelter for migrants and the needy—his father had told him about it. There were stalls set up everywhere, selling backpacks, water, and food.

"Hey, man," a short, stocky, dark-skinned Mexican with a full

Zapata moustache said, coming up to him and Rosa. "You have a pretty little girl there. You want to get her safely across, I'm your guy. I know the best way. Not all coyotes are good, and there are bandits out there, just looking for beautiful girls. I keep you safe. Where you want to go?"

"I'm meeting my cousin," Roberto said. "But gracias." He watched the Zapata moustache walk away, join up with three other men. They glanced toward Roberto, but when they saw him staring back, they looked quickly away. He felt the delicate balance, showing respect to a man he couldn't trust, but making his eyes hard so the coyote and his friends would see he'd cut them if they touched Rosa.

The church, Nuestra Señora de Guadalupe, with a cross atop its dome, stood across the square, many pilgrims entering and exiting, blessing themselves. Bells rang; Mass was about to start. He held Rosa's hand and started toward the steps.

"Hey, *primo*," his cousin Miguel called. They hugged each other, and then Miguel spoke to Rosa. "You're so grown up! Last time you were just a tiny baby in your father's arms. Now you're a princess."

"Gracias," Rosa said, looking at her father to make sure it was okay. Roberto nodded.

"Miguel is our cousin," he said. "He grew up in the same town where we live."

"But now you're on your way to the States, and I've set it all up." Miguel lowered his voice, and Roberto set Rosa on the hard ground so they could talk. She knew not to stray far; he watched her find a stick, then crouch to draw pictures in the dirt.

"You got the money?" Miguel asked.

"Four thousand U.S.," Roberto said. "Half now, half when we get across."

"That's all you have?"

"I'm keeping an extra fifty."

"Hide it well—if they find it, they'll take it."

"Gracias, primo."

"Okay, now you stock up. You need two gallons of water per day per person. Dry meats, too. That's a lot for you to carry, with the niña, too . . ."

"We'll be fine."

"It's hot as hell during the day, but cold at night. You got the right clothes for that?"

"Sí. Papá told me already."

"You could be walking for four days."

"Sí. Yo lo se tambien. Where's the coyote?"

"I pay him," Miguel said. "Give me the money and I introduce you."

"Why don't I pay him?"

"*Primo*, I got you the best coyote. He will take you right away, no staying overnight in a flea-infested *casa de huéspedes*."

Roberto had heard all about them, the stash houses where coyotes kept the *pollos* waiting, up to fifty people in a room. The free shelter was nicer and cleaner, his father had said, but better to stay with the coyote and be ready to leave at a moment's notice.

"The money, *primo*," Miguel said, his hand out.

It rankled Roberto; Miguel was a middleman, matching people with coyotes. He received a cut of the fee and showed no favoritism toward his family. The only benefit was that he'd make sure Roberto and Rosa were taken care of, with the best and most knowledgeable guide, someone who knew the desert bandits well enough to intimidate them from attacking his group.

Roberto and Rosa bought supplies while Miguel waited impatiently. Roberto used half of his extra fifty dollars to buy water and dried beef, sunscreen and a sun hat for Rosa, as well as a sling to carry the heavy water bottles on his back and around his neck. Trying it out, following Miguel across the plaza in the hot sun, he felt like one of his grandfather's oxen and tried not to worry about carrying all this weight through the desert.

"Can I help?" Rosa asked.

"Just take care of Maria," he said. "That will be your job."

"Okay," she said, clutching her doll.

Miguel led them to a truck normally used for transporting livestock. The cab was rugged and old, and the back was fenced in, open to the sky. Already it was nearly full. Some of the passengers were Honduran and Guatemalan, but most were from Mexico. They had been straggling in over the last few days, but the coyote wanted to wait until the truck was full before starting north.

"Okay, now come with me," Miguel said.

Skirting the truck, they walked to a small bar with a front porch. Two men sat in rocking chairs surveying the entire plaza. One was about Roberto's age, the other closer to his father's. They wore faded red shirts and shiny lizard boots. He took in the darkness of their skin, their hooked noses, and their beards and knew they were father and son.

"Hey, *cholo*," the father said to Miguel. "What you bring me?"

"Dos pollos—mis primos, eh? Here's the money," Miguel said, counting out the wad still damp with Roberto's sweat. He handed it over with pride, as if the cash were his and represented years of work and saving.

"Two thousand, that's all you got?" the father asked Roberto.

"Sí, Señor. For me and my daughter. Half now, half later."

"It's two thousand for you, three thousand for la niña," the son said.

Roberto flashed with anger and panic, looked at Miguel. "You said four altogether."

Everyone but Roberto and Rosa laughed. "He's just fucking with you, *primo*," Miguel said.

"Yes, this little angel travels for three. We charge extra because she needs special protection, which we give. Some we charge more, but because you're Miguel's *primo,* well. We give a discount, so your full cost is four thousand. When you get to L.A., maybe you decide to give us a present, maybe an extra five hundred U.S."

"Not up front?" Roberto asked, suspicious.

"No. En serio," the father said. "We try to keep families together. That's why we're the best. We know the way through the desert, over the border, past any *pinche* bandits and Border Patrol—sorry for the bad word, *preciosa,*" he said to Rosa, "all the way to the road where a car will pick you up and take you straight to Los Angeles to your father's house."

"You know my father?"

"My brother helped him cross," the father said. "I told you— family is everything to us. We have helped many Rodriguezes over the years. Ask my name."

"Como te llamas?" Roberto asked.

"Alberto Rodriguez. And this is my son Benito Rodriguez. Perhaps we are related by blood, but for sure we are related by the four-grand total you pay me to get you across. You have my word on that."

"Gracias," Roberto said.

"And now we leave for the first part of the trip. The truck is full, it's time to go."

"Okay," Roberto said. His heart lightened a little. Alberto's words had sounded sincere and true. His father had already told him about this coyote family and warned him never to turn his back, never to trust: all coyotes, even the best ones, were smugglers, in it only for the money.

Never forget, hijo, his father had said, *when you're in the desert and the choice is between your life and his, he will choose his.*

Alberto, Benito, and a third man climbed into the cab. Roberto hoisted Rosa up into the truck bed, then pushed the water jugs after her, and gave his cousin a last hug.

"Buena suerte. Call me when you get to Los Angeles!" Miguel said, with a huge smile that reassured Roberto even more.

"Gracias, primo. Adiós!"

And the truck started up with a roar—the cab might look old, but someone had tricked out the engine, made it very powerful. Roberto put his arm around Rosa, felt the kick of the truck as it started down the main road. Their fellow passengers were settling in too, keeping to themselves, not yet making eye contact. Roberto counted the people, all crammed together.

There were twenty-one travelers, counting him and Rosa. He had twenty-five dollars in the heel of his boot. That, plus the canvas sack and their clothes, were the only material things he carried. The sun beat down, sickeningly hot on their heads and arms.

Roberto shaded Rosa with his body. One man, already unable to take the heat, pulled a knife from his belt and cut the long sleeves off his shirt. He threw them away, into the back of the truck, but Roberto caught them and shoved them into his backpack. You never know what you might need. In that moment he looked up at the blue sky and whispered *suerte*—luck—as the truck rolled out of town and headed for the borderline between Mexico and Arizona.

Julia

They sat in the kitchen, Julia so lost in the tale that when he said the word *suerte*, "luck," she could almost believe that he'd had it, called it forth, that they were five years in the past and their daughters both still with them. She hugged her arms around herself, knowing this was just the story's beginning.

"I know that area," she said.

"*Mande?*" he asked—"What?"

"The Sonoran Desert."

"You said. Hard to believe you ever set foot in that place."

"I was doing research for my thesis."

He stared at her as if he didn't understand. She refilled their coffee mugs just to give her hands something to do. They were shaking because she was remembering the summer she'd been in the desert, when Jenny was ten. Once she'd set the mugs down on the table, she started telling him.

Jenny had been upset to be away from Black Hall and all her friends for July and part of August, baking in tents with only a few special mother-daughter weekends away from the other researchers, in cozy inns in Santa Fe, New Mexico; Marfa, Texas; and San Miguel de Allende in Mexico.

"Mom, I need the beach!" Jenny kept saying. "Beach girls don't belong in the desert. It's summer—where's the water?"

"I know, Jen," Julia said. "Just your luck to have a mother who waited this long to go to grad school."

"I just want to go home to the beach," Jenny said.

"This is part of my schoolwork," Julia said "I could have come alone and left you with Daddy, but I wanted you with me. I wanted you to see the desert."

"It's kind of cool," Jenny said grudgingly. "Did Daddy want me to go?"

"We both want you with us," Julia said. "But he understood."

Jenny was a savvy ten-year old. She loved her father, but she knew he worked all the time. The best lawyer in a small, wealthy town, he had constant and varied work, and he was much in demand on the golf course and tennis courts. If Jenny had stayed home in Black Hall, there would be babysitters every day.

"See?" Julia asked.

Their tent was semi-permanent, made of green canvas. Julia loved it—how rustic it was, how close she slept to Jenny, the canopy of stars from horizon to horizon at night. She loved that she was showing her daughter self-sufficiency and an exciting side of academia. It made her sad, but she even enjoyed the fact her husband wasn't there.

She and Peter still loved each other, but that made the rest hurt even more. They were good parents and decent partners. They fought, but in private, where Jenny couldn't hear. They cared about each other—but in the way friends, or brothers and sisters, might.

Some nights, lying in bed beside Peter, she wanted so much more than easygoing conversation and a quick kiss before bed and sex that felt almost impersonal, more indifferent than passionate. Julia wanted to attack him—not just sexually, but in anger. The rage was powerful, and scared her.

The team was excavating the edge of a mesa where a civilization had once thrived. The mound, known as the Uto-Aztecan Site, contained remnants of a culture—hunting, building, and cooking instruments, caves painted with scenes of tribal movement, the hunt, and Spanish domination. While archaeologists uncovered and catalogued artifacts, Julia and her fellow anthropologists studied the culture, tried to understand the various tribes who had passed through this space—to understand what had caused them to move here.

Jenny had brought her dolls from home, and Julia watched her stage battles against the conquistadors. She had no doubt that her girl dolls would prevail against the armed men on horseback. At night they lit their tent with lanterns and would play on the wood floor, raised up about six inches from the ground, trying to ignore the crawling and slithering noises they heard below. They had seen one rattlesnake at the site, a hundred yards away, but Julia knew the desert night was filled with plenty of other poisonous snakes and insects.

"The Spaniards had every advantage," Julia said. "They rode in blasting. So the Indians had to be shrewd, use their knowledge of the land, to protect their families."

"This girl," Jenny said, intent at play, "found one of the Spaniards' swords." She used a spike they'd cut from a prickly-pear cactus earlier. "And when the conquistadors ride in at night, she fights like this!" Jenny waved the spear over her doll's head. "The girls are too small, so they use magic to help them. All the witches come down the mountain and fight the bad men with their powers, and they win! The invaders are dead and can't hurt anyone anymore."

Julia nodded, and while she helped Jenny form a burial mound among their dirty clothes, she knew the truth of history had gone the other way. The occupants of this mesa had been wiped out in less than a month. Her archaeologist colleagues had found graves filled with ancient bones and skulls, even those of children and infants. She did her best to keep Jenny away from the burial sites, but Jenny was wily, and had spied them as the scientists examined and measured tiny femurs and tibiae and rib bones.

"Ready for sleep?" Julia asked when Jenny had tucked her dolls in for the night.

"What if they come back?" she asked.

"Who?"

"The bad guys. The conquistadors."

"They won't. They've been dead for centuries."

"Their ghosts, then."

"Well, we have our cactus swords to fight them off," Julia said.

"We can protect ourselves," Jenny said. "Even without Daddy."

"Yes, we can," Julia said.

"I know he didn't want to come," Jenny said, "but I wish he'd wanted us to stay home with him."

Julia tried not to react to Jenny's words. Had Jenny, always hypersensitive to Julia's thoughts and feelings, sensed the relief she felt being away from Peter? Or had Jenny sensed her father pulling away, too? Either way, it made Julia sad.

"Why don't you draw him a picture, and we'll both write him letters, and send them out tomorrow?"

"He'll be so glad to hear from us."

"He will," Julia said.

The next day they wrote letters to Peter and handed them to Lupe Alvarez, Dr. Chris Barton's assistant, to put in the mail pouch. Chris was lead anthropologist on the project, and he'd brought many of his students, including Julia, from Yale. Chris's wife, Maxine, and their two kids had come along, so he'd welcomed Jenny and other students' children.

Older kids took turns babysitting, running a sort of summer camp. They drew cave paintings in the sand, scratched petroglyphs on small rocks, sat around the campfire at night, and told ghost stories. The sky was endless, the stars so close, and every night Jenny wished on the first star that her parents wouldn't get divorced. Julia knew because Jenny always made the wish in a stage whisper.

Julia longed to reassure Jenny that that would never happen. But deep inside she wasn't sure what she wanted. Watching Chris and Maxine, she found herself dreaming of a good marriage, two people

who not only supported each other but shared their deepest interests—that's where she and Peter had gone wrong. At night, when
the kids were staring up at the stars and making up stories about
the constellations, Julia would watch Chris slip his arm around
Maxine, watch her rest her head on his shoulder.

One night she heard music coming from their tent and peeked
out to see them dancing in the dark, thinking they were alone.
She'd felt ashamed but had been unable to keep from watching.
The desert night was cold, but Maxine wore a silk slip nightgown;
it glistened in the dark. Chris wore jeans and was bare-chested.
They danced for a long time, and Julia saw the tenderness between
them. When they kissed, it was anything but tender, so she inched
back into her tent and hoped they didn't hear the zipper coming
down.

As she lay rigid in her tent, with Jenny breathing softly in her
sleep a few feet away, tears burned her cheeks. She remembered the
first Campus Dance with Peter, on the Brown green with colorful
paper lanterns glowing all around. It had started to rain, coming
down hard, drenching her dress and his suit, and they'd kicked off
their shoes and pressed so close against each other that they'd felt
naked in the downpour.

Like Chris and Maxine, Julia and Peter had fallen in love in college. How had the Bartons' marriage stayed good while Julia's had
drifted into something so dull? Peter used to hold her face in his
hands and stare into her eyes as if he wanted to enter her, become
one person sharing skin and bones. *Forever,* he'd say. *Forever,* she'd
respond.

She knew it was her fault. She had tried to be too "good"—had
put her own interests on hold so Peter could go to law school first.
Somehow they'd gotten the idea that his work was important and
hers was inconsequential. Peter had fallen into law school almost

by default—he'd finished college without any better plan—while Julia had dreamed of Yale, travel, following the teachings of Ruth Benedict and Margaret Mead, and studying other cultures her entire life.

Peter understood on an intellectual level, but by the time Julia actually entered grad school, he was living the life of a shoreline lawyer—he wanted her to golf and play tennis with him, have dinner parties with other lawyers and people who belonged to the Black Hall Beach Club, instead of devoting herself to rigorous study.

"We've outgrown that," he said. "We busted our asses in college—now we can relax."

"What are you talking about?" she asked. "I haven't outgrown anything—this is what I love."

"I know you love reading about anthropology, and there's no reason we can't take an Abercrombie and Kent trip to Machu Picchu—or Samoa, wherever it was Margaret Mead studied, wherever you want to go. But you don't have to prove anything."

"I know," she said.

"So why, when everything here is perfect, are you taking this on?"

"Because when I told you I wanted to be an anthropologist," she said, "I meant it. Luxury travel isn't the same thing."

"You don't have to be sarcastic," he said.

She agreed and apologized. But she kept at her work, knowing Peter considered it unnecessary and inconvenient, and slowly they began to have quite a different marriage than the one they'd started with.

Now, talking to Roberto, she told him about being in the desert with Jenny, how she and Peter had never been the same after that.

"We stayed together," she said. "But we were not happy."

"But you had so much," Roberto said.

"It seems that way," she said. "And we did in many ways. But not enough of the right things."

"What are the right things?" he asked.

"I don't know how to put it—we were broken. We were good parents to Jenny, but we weren't good enough to each other. We stopped loving each other the way we used to. Before he died, we were planning to divorce."

"You don't believe marriage is forever?"

"Not when there's too much hurt."

He nodded, as if he understood something about that.

"What about you?" she asked to cover her awkwardness. "Do you have a girlfriend, are you with someone?"

"No," he said. "No one."

They drank coffee as the sun rose higher over the mountain, filling the lemon grove with a golden glow. Julia's stomach flipped; they'd gotten off course, and she still hadn't told him her plan. Serapio walked from behind the barn, obviously looking for Roberto. A rattletrap Honda pulled up, and three workers climbed out and stretched.

"Time for work," Roberto said.

Julia paused. She knew she could have gotten him to stay—he would have considered it impolite to walk out while she was talking. But thinking about Peter had made her more emotional than she'd expected; all she wanted was a long walk on the beach with Bonnie. She could tell Roberto the rest later.

"Thank you for the coffee," he said.

"Thank you for talking to me," she said.

He paused, as if he wanted to say something more, but instead turned and walked into the orchard.

Lion

Lion knew the last week of October meant craziness in Malibu. When had people started decorating their houses as if for some kind of warped orange-and-black Christmas, trying to outdo each other with hideous and cheap commercially produced ghosts and goblins? Where was the originality? Half the town worked in the industry—if they were going to do it up, they might as well have Industrial Light and Magic come in and create a worthy spectacle.

For Lion, living in a crumbling mansion of dusty dreams, he saw no reason to gild the lily. Decorating for Halloween wasn't for him. He had the money to hire a studio set decorator and create a true haunted house, but it seemed a waste. If he felt like it, he'd dress up like Dracula on the actual night and hand out Italian chocolates. This might be the very year he'd do just that. His mood had changed recently.

Having Julia just across the mountains made Lion feel young again. Perhaps it was because of all the happy times she'd spent with him as a little girl, when he was dashing, daring, and indestructible the way only certain youthful male movie stars can be.

In those days he could walk down the beach at the Malibu Colony and be one hundred percent sure every eye was on him and every whisper was about him. What an ass he'd been! To think back and remember that level of hubris—God, a midday vodka was in order. He poured Grey Goose into a Steuben glass tumbler and toasted himself in the mirror, gray hair and all.

Julia had always kept him grounded. To her, he was just Uncle Lion. The fact he'd sometimes show up in a movie or in a magazine amused and delighted but never impressed her. She might not realize this now, but she was just the medicine he needed. With Graciela away, and his star fading a little more every awards season when he saw all the new faces up for nominations, he'd been feeling down on himself and his absurd profession.

But all he had to do was call, and Julia would come over or invite him to the Casa. It was lovely, the way he imagined it might be if he and Graciaela had a grown daughter. Today was gray and quite chilly. It called for a wood fire, which he built himself—the legacy of his New Hampshire boyhood. He'd called to ask Julia what she was doing, and she said she was in the midst of a project.

"How industrious!" he said.

"It is, sort of," she said.

"You intellectuals," he said. "Why don't you come over here and work on it? It will make me feel so smart just to watch you."

She'd laughed and said she'd be right over.

Julia brought her laptop and a stack of books and maps and set herself up in his study. The fire crackled on the hearth. Bonnie lay in canine bliss staring at shapes in the flames. Perhaps she imagined they were badgers to chase through the woods. Lion saw the same licks of fire and imagined they were his enemies in hell, all the actors who'd gotten the roles and awards that should rightfully have been his.

He sighed happily.

"What are you thinking?" Julia asked.

"Nothing. Just evil things."

She smiled and went back to her laptop, clicking away on the keyboard. He set out the backgammon board and she didn't even look up.

"You're not even slightly curious about the wicked thoughts rattling around in my head?"

"Do you want to tell me?" she asked, leaning on her elbows and finally giving him some attention.

"Yes. I am remorseless. I'm filled with resentment for everyone who has more than I, and I imagine terrible things happening to them."

"Who has more than you, Lion?" she asked kindly, and he could tell she meant it. He felt a twinge of shame.

"Oh, darling, don't listen to me. I'm just feeling sorry for myself."

"Material things don't make you happy," she said. "Right?"

"Right. And what are those awards"—he cast a glance toward the mantel, where his one Oscar, several Golden Globes, and one Palme d'Or stood amid framed photos of various leading ladies—"but objects that will outlive all of us?"

"Why are you so blue, Lion?"

"I didn't think I was," he said. "Having you here makes me happy. But I suppose it also reminds me of who I am missing."

"Shall we say her name?"

"No," he said. "Let me maintain the fiction that you suspect nothing. But we can toast her." He raised his vodka and she raised her coffee and they drank to Graciela.

"Love in any form is still love," Julia said.

Sometimes she surprised him. He knew of her deep grief, had seen it pouring off her skin, and realized she had closed her heart to all but family and the closest friends. But then she could say something like that.

"What are you doing there?" he asked, gesturing at her books and laptop.

"Revisiting some old research, mainly. Remember the year Jenny and I went to the desert in Mexico?"

"Of course. Your uncle was very proud of you, getting your master's. I was worried about scorpions crawling into your sleeping bags."

Julia laughed.

"Are you writing an article?"

"No, I'm mainly remembering what it was like to be in the Sonoran Desert. Retracing my steps, in a way."

"Hm," Lion said, watching her go back to work. Retracing one's steps—he was familiar with that activity. Only he called it obsession. Well, that might be overly dramatic, but he did find himself reliving moments spent with Graciela. If he closed his eyes, could he feel Graciela beside him? Could he touch her face, kiss her throat? Could he hear her whisper, "Why can't humans be allotted two great loves in the same moment, at the same time?"

"Oh Lord," he said out loud, causing Julia to glance up in surprise. She smiled, as if she knew he was dreaming. The truth was, he felt sick of Graciela's poetic words about two great loves. John and Lion, he got it. But he wanted to be her one and only—he always had. He didn't feel her presence, couldn't hear her voice, couldn't laugh with her.

He wondered why Julia was reliving old days in the Mexican desert. Did re-creating those weeks of research somehow bring Jenny back? Lion stared at her, bent in concentration over the computer screen, and knew they were survivors on the same ship— floating on the open sea without the people they loved most.

Julia

Halloween passed, and Julia felt relieved. She'd had to steel herself for the day itself. Jenny had always loved Halloween, and in the last years of her life had taken to hanging tiny ghosts made from cut-up worn white pillowcases from the dead elm in the middle of her meadow.

Malibu seemed festive and celebrated the holiday with many

lights and decorations on houses all along the Pacific Coast Highway, and in the Malibu Country Mart, and with tons of pumpkins piled around the Feed Bin at the foot of Topanga Canyon. Julia stocked up on candy, but no trick-or-treaters made their way up the long driveway to Casa Riley.

The weather had been chilly for about a week, but now the sun was beaming again, every day in the mid-eighties. Julia received a letter from John saying how much he enjoyed being in Ireland during the fall; the cold rain was inspiring him to stay in the library and write. She also received a letter—not just an email—from Chris Barton.

She had written to him about Roberto and Rosa, told him all she knew so far, and asked if he had any ideas on who might have information about a migrant child who had been lost in the desert.

Dear Julia,

What a pleasure to hear from you after all this time. I keep waiting to see your application for an associate position in the department, but so far no go. Sorry for taking so long to get back to you. I've gone from the desert to the jungle, and electronics are no more workable here than they were in Sonora. In a sense I'm backtracking from our expedition, into Mayan culture and various expansions, but this isn't a scholarly paper, so we'll leave that for now.

There are a few places you can try in your search for Rosa. I'm sorry, but the first is obvious: the Pima County Medical Examiner's Office. Assuming your migrants crossed west of Nogales, Arizona, the desert is brutal and takes more lives than it spares. The morgue has a terrible backlog, but I'm sure would be helpful if you could provide the right information.

Five years have passed—a long time not to hear news of the child, if indeed she survived. If she had, her father's illegal status would make it difficult, if not impossible, for the authorities to contact him.

Knowing the name of the Border Patrol agent who detained Roberto and went to look for Rosa is helpful. He will have records of that search, and may be willing to share them with you. I would try him, or his supervisor, and see what you can come up with.

Another option—it might sound more hopeful but is not necessarily—would be the Reunion Project. It is located in La Jolla, California, and I highly recommend you visit my colleague there—Dr. Juan Rios. He is an applied anthropologist who went into forensics after so many migrants began dying in the desert and mountains. He gathers data from morgues, Border Patrol alerts, and individuals looking for information about family members or friends. His goal is to bring people together—alive if possible, but if not, and more often, so they can bury the remains of their loved ones.

I hope this helps.

Maxine is back in Connecticut right now but will be joining me for the holidays. I'm sure it's a long shot, but if you find yourself hankering to lay your eyes on a seventh-century Mayan tomb, come down and see us. The kids will be here, too. You'll never believe it, but Henry is working with me. Remember how bored he was eleven years ago? I'll never forget Jenny getting him to scratch out a petroglyph in her rock collection— he drew an eagle, and was quite happy. The only time we really saw him enjoy himself that summer—he was dead set on making us regret bringing him along. He finished Harvard last spring and is taking a year to decide what's next.

Anyway. Call Juan—I'll write him and tell him to be
expecting you.

                                        Fond regards,
                                        Chris

She followed Chris's advice and sent an email to Juan Rios. She also reached out to the U.S. Border Patrol, asked for Jack Leary, and was told that he had retired. She decided to wait until she heard back from Dr. Rios before talking to Roberto again.

They always waved and called hello, had short conversations about the weather or Bonnie or the property. During the cold week, she'd seen him in a heavy jacket, walking through the orchard to check every tree. He would stand at the base, laying his hand on the trunk, gazing up into the branches as if looking at each leaf, each lemon.

They hadn't had frost, but she remembered from childhood that citrus was sensitive, and she knew he was monitoring the fruit for possible damage. He made his survey each morning after dawn and each night just at twilight, so she got used to seeing him striding through the orchard, touching each tree as if greeting an old friend, making sure all was well.

A six-foot-high stone wall surrounding the pump had mysteriously cracked along the base. Perhaps there had been an earthquake that Julia hadn't felt, or maybe the concrete was just old. One morning in early November, when the sun was hot again, she walked Bonnie along the coast path and heard the whir of a power saw.

Heading in the direction of the noise, she saw that Roberto was building a wooden frame to prop up the wall. He had constructed the brace to rest firmly on the ground, with lengths of two-by-fours angled up to the wall's top. When he finished nailing the last board, he wiped his forehead with a bandanna and turned to the masonry tools he'd set out.

She crouched in the shade with Bonnie, petting her fur and

thinking of Jenny. Jenny had always helped untangle the burrs and twigs caught in Bonnie's lovely, lush coat. Sitting quietly, Julia worked out some of the brambles while Bonnie panted contentedly beside her. They watched Roberto work alone; she wondered where Serapio and the others were.

He was tall with broad shoulders that filled his white T-shirt, and his close-cropped hair and beard looked almost black in the bright light. He worked steadily, stopping to appraise what he had done so far, testing the wooden supports to make sure they would hold, examining the wall itself.

Julia liked sitting there, watching him. Now he was mixing the concrete, pouring sand and cement from burlap bags into the mortar box, directing the garden hose, the water a silver arc pouring into the mixture. The heady smell of lemons surrounded her. Holding Bonnie close was like hugging Jenny. She thought of all the threads stitching everyone together, the inquiries she had put out, feeling as if Jenny were guiding her to find Rosa.

The light shifted—the sun rising higher over the eastern mountains—and the shade disappeared. Roberto glanced over, saw Julia and Bonnie reclined in the grass thirty yards away. He waved and Bonnie took it as an invitation—she went bounding over, and Julia followed.

"Hi there," she said, walking over. "We were just feeling very lazy, watching you work so hard."

"Not so hard," he said, laughing. "La, Julia . . ."

"Where are the other guys?"

"Serapio's mother is sick, so he is with her today."

"Oh, I'm sorry. Is it serious?"

"I hope not," Roberto said. "She had a heart attack in August. They worry about her."

"I can understand," Julia said. "She lives in L.A.?"

"East L.A., like Serapio, like me. They have a big family, and the children take turns staying with her. Today is Serapio's turn."

"What about your other helpers?" she asked. "This looks like a big job."

"I didn't go to find day laborers, because I want to fix the wall myself." He smiled. "I caused the damage, I repair it."

"You caused it?"

"On Monday," he said. "The pump broke down, and while I was fixing it, I smashed right into the wall with some copper pipe."

"It could have fallen on you!" she said.

"I'm too fast," he said, smiling.

"That's good," she said.

"Anyway, it's still standing. The crack isn't too bad, but I want to fix it before it gets worse."

"I'm sure you'll do a great job," she said. "I'll let you get to it."

He hesitated. "Everything okay?" he asked.

"Yes. Bonnie and I love it here. We never want to leave."

"I hope you don't," he said.

His remark surprised her, filled her with unexpected joy. She couldn't disguise her feelings and felt the blush spreading across her face. It was odd; they existed nearly side by side at Casa Riley, and they were connected by their daughters, but beyond that she had no idea of how he felt about her.

"Really?" she asked.

He nodded, taking a step toward her. He stared at her, his eyes golden brown in the sun, and for a minute she felt he was going to kiss her. She wanted him to. He reached up as if to touch her face, then noticed his hands were gritty with cement. They both laughed nervously.

"I'd better let you get back to work," she said. "Before the mortar dries."

"Yes, good idea," he said.

"See you later," she said, starting to walk away. Bonnie lingered, as if she didn't want to leave him.

"Julia, I have a question," he said. She turned back, saw him standing especially tall.

"Oh," she said. "Sure, what is it?"

"Do you like Mexican food?"

"I love it."

"Would you ever have dinner with me?"

"Yes," she said, smiling. "That would be wonderful."

Roberto

When he woke up that morning, if someone had told him he would be having dinner with Julia that night, he would have called him a liar. He barely knew what had come over him—he thought of her all the time, dreamed of her at night, but the difference between imagination and reality was huge. Yet she had said yes, and in a few minutes they'd be leaving the Casa.

First he had washed his truck, vacuumed the inside, then gone into his cabin to shower and scrub his nails clean. He dressed in clean dark jeans and a black T-shirt. His belt was black leather with a silver buckle, and he wore his best shoes, a pair of black work boots he hadn't scuffed up yet.

Julia came down the driveway in a blue dress and soft white shawl. He watched her walk and could barely breathe. His father would kill him for this, crossing the line and asking the boss's niece to dinner, but even if he died tonight, Roberto would never forget this moment: the way Julia glowed, beaming as if she'd never been happier to see anyone.

He held open the truck door for her. "You look beautiful," he said.

"Thank you. You look very handsome," she said, kissing his cheek as she climbed in.

Driving down the steep road, he still felt her lips on his skin and thought the top of his head might explode. He forced himself to pay attention to driving, and not keep glancing across the seat toward her.

The restaurant he'd chosen was a long way off. He didn't want to take her to any of the gringo places in Malibu or Santa Monica, but instead to a real, authentic spot that served the kind of food he remembered from home.

They drove south along the ocean, and then onto the 10 freeway heading east. His radio was tuned to a Spanish station. When he realized that she might prefer her own kind of music, he reached for the dial, but she put her hand on his wrist.

"Don't change it. I like it," she said.

"It's different for you?" he asked.

"I grew up with Latin music," she said. "My family loves it and so do I."

Roberto nodded. That made sense—he'd often heard Juan Gabriel's voice coming from speakers in the Casa.

The night was warm, so they kept the truck windows open. The breeze tossed her hair, and he smelled her perfume, and it made him think of a field of fresh grass and wildflowers. His truck key was in the ignition but all the rest dangled from a long chain. Julia leaned over, touched the chain, and her fingers found one small plastic key ring with a faded pink heart attached.

"I like this," she said.

"So do I," he said.

"Someone special gave it to you?"

He nodded. "Rosa," he said. He remembered the day—his birthday the year before they left Mexico. His grandmother had taken her to the market, and she'd bought the little key ring. Beneath the heart it said *Te Amo Papá*.

Julia seemed preoccupied, looking through her purse. After a minute she pulled something out, pressed it into Roberto's hand. He looked: a silver key ring engraved with the words *World's Best Mom*.

"From Jenny," he said.

"Yes," she said.

Did she think the way he did, that these objects had been touched by their daughters, given with love? He told himself every day that love was alive, a living and breathing force. This little plastic heart was only a reminder—what made it precious was the fact that Rosa's hands had held it.

The lights of downtown Los Angeles glittered, and the tall buildings glowed with color. It was a romantic sight, and Roberto wanted Julia to see it. When he glanced over, he saw her looking at him instead, and he put his eyes back on the road.

La Casita de las Flores was on North Evergreen Avenue, not far from Roberto's family's house. He parked at the curb, completely aware of the possibility his father could drive by and stop in to see what Roberto was doing here—his father and Esperanza were not shy about letting him know they wanted him to meet a woman. They wouldn't approve of Julia, but Roberto found himself wishing they would show up just so he could introduce her to them.

They walked past the garden overflowing with flowers, into the restaurant—one small room with about ten tables. The walls were painted rose red, the tables were turquoise, and the chairs were yellow.

"Hola, Roberto," said Isabel, the owner's wife. She gazed at Julia with friendly curiosity.

"Julia, this is Isabel. Isabel, my friend Julia."

"Very nice to meet you," Isabel said. "I hope you will enjoy our food."

"I'm sure I'll love it," Julia said.

The minute they were seated, a waitress put a basket of warm chips and two dishes of hot sauce on the table. Isabel wheeled a cart over and made fresh guacamole with avocados, red onion, tomato, and a handful of cilantro.

"That smells great!" Julia said.

"Wait till you taste it," Roberto said. He scooped some guacamole onto a chip and handed it across the table.

"Wow," she said.

When she took another for herself, she dipped it in the hotter of the two sauces, and he waited for her eyes to water.

"I should have warned you," he said.

But she took another. "I love spicy food," she said.

They looked at the menus—all the dishes were in Spanish. "Can I help you translate?" he asked.

"Why don't you order me your favorite dish?" she asked.

"*Ropa vieja* is very good," he said. "Slow-cooked beef, nice and tender. We always had it at home."

"Sounds like pot roast," she said. "Perfect for a November night."

So Roberto ordered *ropa vieja* for both of them. The dishes came out quickly, the meat spicy and fragrant with herbs and chili, piled high beside yellow rice and black beans. He watched Julia's reaction as she took a bite, and felt pleased to see her close her eyes and smile.

"Delicious," she said. After another few tastes she followed his lead and added spoonfuls of hot sauce.

"You really like it?" he asked.

"Yes," she said. "Everything . . ."

"Even the beans?" he asked skeptically.

"Yes, you don't?"

"They're not special," he said. "We ate them every day when I was a kid. I thought maybe you wouldn't like them."

"I like it all," she said, The way she looked at him made him feel electric, as if a current ran though his body. He didn't trust himself to believe what he was seeing or feeling. Her blue dress brought out the color of her eyes.

"I never thought . . . ," he began.

"What?" she asked.

He just shook his head, because he couldn't answer the question. His feelings were too big to put into words—or at least words he could understand. Together they ate their food, and when they'd finished dinner, Isabel brought coffee and flan, and Julia spooned a bit of custard and held it toward him, and he tasted the sweet soft caramel in his mouth.

Julia

November passed in a dream. It became normal to stop by Roberto's work site, whatever he was doing in the orchard, and bring him water or invite him to take a break for coffee. She loved having his friendship, even feeling somewhat deliciously confused by what it really was. The French had a phrase for what she was feeling: *amitié amoureuse*. It translated roughly to a "romantic friendship."

She felt his attention anytime they were near each other. He watched her whenever she went near the cliff path, as if ready to bolt and catch her if she fell. She thought of him while at her desk, continuing to write to the people Chris had suggested.

"Do I seem crazy to you?" she asked Lion the last Monday in November, when he stopped by with a basket of apples.

"Of course! Crazy as a loon, darling. I wouldn't love you as much or know how to be around you if you weren't. It's the non-crazy people I worry about."

"I'm serious."

Lion wore a crisp yellow shirt, navy cashmere double-breasted blazer, and his favorite Hermès long white silk-fringed aviator scarf wrapped around his neck. His wave of white hair gave him an air of fading majesty that he cultivated in subtle ways. Squinting, he regarded Julia.

"If I were to choose one word to describe you, it would be 'happy.' Happier than I've seen you in ages. Does that sound right?"

She nodded, knowing it was true. But if she explained to him how this feeling had come about—her strong attraction to Roberto, her impossible search for Rosa, and how the mystical alchemy of it had all was bringing Jenny back to her—he would know just how crazy she was.

"Well, I'm glad," he said. "Now, Thanksgiving."

Julia had dreaded holidays these last five years, and this one was no exception.

"I'm having the usual gang up to the manse," he said. "Not John and Graciela, unfortunately; as you know, they've decided to stay in Connemara. But a few decrepit actors like me, some young fluff to cheer the place up, some wayward surfers, a dissolute rocker or two, a smattering of Malibu hoi polloi, and far too many Brits. They flock to me for some unknown reason. I could probably manage to scare up some intellectuals so you'll feel more at home."

"I'm at home with you," she said. "I don't care who else is there. But I don't know, Lion. I might have a quiet Thanksgiving here."

He snorted. "What—you, Bonnie, and the wildlife? Even your orchard manager will be going home that day, I'm sure. John always gives everyone the long weekend off."

"Really?" Julia asked.

"Yes."

"Well, I'll think about it," she said. "Could I bring someone?"

"Julia, a date?"

"I guess you could call it that," she said.

"What, you've met someone and dared to keep it a secret from Uncle Lion?"

She laughed. "No—it's Roberto."

"The orchard manager?"

"Yes."

"You're dating him?"

"We're just friends," she said.

"Of course," Lion said. "We'd love to have him."

"Thank you. I'll see if he can make it," she said.

After Lion left, Julia brought some apples to the barn. Roberto stood next to the workbench, taking apart the tractor. His hands were covered with grease, but he wiped them on a cloth at the sight of her.

"What are you doing?" she asked.

"Replacing parts," he said. "So we don't have to buy a new tractor."

"I'm sure John appreciates that," she said. Clear light slanted through windows; she saw dust and bits of hay drifting in air currents. "Thanksgiving is Thursday," she said.

"Sí," he said.

"I'm sure you have plans with your family," she said. "But I was wondering—would you like to come with me to Lion's house for dinner? We wouldn't have to stay long, and you could still be with your family."

"Señor Cushing?" he asked, frowning. "Does he know?"

"Yes. He invited us."

Roberto hesitated so long Julia began to feel embarrassed. What was the problem? He had taken her to dinner, she had thought they were getting close, but maybe she'd crossed an invisible line. Thanksgiving was an American holiday—maybe he didn't celebrate it at all.

"What's wrong?" she asked.

"Nothing," he said.

"I can tell something is. Would you rather not go?"

"No, Julia—I would love to go with you."

"Great," Julia said. She stepped toward him, stood on her toes, and kissed his cheek. He wrapped one arm around her waist, and his direct gaze melted the bones in her legs. He touched his forehead to hers, barely brushed her lips.

"Hey, el pinche inspector es—" Serapio began, bursting in. "Ai, lo siento."

Roberto and Julia moved apart.

"I'm so sorry," Roberto said to Julia. "But the inspector is here. We made changes to the pumping and irrigation system, and he has to sign off."

"I understand," Julia said.

"But Thursday," Roberto said.

"Yes," Julia said. "Thanksgiving."

Thanksgiving morning was sunny and warm, as far from New England weather as possible. Julia felt glad for that. Holidays without Jenny had been excruciating. Everything—the weather, the quality of Black Hall's November light, the silken darkness of Long Island Sound—had reminded her of the sixteen Thanksgivings she'd spent with her daughter.

In the Casa Riley kitchen, she sliced the rest of the apples Lion had brought. She made piecrust and saved a few scraps to make maple leaves to press on top, just as Jenny used to do. Roberto always left a bowl of lemons at her door, so she used one of her grandmother's recipe books to make two loaves of lemon bread.

By the time Roberto arrived to pick her up at three o'clock, she was ready to go. Not sure of what he would wear, she wore black pants and a white silk shirt.

He looked great in black jeans, a white shirt, and a well-worn and rugged leather jacket. They hugged and walked toward his vehicle—an old but obviously recently waxed gray Honda Civic.

"Where's your truck?" she asked.

"I borrowed Serapio's wife's car," he said. "To drive you to Thanksgiving dinner."

"Thank you," she said, getting in.

The trip was short—down one canyon, along the coast highway, up Topanga Canyon and along the steep, twisting road that led to Lion's house. People were arriving all at once. Roberto started to park on the roadside, but a man in a black uniform waved him ahead.

"Looks like valet parking," Julia said. "That's very Lion."

"Mande?" Roberto asked, not understanding.

"Extravagant," Julia said.

One parking attendant opened Julia's door while the other opened Roberto's, speaking to him in Spanish. They seemed friendly, had a short conversation, and Roberto caught up with Julia, smiling.

"They are both Mexican," he said. "This is a good job for them."

"Are they friends of yours?"

"No, Julia," he said. "Just Mexican workers like me."

They walked up the curving stone steps in a steady stream of people. Roberto carried the apple pie and held Julia's arm. She'd wrapped the lemon bread in tinfoil and packed it in a canvas bag embroidered with Graciela's family crest—she knew Lion would enjoy that.

Inside the castle Lion called home, Julia saw half a dozen young actors she recognized, several of John and Graciela and Lion's dearest Malibu friends, and twenty or so people she'd never seen in her life. Roberto seemed relaxed, but tense like a cat: ready to spring if necessary.

"You okay?" she asked.

"All these famous people," he said.

"Most of them aren't," she said.

Lion burst forth from a cluster of tall, skinny young women with asymmetrical haircuts and embraced Julia. Then he shook Roberto's hand.

"What a pleasure, Roberto. So glad you could join us," Lion said.

"Thank you for inviting me," he said.

"It's my pleasure," Lion said. "Let's get drinks."

They went to the bar, tended by two Latino men. Roberto spoke to them in a friendly way. Lion ordered martinis for him and Julia and cocked an eyebrow at Roberto. "Martini?" he asked.

"Cerveza," Roberto said, and accepted a beer from the bartender.

"What shall we drink to?" Lion asked, raising his glass.

"Things we're thankful for," Julia began, but just then an actor known for playing James Bond wrapped Lion in a bear hug, and Julia and Roberto found themselves clinking glasses alone.

"Salud," he said.

"Salud," she replied.

The house smelled of turkey, stuffing, and all the delicacies of a

New England Thanksgiving. Julia and Roberto began to walk through the rooms, and she showed him all the things she'd loved as a child: the suits of armor, the chariot wheels, the stone and bronze Buddhas, the Tang dynasty gong, the fountains in almost every room, the fireplaces large enough to roast oxen, the gallery of still photographs from Lion's films, including many with Graciela.

"Doña Graciela," Roberto said, leaning closer to see Graciela and Lion in a shot from *The King Goes Rowing*.

"They were young there," she said. "They filmed it in Cambridge, and he was the king of England, in disguise, in love with a student. Have you seen any of Graciela and Lion's movies?"

"No," he said.

"We'll have to watch one," she said.

"Claro," he said. "They were in many together?"

"Yes," she said. "They were known for their work, and also being friends off screen."

Just then she felt an embrace from behind. Turning to see, she found herself surrounded with people she vaguely knew from many visits here. Doug Longwood, the man who had hugged her, was a British film producer who lived in the Colony.

"Well, what a lovely surprise to find you here, Julia!" he said.

He introduced her to his date, Melinda, and a tall dark-haired boy named Magnus, and refreshed her memory on the others.

"Good to see you all," she said. "This is my friend Roberto."

A few of them said hello and shook his hand, but Doug looked right past him as if he hadn't even heard his name. Julia glanced at Roberto, but he was back to looking at the photos.

"I was just saying to Roberto," she said, "that Lion and Graciela made many films together."

"Which is your favorite?" Doug asked.

"Oh, Roberto hasn't seen them yet, but we're going to watch—"

"I meant you," Doug said.

"All of them, I don't know."

"This one looks good," Roberto said, pointing to a still of *The Washington Affair*. Graciela and Lion had played American spies who'd discovered that a group of White House aides had kidnapped the First Lady. The shot showed the pair with machine guns blasting, a bloody scar on Lion's face from where one of the kidnappers had slashed him.

"He likes shoot-'em-ups," Doug said in his East London accent, and laughed. He spoke about Roberto without looking at him, as if he were not right there.

"What is that?" Roberto asked.

"Bang-bang," Doug said.

"Do you work in the movies?" Roberto asked.

Doug kissed Julia on both cheeks, then he and his friends drifted away without responding to Roberto. To Julia it felt like a punch in the stomach. She started after him, but Roberto held her arm.

"It's okay," he said.

"No, it's not," she said. "He was so fucking rude!"

"Julia," Roberto said. "It's fine."

"Do you want to go?" she asked.

"I'll stay for you," he said.

"No, I want to leave," she said.

Roberto acted as if he wasn't hurt, but she knew he had to be. Hurrying through the house, Julia didn't even stop to find Lion. He caught up with her and Roberto at the door, looking stricken.

"What happened?" he asked.

"Nothing," Roberto said quickly.

"How did you know something happened?" Julia asked.

"Doug Longwood made a comment. Roberto, I'm sorry."

"It's fine," Roberto said.

"Class still means something to him," Lion said. "He's a very arrogant, ignorant Englishman who hasn't had a hit movie in decades. I'll leave it to you to figure out why he behaves the way he does."

"He's insecure," Julia said. "But he's still a fucking asshole."

The ice was broken; all was well, except it wasn't. The valet brought the Honda and Roberto drove Julia home. She felt so sad, defeated somehow; the fact that he had dressed up and borrowed a car for the occasion made her want to cry. She reached across the seat and held his hand. He squeezed hers.

"I wasn't really in the mood for a big party," she said. "Holidays are hard for me."

"You miss Jenny."

"Yes," she said. "And you miss Rosa."

"Sí. Not so much for Thanksgiving, it's an American holiday and she never knew it. But Navidad is coming, and Three Kings Day . . ."

"Roberto," she said, still holding his hand when they pulled up in front of Casa Riley. "I've been working on something and I've wanted to tell you about it. Can you come in, or do you have to get to your family's house?"

"I can come in," he said.

When they entered the house, Julia turned on lots of lights. She wanted the house illuminated for what they were about to discuss. They went into the living room, and she lit the table lamps, the wall sconces above the fireplace, and the small brass lights John had installed above every painting.

They sat on a small sofa, at either end. Julia kicked off her shoes and drew her legs up so she could face him directly. The seaward windows were open, and a warm salt breeze blew off the ocean.

"Weeks ago, you started telling me about when you and Rosa crossed the border."

"I'm sorry," he said. "I know it was hard for you to hear."

"It was," she said. "Because I can't imagine what you went through."

"Gracias, Julia," he said.

"And I want to help."

He gave her a sad smile that barely touched his eyes. "I know," he said. "But there is no help."

"I think there is," she said. Her heart was beating fast, and she walked over to the writing desk and brought back a pile of papers. "I've been researching. Being an anthropologist has some advantages. I know people who can get information for us."

"What good is information?" he asked. "Rosa is gone!"

"I reached out to a colleague, Chris Barton," she said. "And he put me in touch with Dr. Juan Rios, who runs something called the Reunion Project. Also, I remembered the name you mentioned—Jack Leary. He's retired, but there's a way to look him up."

Roberto had stiffened, his jaw set and his back straight—as if he wanted to bolt out of the room.

"For what?" he asked finally. "Why would you talk to him? Or any of them?"

"To find Rosa," she said.

He looked at her with what seemed to her to be a mixture of despair and fury. "Find her? I couldn't, how could you?"

"I want to go there."

"Go there? The desert, where we were—you have no idea. It's not like your *expedición antropológica*, Julia. Nothing will help. Thank you for asking, but no, Julia."

"Why?" she asked.

"You don't even know the full story," he said. "I've told you the smallest part. If you heard the rest, you would never think of going there."

"Then tell me," she said as the sea breeze rustled the curtains. "And let me decide."

chapter five

Roberto

How to explain to Julia? The feelings were as strong as if he were still riding in the truck, back breaking every time the wheels hit a rut. He cushioned Rosa against his chest, fed her sips of water, cursing the coyotes Alberto and Benito Rodriguez for setting out during the hottest part of the day.

The desert was flat and endless. He couldn't believe any land could be so vast—it made the fields of home, ringed by hills and trees, seem small. Heat shimmered over the ground in all directions.

Rosa got sick and he didn't know what to do. Hold back the water and she'd dehydrate; give it to her and she'd throw it up. She clutched Maria, begging the doll to spread her wings, use her great-grandmother's magic, get them there safely. Which "there" was she wishing for, Roberto wondered—his papá's house or his grandmother's shack back in Mexico? The truck just kept rumbling, on and on for miles. Roberto began to feel *náuseas* and sleepy himself, but he fought the feeling.

Some of the other migrants slept or passed out, collapsed in a heap against one another. He reached over and shook one who looked particularly pale. The man woke up, vomited off the back of the truck. Exhaust fumes were making everyone dizzy. The sun finally started to go down, a red ball in the west.

Rosa whimpered while Roberto rocked her. "There," he said, pointing at the sun. "That's where we are going. Los Angeles, as far west in El Norte as we can get, at the edge of the Pacific Ocean."

"I want the water!" Rosa cried.

"Here, niña," he said, pouring a capful into his hand, letting her lap it like a cat. When the sun disappeared below the horizon, the desert glowed rose, purple, and amber. His grandmother had amber earrings and a pendant. A blue *mariposa*—butterfly—frozen in time in the pendant, and staring across the wide Sonoran landscape. Roberto was awake, but he dreamed he saw thousands, millions of blue butterflies migrating north like them.

Suddenly, the truck stopped. Without being told, Roberto knew the border was near. Anxiety rippled through the group, everyone rousing one another, gathering their belongings.

The coyotes climbed out of the cab. Now Roberto saw their weapons—pistols in holsters on their hips, automatic rifles strapped across their chests. Alberto, the father, barked out directions.

"Stay close, don't trail behind, drink your water," he said. Benito and the third coyote, Pedro, would lead the *pollos* north while Alberto drove back to Altar. "La Migra has night goggles and they can see better than God, and you'll hear and then see the airships, big lights all over. When you hear that noise, duck under bushes, tumbleweed, any rock you find. Each person for himself. Once they see us from the air, they send trucks. And keep in mind—there are always vehicles on patrol."

"Here's what else you have to worry about," Benito said. "Rattlesnakes, scorpions, coyotes—the other kind, with teeth—bats, rats, ring-tailed cats. Those cats look cute but they fucking bite. Spiders and Gila monsters, more venomous than *cascabeles*." Rattlesnakes.

"You might not see the border. La Migra built a fence, but that's east of here. They make their fence strong around the cities, make it look good, but that's why we're in the desert. We're smart." He touched his head. "We go to the more rural places to cross, where there aren't so many roads. Now listen. We're walking next to Tohono O'odham land. Don't think the tribe wants us here any more than the border agents. Someone looks your direction, hide. Otherwise they make a call, we get picked up by ICE in less than an hour. *Suerte*."

They started walking. Roberto carried Rosa and she held him even more tightly. Everyone went single file or two by two. Roberto felt strong; his legs had cramped up during the long truck ride, and it was good to stretch out his muscles, take long strides.

The group came upon a drag—a wide, smooth swath made by La Migra trucks pulling chains behind them to create an even surface. Every footprint, even those made by mice and roadrunners, showed up clearly.

Benito walked behind, sweeping away tracks with a broom made of twigs. Everyone knew La Migra were expert at "cutting sign," a method of tracking they'd learned from the Sioux and Tohono O'odham tribes. They even employed Shadow Wolves, a unit of the Customs Patrol made up of Native Americans.

Once the sunset's unearthly glow disappeared, they walked in pure darkness, one foot in front of the other, trusting the desert's flatness. The ground began losing heat, and Roberto pulled his fleece and Rosa's from his pack, zipped them on. Then the moon rose: pure white light, softer than daylight but illuminating every footstep, person, and rock. Rosa walked beside him, holding his hand. He figured it would be better for her to walk now than in tomorrow's heat. But as the night grew late she began to stumble. She tried to be brave and strong, but she was exhausted. He lifted her up.

In the moonlight Rosa's black hair gleamed against Roberto's shoulder. He shifted her from one hip to the other. The longer he walked, the heavier the water jugs became. Rosa had fallen asleep. Walking on hard earth, he heard sounds: an almost constant buzzing, as if rattlesnakes were everywhere. He saw movement out of the corner of his eyes, watched the sweeping S movement of a sidewinder slithering away into the silvery darkness.

Bats circled his head. He waved them away from Rosa's hair. The temperature dropped. While the day's temperatures had risen over one hundred degrees, now the air felt frigid. Rosa shivered in his arms. Roberto dug into his pack, removed the denim sleeves the other migrant had cut off, and slid them onto his daughter's arms, over her fleece jacket.

The group walked for hours. Eventually the guide said it was time to rest. They found a spot near a dry creek bed that seemed to offer some cover: there were boulders and tufts of brush. The coyote said to stay away from the brush, it was where snakes preferred to gather, but that if ICE or the Shadow Wolves were to approach, then take cover and forget the sidewinders.

Roberto lay beside Rosa. The night was so cold their teeth were chattering. Her upper body was warmed by the fleece and the extra sleeves, but he hadn't prepared for her bare legs. Even his own ankles stung in the cold. He took off his jacket and covered their feet.

Twenty feet away the man who'd sliced off his sleeves was shivering so loudly he sounded like a stampede. Roberto felt bad, but he couldn't offer the man any help. All his resources had to go to Rosa.

Trying to sleep, he thought of his father, who had made this journey—alone, without a child in tow—and tried to imagine how it had felt to leave his son behind. Roberto knew how much his father loved him—loved the whole family—and knew he would never have done this unless he believed with all his heart he was creating a better life for all of them.

And now his father had a green card, giving this journey hope and meaning, and he lived around the corner from Mariachi Square. To comfort himself as much as his sleeping daughter, Roberto hummed "Contigo" in a low voice, imagined sitting on his father's porch in East L.A., listening to the mariachi horns play their passionate and melancholy music; and holding Rosa, he finally drifted off to sleep under the bright moon.

The day started before dawn. The group drank water and ate their dried meat and fruit, then began to walk before the sun rose. Without mercy, heat seared through the gray light. The ground burned Rosa's feet through her lime-green sneakers, so Roberto carried her again. He asked her if she remembered the moon last night, and she didn't, so he described it to her, the way the whole desert had been painted silver, even the prickly pears and round boulders.

Usually she loved his stories, but today she couldn't concentrate on his words. The morning hours advanced, and Roberto's head ached as if a metal band were being tightened around his skull. Rosa cried softly, delirious and calling for Roberto's grandmother. Roberto lowered Rosa and made her drink water. She guzzled it and promptly threw it up, so he asked her to take small sips, even smaller than the ones she would give to Maria.

One night and half a day in the desert, and already two gallons of water were gone. Roberto looked around. The land was a garbage dump, strewn with plastic bottles, candy wrappers, piles of human excrement, and women's panties. It was true, what his father and other migrants had said: the desert was not just a wasteland, but evil, filled with evidence of rape. He left his plastic jug in the dirt, lifted Rosa, and caught up with the other walkers. Pedro had waited, and when Roberto passed, the coyote swept away the track with his twig broom.

No one spoke. They saved their energy for the trek. Roberto noticed husbands helping wives, wives helping husbands. An older man's lips turned white, and he sat heavily on the ground. Some people tried to help him. He clutched his arm and shuddered as he took his last breath. Roberto kept walking so Rosa wouldn't see. No one stayed behind to bury him. They hadn't a shovel or the strength.

Two hours later, with the sun at its peak, Benito decided it was time to rest again. Where? Roberto wanted to ask. In what shade? There was nothing—no tree, cactus, rock. A mountain range rose in the distance—it looked a hundred miles away.

The migrants drank more water, tried to settle down for a siesta, covering themselves with jackets and packs in an attempt to create shade. Roberto lay north-south on his side on the scorching hot dry earth and tried to angle his body to make shade for Rosa.

Her lips were white, like the old man's. She wanted to drink the whole water bottle, but he wouldn't let her. While she sobbed, he portioned out one capful after another. He took her pulse. Her skin felt clammy. Once she'd drunk four capfuls of water, slowly, he settled her down so she was completely in the shadow of his body.

"Abuela," she cried, hallucinating for his grandmother. "Delfina, Alma . . . ," her best friends. "Tino," the pet goat Roberto had told her about, that he had had long before she was born, when he was a little boy and his grandfather had given him one kid from the herd. And how Roberto had named him, played with him, and one day, returning home from school on his seventh birthday, smelled a feast, a special meal for the whole family—only they had cooked Tino—the only animal they could spare.

Hearing Rosa cry for Tino constricted Roberto's throat. He held his daughter tightly, his sweat sticking to hers, thinking of that little goat and how he'd loved it, and how he'd had to pretend to his grandfather to be happy for the birthday feast, and to hide the hatred he felt for the old man for killing his pet.

Jack Leary
2007

Jack's grandfather on his mother's side had been a Texas Ranger, patrolling the hills along the Texas-Oklahoma border looking for every type of criminal hiding in the caves and holes. He still had Grandpa's Colt .44 and his nightstick, more like a baseball bat, really, and also his sap—that's what they called it, a flexible six-inch weapon covered in braided black leather and well soaked with the blood of the many bad-guy skulls his gramps had conked.

While Grandpa Tecumseh Shane had been a hard-core, hard-assed redneck mountain man and expert tracker, Jack's other grandfather, Brendan Leary, had been an FBI agent in Boston, working white-collar paper cases on con men who targeted the vulnerable through church groups and immigrant populations. That's where Jack got his desire to work for the federal government—the combination of power and good benefits. Marriage to Louella and memories of his grandfather Brendan had drummed into his head a better reason for working for the Fed: the potential to help people.

Driving his Explorer through the desert that late afternoon, he kept his eyes open for any signs of cutting the drag. The big machines had been through here earlier hauling chain and pipe, smoothing out the dirt and sand so any footprint would show up clearly. The dashboard thermometer registered 120 degrees out there. It wouldn't be the first time he'd saved someone's life in the heat; sometimes the migrants staggered onto the road, begging him to stop.

His SUV was equipped with a radio mounted by the driver's seat, and a shotgun rack behind his head but separated from the back by wire mesh. The rig was heavy, with four-wheel drive strong enough to haul a semi out of the sand. He had the AC blasting, a coffee in the holder, water jugs bungeed in back just in case he came upon some wanderers.

Jack had worked for the United States Border Patrol for twenty-five years, and he could see retirement on the horizon. His job was to guard the U.S.-Mexican border and work in conjunction with ICE: Immigration and Customs Enforcement. When he'd first started, ICE was the INS—Immigration and Naturalization Service. The change in last words from "service" to "enforcement" said everything about the new attitude.

Some of his colleagues in the Tucson Sector of Arizona called the illegals "wets" for wetbacks, back from when most of them tried crossing the Rio Grande. Now, with urban entries heavily guarded, and the eight-hundred-mile fence, floodlights, sensors, and helicopter patrols, the migrants had started moving through the most deadly, less-patrolled sections of desert.

He rode along, eyes sweeping from side to side. He had a gift for tracking from his grandfather Shane, but his sensibility was more in line with his grandfather Leary. His Irish ancestors had fought and died their way across the Atlantic in steerage, many of them dying of disease on an island in Canada's St. Lawrence River before ever achieving their goals of "a better life."

Assimilation was a hell of a lot easier for the Irish, white-skinned and blue-eyed, looking the Anglo part, fitting into society and getting good jobs—patronage jobs in the case of his Chicago and

Oklahoma City ancestors. They started out as janitors in City Hall, worked their way up to cops and finally the FBI.

Love of family, that's what killed him. These people were literally dying to be together, to make enough money to feed their elderly and young, just as his had done. He was always on the lookout for terrorists and drug smugglers, but most of what he found were poor families. His wife, Louella, reminded him of that every day. She said that inside he had more in common with the Mexicans and other Latin Americans he picked up than he did with his bosses.

He didn't exactly go around talking about his philosophy. The Border Patrol and ICE had plenty of closet kind-hearted agents, but more and more it attracted kids who watched *Border Wars* on TV and wanted to chase down the wets and send them packing back to where they came from, preferably with lumps and bruises to remind them of what awaited should they decide to attempt another crossing.

The sun was setting; he took his Ray-Bans off and in the last golden light saw it: a crescent-moon-shaped heel print on the track's edge. He pulled over the Explorer, got out for a closer look. The coyote had swept up. He was smart but daring: this stretch of land was brutal, and very few groups attempted to cross here. Patrols in this area were relatively light, and the coyote would know that.

If he hadn't left that heel print behind, Leary would have missed it entirely. He scanned the desert in the direction the print was heading. Then he locked his truck and set off that way himself. He left the shotgun behind but had his pistol and hollow-point ammo in his holster.

Even at sunset, the heat hit him like a wall. Only travelers who lived far below poverty level were desperate enough to risk their lives this way. Now that he was walking, he saw another set of not-quite-erased footprints: tiny ones. He thought of the little kid and walked faster.

He saw the mound in the distance, crows and turkey vultures
all over it. He had his service radio out and was calling headquarters before the smell reached him. Did the wanderers know they had
crossed the U.S. border, that they had already arrived? Had their
coyotes arranged for pickup? He searched the immediate area, still
thinking of that little footprint.

"I've got a body here," he said to Jeannie, the dispatcher. "And
it looks like more dead up ahead."

"Do you think the others are making for Route 2?" she asked,
knowing the area as well as he did.

"Yeah, that's what I figure."

"You want to stay with the body, and I'll send Chandler and
Leone to intercept the rest of the group up on the highway?"

"No," Leary said. Chandler and Leone: two of the new guard,
not just ready but eager to bust heads and send everyone packing
back to whatever place so hellish they'd risk crossing this desert
trying to escape.

"Then what?"

"Have them come here. I'll plant a flag by the body—they'll see
it with their flashlights. I'll drive north and look for the others."

"Jack," she said. "They're closer to the highway. I'm sending
them, okay? A helicopter, too. They'll find them."

He couldn't argue the point. Chandler and Leone were already
on the way, and there was nothing he could do about it.

Roberto
2007

Roberto and Rosa drank all their water, and even in the heat of the
late-day sun, her skin felt damp instead of hot and dry, and that
scared him. He carried her with both arms stretched out—she was

too weak to grab his neck now. Other members of the group had fallen behind—were resting or sleeping or maybe dying. Benito and Pedro led Roberto and ten others deeper into the desert, toward a distant V of rocks rising out of nowhere.

"What is out there?" Roberto asked.

"That's our landmark. Tells us we're close to the pickup spot," Benito said.

"The border?"

"We crossed it, man," he said, holding up his GPS. "You're in the United States."

Roberto expected to feel exultant, but he felt panic. "My daughter needs water."

"We all do. Keep walking."

"Where's the pickup?"

"Through those rocks. Two more miles and our contact is already there with his van running and waiting for us."

Two more miles once they passed those rocks, Roberto thought. The sun began to slide down, but nothing cooled his body or feet, and Rosa's eyes were closed; she had white foam in the corners of her mouth, but when he kissed her forehead, she opened her eyes.

"Did you hear the man?" he asked.

"He talked too fast," she said.

"We're almost there, *preciosa*," he said.

"Daddy, it's too hot," she said, practically the first complaint he'd heard from her, and he kissed her forehead again.

"When we get there, we'll have all the water we want, and Papá has air-conditioning, and you'll be so cool," he said. "You'll need your fleece."

"Where's Maria?" she asked.

"In the pack," he said.

"Will you give her to me?"

"Soon, *cariño*. We just go through those rocks, and then to the road, and then we'll be fine and you can have Maria."

"I want her, she'll fly us to Papá," Rosa said, and began to cry, and again Roberto panicked because she had no tears on her cheeks.

The coyotes walked faster, herding the ten of them along. The sun dipped down, and as they approached the rocks he noticed deep shadows.

"Hey, can we take a rest here?" he asked the coyotes.

"Listen, you hear that?" Benito asked, pointing overhead. "Helicopter. Border agents in the airship looking for us. It's getting dark, so we have a little cover, unless they're using heat sensors. Two miles and we get into the van, and we're all on our way to L.A."

Roberto strained his ears, couldn't hear anything but the desert wind. Holding Rosa, he almost wished for the helicopter—no, he *did* wish for it—he wanted ICE to come, find them, and take her to the hospital. But then he thought—two miles. They could make it.

"We'll be at Papá's house tonight," he said to her.

"The mariachis?" she asked.

"Yes!"

She was okay. If she remembered the mariachis, and wanted to hold Maria, she was going to get through this. Roberto told himself that, even while cursing himself for doing everything wrong. He should have carried more water, he should have found a better coyote with a smarter route, he shouldn't have taken Rosa on this journey—his father had been so much smarter, had left him behind when he was a child.

Passing through the rock formations, Roberto tensed up. For a minute he thought the coyotes had led them into a trap—this would be the right place for bandits. But they made it through, and now there were just two miles to go. The tall rocks looked purple and gold and cast long shadows, and then as the sun disappeared, there were no shadows.

Suddenly everyone got a second wind. Benito and Pedro were dehydrated too, but they started to trot, and the remaining ten walkers kept up. Roberto ran along with them, holding Rosa as if she were light as air, knowing it was less than two miles to go. He counted his steps, lost track, forced himself to keep making progress. She squirmed, nearly dropping from his arms. Roberto fell behind, focusing all his attention on each step, staying strong and holding Rosa tight.

"Daddy, I'm going to be sick," she said.

"It's okay," he said. Let her throw up all over him, he didn't care. He just had to get her to the road, and the van, and there would be water.

"Hurry, faster!" Benito called. "Hear those engines? Fucking ICE SUVs!"

"Daddy, put me down," she cried.

He ignored her, tried to keep up with the others. There were rocks in small formations, and the ground had turned from hard earth to small pebbles. She retched and cried, sick and embarrassed, and calling "Abuela, Abuela . . ."

She wanted his grandmother. He stumbled on a stone, nearly twisted his ankle, fell to one knee and skinned it right through his jeans. Rosa tumbled from his arms, but he caught her, let her stand wobbly on her feet for a minute, vomiting spit and bile into the sand, leaning against a round boulder.

"Wait!" he yelled to the others.

The moon rose, turning the desert bright as morning. Now he did hear noise—but not SUVs, just regular traffic. Up in the distance he saw one set of headlights, bright white car lights parked along a road.

"That's it," he said to Rosa. "We get there and we're home."

"Abuela," she wept. "Maria."

Roberto watched the figures getting smaller. He narrowed his eyes and swore he saw the van. All he had to do was get Rosa to the road—another half mile at the most. He tried to stand, and nearly passed out. "Come on, baby," he said, trying to lift her. "Just that far, see the van?"

She curled up in a ball by the boulder, where it felt cool. Roberto watched his fellow travelers reach the road, start climbing into the van. He didn't think—he just acted. They weren't going to leave Rosa and him in the desert. He knelt down, pressed Maria into Rosa's hands.

"Five minutes, love," he said. "That's all. Stay with Maria, and I'll be right back. Don't move. Promise me you won't move."

"I promise."

He'd cracked his knee, maybe broken something, but he had never run faster in his life. The moon shone bright on Rosa's boulder—a beacon of gold blaring from the bleak and empty land. The faster he ran, the more dangerous he felt. He'd kill the driver if he tried to leave without them. He'd jump on the windshield and make them stop, grab Pedro's pistol, hold it to his head and walk him back to the boulder to get Rosa.

The road looked smooth. He tripped over a stone, and his ankle twisted. The van's headlights were on, the door was open. All ten of the migrants were already inside; he saw Pedro and Benito climbing in last.

"Wait!" he yelled. The moonlight caught the metal of their guns. Or jewelry. Or bracelets. His eyes were used to the bright moon, and hadn't picked up the two dark shapes behind the van. SUVs.

The metal on Benito and Pedro and all the others was handcuffs.

"We got another one," a voice said in English.

"He wanted us to wait," another voice said, laughing. "So we waited."

Roberto couldn't understand the language but he knew La Migra when he saw it. He turned and bolted—straight back the way he'd come, heading for the moonlit boulder. He could see Rosa's tiny shape curled up at the base, her little feet in her lime-green sneakers, and he heard the hissing and howling of night creatures, and he bellowed, "Rosa!"

"Stop right there! Put your hands up!" the voice yelled.

"Mi hija," Roberto shouted. "Ella está ahí, tengo que rescatar a mi hija!"

"You're in America, speak English now."

The shotgun butt cracked him across his skull, and he never even felt himself hit the rocky ground. He didn't die, but in that moment his life ended.

chapter six

Julia

At the Casa, listening to Roberto, she heard how the border agents had arrested and detained the group. Roberto couldn't get any of them to look for Rosa. But once he was at the detention center, waiting to be processed, something like a miracle happened. A border agent named Jack Leary walked into the holding cell and asked if anyone there had a child. For a minute Roberto had thought he had found Rosa, but no—he had just seen her footprint. Roberto told him what had happened. Leary went straight to look for her, but by the time he got to the big rock, Rosa was gone.

It took two days for Roberto to be processed—arrested and deported to Mexico across the river from Nogales. He went straight to Altar, and found his way along the same route taken by the coyotes. Landmarks had been burned into his memory: a saguaro cactus shaped like a horse, piles of plastic water bottles left by previous groups, the body of the man he and Rosa had traveled with, and finally the boulder where he'd left his daughter.

He made it to the highway, and this time there was no La Migra waiting for him. A trucker picked him up and drove him to the next town, where he'd called his father. And his father drove down from Los Angeles to get him.

After he finished telling her, Roberto left the kitchen, and she watched him cross the courtyard, pass behind the barn. The sprinklers went on, filling the dry air with mist. It was late in the day for irrigation—usually Roberto took care of it before the sun crested the mountains.

Julia couldn't breathe. She could see the moonlight on the endless desert, Rosa so tiny in that wild landscape. It was as if Roberto's memory had become her vision. She could feel Roberto's heart pounding, his panic in those minutes without Rosa in his arms, running back to her. Just a few more yards—all he'd had to do was make it to the rock, and Rosa would be safe now.

Stepping onto the terrace through the mist and darkness, she saw Roberto checking on the sprinklers. She walked outside, through the lemon trees to find him.

"Roberto," she said.

"How can you look at me after what I just told you?" he asked. "I let my daughter go."

"It wasn't your fault."

He kept his head down, as if he couldn't bear to see her eyes. She touched his face, turned it to meet his gaze. Then she reached for him, holding him close. He embraced her and his head came to rest on her shoulder. Around them the water hissed. Her feet felt wet in the soaking earth.

They broke apart, and his shoulders slumped. She could feel the shame pouring off him.

"Thank you, Julia, for listening to me," he said. "You're the only person I've ever told that story, all of it."

"I wanted you to tell me," she said. "And I understand."

"Thank you for saying," he said. "But impossible a woman like you would ever be so reckless, take your daughter into danger, leave her even for a minute."

Julia's head buzzed with thoughts and memories. But she took a deep breath of the mountain and sea air, and touched his arm. "I have blamed myself for five years," she said. "As long as you have suffered over losing Rosa, I've felt the same about Jenny."

"That was not your fault."

Julia smiled sadly. "I said the same thing to you, but it's hard to take it in and believe it, isn't it?"

"Very. But different for you—you didn't leave Jenny, you . . ."

"Roberto, I failed her. I must have, because why else would she have done what she did?"

Now he held her, rocking her while she tried to breathe.

"I knew she was so sad, she missed her boyfriend, but I had no idea she was so desperate. I never imagined, we were close and talked about everything, but I missed the signs. She must have been trying to tell me, because that's how we were. But I didn't hear her."

"For her, it might have been too hard to tell you," Roberto said.

"I would have helped her."

"Maybe she didn't want help," Roberto said.

"But Roberto, I still don't know and I never will! Evidence adds up to one thing for the police, but I'm her mother. I can't believe Jenny would do it. She's my girl, she wouldn't leave me that way. She wouldn't do it to herself! But then there's the evidence. It's so hard to think about, I pushed the thoughts away. I broke our connection."

He nodded, as if he understood.

"But it's not broken forever," she said.

"What do you mean?"

"Little by little," she said, "Jenny is coming back to me. It started when you first told me about Rosa, when we were sitting on the house steps that night. I actually felt her with me."

"En serio?" Roberto asked.

"It sounds crazy, right?"

"Maybe a little," he said.

"I know, it feels that way to me. But I swear, it was as if she were right there, sitting next to me."

Roberto stared at her with wide brown eyes and took her hand. Lemon trees surrounded them, their branches arching low over their heads. She smelled citrus, felt the leaves brush the top of her hair. He put his arms around her and kissed her, long and slow. When he stopped, her heart was pounding.

They held each other for a long time before he let her go. She felt him watching her head toward the house before he turned in the opposite direction. By the time she glanced back, he had walked into the rows of lemon trees, disappeared into the night's ghostly mist.

The next morning she woke up and saw that Serapio's wife's car was gone—he must have returned home to East L.A. He'd left without saying goodbye.

She drove along the Pacific Coast Highway with the radio on. She kept it tuned to Sirius E Street, and listened to Bruce Springsteen. He was singing "Further On (Up the Road)," but it could have been anything. He'd become a companion and guardian angel during these years alone. The way Bruce sang, whether it was a rock song or a ballad, she knew that he understood suffering. His music had kept her company cross-country, and it was keeping her sane right now.

Pulling onto Westward Beach Road, she went past the Sunset

Restaurant. The road hugged the bluff, and she took it all the way to the last lifeguard station and got out. Bonnie ran straight for the tide line. It had always been this way. In Connecticut, walking along Griswold Point, she'd investigated all the kelp that had washed up between tides. Her limp was worse, and her coat had lost some of its luster, but on the beach she was still the puppy Julia and Peter had brought home for Jenny.

Julia left her shoes in the car, rolled up the legs of her jeans, and walked behind Bonnie in the hard sand. The waves here were the most beautiful she'd ever seen. Great curling tubes of blue-green glass breaking into white foam that spread across the packed sand and rolled back into the Pacific.

She walked barefoot through the foam, cold on her feet—much colder than the Atlantic and Long Island Sound—deep enough so the waves splashed her pants. She felt the waves wanting to pull her out, into the ocean, picking up smooth rocks and bits of broken shell.

Offshore four dolphins swam north, parallel to the beach. Bonnie heard one exhale from its blowhole, and began racing back and forth along the sand, barking. She jumped into the water, swam out twenty yards, but was no match for the dolphins. Julia sat on the sand, watching. The dolphins were long gone, but Bonnie swam in the waves, buoyed by the sea.

Julia slipped off her jeans and T-shirt and walked into the ocean in her underwear. The water felt cold on her legs, but she dove straight in—a habit from her childhood, growing up at the beach. Sometimes people would give themselves time to get used to the water, but not Julia. She'd taught Jenny to do it the same way.

She and Bonnie drifted in the current and were lifted by the waves. The rip ran swiftly along the beach. It carried her and Bonnie parallel to the sand, all the way to the next lifeguard tower.

Because it was off-season, the guard stations weren't manned. But Julia was a strong swimmer, and she loved being in salt water more than anywhere else on earth. It restored her.

The ocean and sun brought Julia back to herself. As she swam hard, then let go and floated, face up toward the blue sky, she wondered what objects Roberto had to remind him of Rosa. She wondered whether he'd found her doll, Maria, when he'd gone back to the rock months later.

She and Bonnie climbed out of the ocean fifty yards along the beach from where they'd first gone in. Julia walked back to her towel but didn't pick it up and just stood there drying in the sun. She had a long day ahead of her, and she wanted to hold on to this bright feeling of stepping out of the ocean.

She drove home and got ready. Sprayed Bonnie with the hose, combed out the worst tangles of seaweed, dried her with a towel. Then she stood under the outdoor shower—such a luxury—standing in the sun as she rinsed all the salt water off. She washed her hair with her aunt's lemon shampoo—the label said *Casa Riley,* and Julia knew she'd had it made with blossoms and fruit from the orchard.

Inside she changed into a blue cotton shift and threw a navy sweater over her shoulders. She slipped her feet into a pair of ballet flats, momentarily wondered whether to take an overnight bag. She packed one, just in case.

She looked at Bonnie, debated on whether to take her, too. She knew she'd be busy, and didn't want to chance neglecting her. Although she might have asked Roberto to feed and walk Bonnie, he'd gone home for the long weekend. She picked up the phone.

"Darling, you missed a delicious dinner," Lion said when he answered.

"I know, I'm sorry," she said.

"It's appalling you got stuck with that pompous ass. Did he really drive you away?"

"No. Honestly, Lion—Thanksgiving was such a Jenny holiday . . ."

"Say no more. I completely understand."

"Actually, I'm calling to ask a favor."

"Hmm?"

"I have to drive down to San Diego. I have a project in mind, and I'm not sure how long it will take. Would you mind feeding Bonnie?"

"Not at all, love. I'll drop by the Casa soon and give her lunch and a walk. Will, um, someone be going with you?"

"Roberto? No," she said.

"Sweetheart, a solo road trip can be just the thing. Do you have some thinking to do?"

"Maybe," she said, and laughed. "But I'm fine, Lion—I promise. And thanks for Bonnie-sitting. I won't be gone long."

"Whatever suits you," he said. "Consider her fed. Two old dogs—she and I will have a lot to talk about."

"Thanks," Julia said, and they hung up.

Bonnie, worn out from the excitement of the beach and her swim, was lying in the shade on the terrace. It overlooked the canyon and sea, and Julia saw Bonnie watching the red-tailed hawks ride the thermals. Julia leaned down and kissed her goodbye.

"I'll be back soon," she said, knowing Lion would soon be there to take her on a midday walk.

Bonnie gave her a baleful look. They understood each other. Living alone for so long, they'd developed a language between them. She let out a small but not overly protesting bark.

As Julia backed out of the driveway, she saw Roberto in the orchard—he'd come back after all. He was on a ladder, pruning branches. Their eyes met and they waved. She braked, and for a minute thought of telling him where she was going. But instead she stepped lightly on the gas and kept going.

Roberto

Wherever Julia had gone, Roberto hoped she would return soon. He thought of her nonstop.

Señor Riley always gave him and Serapio Thanksgiving weekend off, but Roberto needed to work. The orchard ate up hours, and while he stood on the ladder he kept picturing Julia back from the beach, walking into the outdoor shower. Roberto, on his ladder, had been unable to tear his eyes away.

She stood behind the latticework, so he couldn't see much except squares of sunlight on her bare arms and shoulders, but his imagination did the rest. He heard the water spray onto her skin, saw her raise her lean arms to lather shampoo on her head, could almost feel the warm water running down her smooth body.

He had planned to wait till she dried off and got dressed to go to her, take her into the orchard, kiss her again, tell her what last night had meant to him. But she had driven away before he could climb down from the ladder.

Around noon, when the sun blazed a path across the Pacific, he heard a car coming up the drive. For a moment he thought it was Julia and he couldn't wait to go to her. But the car engine was too powerful to be her Volvo, and when the maroon Jaguar XKE skidded into the turnaround, he saw it was Mr. Cushing, who then walked into the house without knocking.

Roberto wondered if something was wrong. After rinsing his hands under the hose, he hurried to the kitchen door and looked inside. No sign of anyone. He knocked loudly.

"Hola!" Roberto called.

He heard Bonnie barking from somewhere inside, maybe on the big circular seaside terrace. Then footsteps, and Mr. Cushing and Bonnie entered the kitchen at the same time.

"Señor Cushing, Julia has gone out," Roberto said.

"Yes, Roberto. She told me. Call me Lion, for godsakes." He rummaged around one of the lower cabinets. "Where the hell does she keep the dog food?"

"I'll get it," Roberto said. His stomach dropped—why hadn't she asked him to feed Bonnie?

Roberto went into the pantry, knelt by the cupboard beside the sink. He had carried the groceries in, placed Bonnie's food here himself—a case of canned beef and a three-pound bag of dry food.

"Oh dear," Mr. Cushing said. "What does Julia give her? Half wet, half dry?"

"Yes, that is right. Is she coming back soon?"

The old actor looked at him with kindness. "Um, I don't know, Roberto. She didn't seem to know herself." He stuck a can under the electric opener and zapped the lid off.

"But she will stay away tonight?"

"Yes. Meanwhile, she asked me to feed and walk Bonnie."

"I would happily do that for her," Roberto said. "Since I am here anyway." He felt stabbed that she hadn't asked him, that after last night she would leave without saying goodbye.

Lion seemed to be watching him with a glint in his eyes as Roberto took the can of food from Lion's gnarled old hands and mixed it in an aluminum bowl with a handful of kibbles.

"That's very nice of you," Lion said. "Thank you. I'll let her know you're on dog patrol. Will you take Bonnie out tonight and in the morning?'

"Sí, for sure," Roberto said.

"Muchas gracias," Lion said.

Roberto and the old actor watched Bonnie eat. He had the sense Lion felt the same emotional current he did; they knew what Bonnie meant to Julia.

"Did she say anything about why she left?" Roberto asked.

"Not really." The old actor's eyes gleamed. "Something about a project. But I'll tell you one thing, Roberto."

"What?"

"She was driven mad by Jenny's death. Did she tell you about what happened?"

"Sí," Roberto said.

"It practically destroyed her. You can imagine. But I see a difference in her in the last few weeks. A real transformation."

"What is that?"

"She's alive again. She feels happy." Lion clapped Roberto on the shoulder. "And it's because of you."

"Me?" he asked.

"Yes. She likes you and you make her happy."

Lion walked toward his car and climbed in. The motor started with a lusty roar. "The least we can do is take care of her while she's here," he said.

"We can do that, Mr. Cushing," Roberto said, forgetting.

"Call me Lion!" he said. "You make me feel even more ancient than I am."

"Okay, Lion," Roberto said.

"I'm the oldest man in Hollywood, but I don't feel it!" Lion called as he tooted the car horn and sped down the driveway.

Julia

The Reunion Project facility was in La Jolla, adjacent to Scripps Institution of Oceanography, far removed from the U.S.-Mexican border. Juan Rios had told her they would be open Friday and all weekend, and for her to come anytime. The building had a glass door but no windows and looked exactly like what it was: a morgue. That it was used for research, and for reuniting families, couldn't take away that fact.

She parked her car in the lot next door, walked to the tall glass doors, and buzzed. The receptionist had her name on a list and told her Dr. Rios would be with her shortly.

He came out a few minutes later. Short and compact, he had graying black hair and tortoiseshell half-specs were dangling from a cord around his neck. He wore a rumpled blue oxford shirt and khaki pants, and he greeted her with a hug, like a long-lost friend.

"Chris speaks so highly of you!" he said.

"And of you," Julia said.

"We go back a long way," Juan said. "Grad school, when we did our field study together."

"Chris tends to make work fun," Julia said.

"You worked with him at the Uto-Aztecan mound, didn't you?"

"Yes, eleven years ago," she said.

"Well, I'm glad you got in touch."

"I know you're very busy."

"Not at all. That's what we are here for," he said. "But if you don't mind, let's grab a bite before we get down to work." He patted his belly, which was spilling over his belt. "Small, frequent meals. That's what my wife keeps telling me."

They climbed into his vehicle, an old Jeep that looked as if it spent more time in the mountains and deserts than on the well-kept roads of La Jolla. He drove her past the ocean, waves breaking on the rocky coast, and past Children's Pool, a seawall built in 1931— he told her—to create a protected place for kids to swim.

"It's been taken over by seals," he said. "That's Seal Rock, just offshore, and they seem to think Children's Pool is a good place to birth their pups and keep them safe from what's out in the ocean."

She stared down at the glossy creatures, their pelts gleaming in the sun. No children were in the swimming area. They drove a few miles and parked in front of Rimel's—a tiny restaurant, warm and cozy and filled with beautiful paintings.

"Everything is good," Juan said as they sat down. "It's all fresh, the catch is right off the dock, and if you like fish tacos . . ."

"Done," Julia said.

They drank iced tea and talked about Chris and Maxine, how Julia had wound up studying with Chris at Yale, how Juan had gone into anthropology because he was Mexican and wanted to study the layers of culture and movement that gave his country and its people their identity.

The food arrived, and Juan was right: the fish tacos were delicious—fresh halibut, salsa, and crisp white cabbage in a corn tortilla. They ate quietly and drank iced tea in the gentle daytime darkness of the small restaurant.

"The Children's Pool," she said. "Did you show it to me for any reason?"

"No," he said. "It's just a La Jolla attraction. Why?"

"I was thinking about fences and walls, and how they don't really do the job, and how they relate to your work now."

"Very perceptive," he said. "Fences and walls."

"Keeping out the unwanted."

"Unwanted—that's a good way to put it."

"Tell me about your work now, Juan. It's called the Reunion Project?"

"Yes," he said. "But in general, not happy reunions. I work on border-crossing deaths."

"What do you mean?"

"We collect bodies and bones from the desert, try to match them with dental records, DNA, even clothing and belongings, and let families back in Mexico know the fate of their loved ones. Six hundred to a thousand deaths a year, mostly in the hot months."

"How did you go from papers and fieldwork on cultural anthropology to studying border-crossing deaths?"

"It's still anthropology, but applied in a very specific way. The border has changed drastically since I was young."

"How?"

"There has always been migration. That goes without saying when you have a rich country like ours sharing a border with a country as poor as Mexico."

"It's a given," Julia said

"Yes," he said. "The U.S. wants to protect the border—Operation Gatekeeper and the fence. The first phase took place just a few miles south of here—from the Pacific Ocean into San Ysidro—the border between San Diego and Tijuana."

She listened intently.

"That's when migrants began heading east, crossing through the Otay Mountains and the desert beyond—and dying in great numbers."

"That made you change your focus?"

"Yeah," he said. "The sheer numbers. Fresh skeletons. And then we'd go into town and see families walking around with pictures of their sons and daughters and husbands and parents—it got to me."

"It would get to me, too," she said.

He nodded. "Some Mexican and Central American families say goodbye to their children, parents, expecting to hear from them when they arrive in Phoenix, L.A., New York, wherever. But they never hear. And I couldn't imagine how they felt, and how they lived with it year after year. I'd seen the bodies in the desert, and I knew there had to be a way to match them with their families. So I joined up with other anthropologists working on similar projects in Texas and Arizona."

"Do you think we'll find out about Rosa?"

"I've already started trying," Juan said. "Let's go back to my office."

He paid the bill and they walked into the shaded parking lot, climbed into the Jeep, and headed back to the morgue. Julia closed her eyes because she had a picture of smiling, dark-haired Rosa in her mind, from Roberto's stories of her, and she wanted to hold on to it as long as she could, before they entered the building of bodies and bones.

After walking through the reception area, they came to a locked door with a sign that said THE REUNION PROJECT. Juan punched in a code and they entered. The hallway smelled of pine and lemon, but the scents didn't quite cover the chemical odor beneath.

When they got to Juan's office he dragged a second chair beside his and invited Julia to sit beside him at his desk.

He tilted the computer screen toward her. Several windows were open, including one that bore images of differently shaped skulls.

"We work with medical examiners in lots of jurisdictions," he said. "We start with fingerprints and dental records, of course, but sometimes the body is too decomposed, or has been separated by animals, and we're left with only bones and shreds of clothing."

He glanced at her, as if to see how she was taking this. She nodded, wanting him to continue. "Tell me more," she said.

"One of the problems in making identifications is that the bones are often so degraded by the time the coroner gets them—predators and the desert heat destroy all but slight traces of mitochondrial DNA. That can narrow an ID down to a particular family, but it's not enough to positively identify an individual. So we're getting creative."

"What are those skulls?" she asked.

"Some of my colleagues and I are working on a genetic map of Mexico, Guatemala, and Ecuador. Skull shapes, bone length and density, other factors are helping us narrow down where the dead came from. People from different regions in those countries have skulls with vastly different characteristics. So we can determine one crosser began in Oaxaca, while another comes from Veracruz."

"And that helps you learn enough to notify the families?"

"Not alone but sometimes with other evidence, such as a piece of clothing. In one case, a distinctive pair of sneakers, with initials drawn on the cloth, inside a heart."

"Lime-green sneakers," Julia said.

"That's what Rosa was wearing?"

"Yes. Her father told me."

"We can enter that into our database," he said, typing in the words. "I've already gotten started, based on what you emailed me. Is there more?"

"She had a doll," Julia said. "Her great-grandmother made it for her."

"What about her mother? You haven't mentioned her."

"The parents never married. They were young when she was born, and Roberto raised her with his grandmother."

"And where was Roberto's mother?"

"She died."

"Okay. So Roberto was picked up by La Migra, and then what happened?"

"While he was in detention, a border agent—Jack Leary—came looking for him—he'd found a child's footprint in the sand and connected it to Roberto's group. He wanted to check it out. Roberto gave him the best directions he could."

"The agent went looking for her?"

"Yes, right away, but she was gone. Still, Roberto had to see for himself. It took two days for him to be deported back to Mexico. He went straight to Altar and retraced the route the coyote had taken, crossed the border again on his own."

"He found the rock?"

"Yes, but no sign of Rosa."

Juan typed all this into a report, and she watched him hit Send, sharing it with other members of the Reunion Project throughout the Southwest. "You never know what will come back," he said. "I've already checked our database for skeletal remains of young females in that particular sector."

"Did you find any?" Julia asked.

"Yes, too many," he said. "But none that fit the criteria you gave me. All the girls were older, and the times of death don't fit; they were either before or after 2007."

"What did they die of, the girls?"

"Heat, dehydration, mostly. One was bitten by a snake—there are twenty-five varieties of poisonous snakes in that section of desert."

"Roberto said Rosa was so dehydrated, she was delirious. Talking about her flying doll, and a pet goat, and her great-grandmother."

"That's what happens," Juan said. "Her system was starting to shut down."

"Then why wasn't she found?"

"I don't know," Juan said. "An incredibly large percentage who try to cross get caught by the Border Patrol, but we know she wasn't. For those who don't, the chances of survival vary according to age, strength, health—even luck. We have to assume she died, but that's what's so cruel—there's no evidence that she did."

"And people were searching for her, so soon after. Roberto went back. And that agent, Jack Leary."

"I looked him up," Juan said, "after I got your email. I thought maybe I'd give him a call at Border Patrol headquarters in Tucson, but he's retired, unlisted number."

"I tried the same thing," Julia said. "Maybe there's another way to track him down."

"How?"

"Facebook."

"A badass border agent on Facebook?" Juan asked. But he did a search, and out of the hundred or so Jack Learys, only one looked weathered and old enough to have been a seasoned Border Patrol agent. His photo showed him and a petite blue-eyed woman with a long gray braid, holding each other tight and smiling for the camera. They stood in a yard, an adobe house and cacti behind them. It said they lived in Yuma, Arizona.

"That has to be him," Julia said. "Roberto said they crossed in Arizona." She reached past Juan, clicked some keys to type her password, and her own page popped up.

"There you are," he said.

"I joined because of Jenny," Julia said. She quickly typed a message to Jack Leary.

> Hello, you don't know me, but I'd very much like to discuss one of your old cases with you—Rosa Rodriguez. Please call me.

She gave her cell phone number and clicked Send.

"Jenny?" Juan asked.

"My daughter," she said, and smiled, and she left it at that.

She had planned to spend the night in Del Mar, just a few miles away from La Jolla, and return here tomorrow. By then Juan might have responses from the emails he'd sent. But now she had another destination.

"Will you stay in touch?" she asked, gathering her things. "Let me know what you hear?"

"Of course," he said. "It's an old case, but don't give up. We'll do what we can."

"Thank you so much for everything," she said.

They hugged, and she walked to her car. The sea air was fresh and cool, with a strong breeze coming off the ocean a few blocks away.

She dialed Lion's number on her cell phone.

"Hello, darling," he said.

"It's me."

"I know. The beauty of caller ID. How are you?"

"I'm good. The trip is going well. How are you?"

"First of all, Bonnie and Roberto are fine."

"And you?"

"Grrrr," he said.

"What's wrong?"

"I'm reading Nabokov. He dedicated *Speak, Memory* to his wife, Vera. That means he loved her, obviously."

"I'd say so."

"It burns me that your uncle writes all those scholarly books and dedicates them all to Graciela. It's like a slap in the face."

"What are you talking about?"

"He's married to her—isn't that enough? Does he have to proclaim his love in print, too? I'm just an actor—what can I do?"

"You've played some of the most beautiful love scenes on screen with her, Lion. Why are you so sad today?"

"I don't know," he said. "It gets to me once in a while."

"You are loved and adored by many, including me," she said.

"That is of no comfort whatsoever. That kind of love is nice, but it doesn't make you want to get up in the morning, no offense."

"Well, I'm calling to say I'll definitely be away tonight. You have to get up in the morning to feed Bonnie, right?"

"Oh. No. As a matter of fact, Roberto offered to take over Bonnie duties. He's such a nice man."

"He is," she said, her skin tingling just because Lion had mentioned his name. "Did he say anything else?"

"About you? Yes. He was concerned that you'd left without telling him."

"Oh."

Long silence. She had turned on her engine and was programming the GPS for route guidance to Yuma, Arizona, but Lion's silence made her stop. She could almost hear him smiling through the phone.

"Well," Lion said finally. "I assume you'll want to call to fill him in on your plans."

"Could you do it for me?" she asked. She didn't want to explain to Roberto where she was or what she was doing.

"Of course," Lion said. "But I'm sure he'll be sorely disappointed."

Julia didn't reply.

"Darling, when it comes to matters of the heart, I am your man."

"Thank you, Lion," Julia said.

"Okay, love. Drive safely, wherever you are. And come home soon."

"I will," Julia said.

After she hung up, she finished programming her GPS and realized that without traffic, Route 8 would get her to Yuma in under three hours. She headed for the highway out of San Diego and saw the Pacific Ocean disappearing in her rearview mirror.

Roberto

With the sun setting behind the Channel Islands, Roberto fed Bonnie and took her for her evening walk. He followed the path Julia liked.

Working in Malibu, Roberto was mostly focused on the job, all the details of keeping the orchard running. But Bonnie walked slowly, and so did Roberto, so he tried to see the landscape as Julia did.

It was beautiful here. He looked down the long canyon, shadows painting the chaparral shades of green and gold. At the bottom the ocean spread to the horizon. Waves broke near shore. He saw surfers—tiny black dots from this height—waiting for their chance. Out beyond, the ocean was dark blue with silver currents running through it, like independent pathways to secret destinations.

The curve of the coast was visible, mountains ranging down to the edge of the sea. He never spent time looking around like this. He'd grown up in the country, surrounded by nature, but he just took it for granted. In Mexico he had worked hard in the fields and orchards, walked home to eat and sleep, or to go to school, and then taken the same path back to work the next day. Landscape was something to be gotten through—crossed, like the desert—not enjoyed.

Bonnie stood beside him, pressed against his leg. He rested his hand on her head. She trusted him. He wondered about Julia. She had driven off so suddenly he hoped he hadn't upset her too much. Maybe she had to get away from him. He knew he had offended her by kissing her. Maybe he had misread her signals.

Bonnie had started walking again, so Roberto followed. They went slowly, and he breathed in the cool sea air, and wondered what it would be like if Julia were here, if she were walking beside him. They rounded the corner, came upon a herd of mule deer grazing. Bonnie chased them, barking.

Roberto watched Bonnie with admiration. She was bred for herding, and he saw she had a great heart, and in that moment when she ran so bravely after the deer he saw the young dog she once had been.

He wished Julia were here, so he could take back what he'd said, and filled the spaces with what he hadn't said. When Bonnie returned from her chase, she looked up at Roberto for approval, and he petted her head.

"Good dog, Bonnie," he said in English, because that was her language. "You are a very good dog."

Julia

Route I-8 ran due east from Sunset Cliffs in San Diego, and when it dipped south below the Anza-Borrego Desert State Park, it practically touched the Mexican border. There was a big sign over the ten-lane highway proclaiming BORDER FRIENDSHIP ROUTE as the road began to climb into the craggy mountains. She passed signs for La Posta and Campo Indian reservations and drove for a while as the sun began to set.

Descending through a pass between two peaks, she entered the Imperial Valley as traffic slowed down. She saw flashing lights up ahead. As they crept along, Julia saw three state trooper cars, a U.S. Border Patrol SUV, and a Dodge Charger.

There was an overpass above the highway, and when she drew beneath it, she saw two men in handcuffs being led into one of the police cars. They had light brown skin and their postures made them appear defeated—round shoulders, heads down. She stared, thinking of what Juan had told her, and wondered how many times the men had tried crossing before.

When she reached Calexico, she decided to stop for the night. She hadn't heard from Jack Leary, and continuing on didn't make sense unless she did. The city was on the border, directly across from Mexicali on the Mexican side. Driving into town, she found the strip of motels and restaurants, and through her open window she heard mariachi music.

Pulling into the Flores Blancas motel parking lot, she saw a stage set up by the entrance. The mariachis were dressed in black, with white braids on their lapels and around the brims of their sombreros, and their guitar and horn music was bright and happy.

She sat in the car for a minute thinking of Rosa, of the promise Roberto had made her: that they would live near the square where mariachis gathered. Her scalp tingled, almost as if a little girl with lime-green sneakers and a winged doll named Maria was nearby.

The desk clerk gave her a choice of rooms—all were named for white flowers. Oleander, Lily, Geranium, Rose. Julia chose Rose, and when she reached the room, she saw the theme had been carried forth: from the wallpaper to the bedspread, everything was covered in white roses. She checked her phone in case Leary had called, but he hadn't. So she headed down to the outdoor terrace for dinner.

The café was set beneath enormous ficus trees with glossy green leaves and pale gray bark. White lights filled the branches and leaves, and candles in pressed-tin lanterns were on every table.

Colorful flags of turquoise, vermilion, emerald, crimson, and dark pink hung on a wire strung all around the seating area, and fluttered in the slight breeze. The air was still hot, even after sunset. The menu had *ropa vieja*; remembering dinner with Roberto, she ordered it. Patrons called out requests, and the mariachis began to play "Contigo."

Waiting for her food, she remembered her uncle's letter. She pulled it from her bag and began to read.

Dearest Julia,
Greetings from Clifden, capital of that most beautiful place on earth—Connemara, Ireland. To be here is to know our

ancestors, to hear their whispers, and to feel their desires. How you would love it, my dear. You must visit one day.

Meanwhile, Graciela and I thank you mightily for looking after the Casa while we're gone. I trust all is well, or you would have called. You are in good hands with our orchard manager, Roberto, and of course Lion is just down the road. Graciela and I have such happy memories of your visiting as a child, and we hope you are rediscovering the pleasures of Malibu in general and Casa Riley in particular.

Speaking of "Riley," our namesake, my research into John Riley's roots is going well. I hope to have a new book finished by the end of next year. While Clifden is exceptionally beautiful, on the rocky shores of Clifden Bay—and in the virtual shadow of Croagh Patrick, Ireland's holy mountain— I've uncovered much evidence of the suffering that led our forebears to escape the potato famine and immigrate to the United States.

John Riley himself is a prime example. I'm telling you this because I know, as an anthropologist, you have a special interest in the patterns and movements of human development, and here we have a case history in our own past. Because of the famine, which was so deadly many of the Rileys died of starvation, John joined the British Army. Can you imagine that? The conflict he must have felt, an ardent Irishman, joining with the enemy just to survive?

Perhaps this is a book you should research, Julia. More to the point, would you be interested in helping me? As I've told you often enough, and as is well documented in art and lore, after Riley immigrated to the United States, he fought in the Fifth U.S. Infantry Regiment against Mexico in the Mexican-American War.

Recognizing the injustice of taking Texas and other land from Mexico—and I'm sure identifying with Britain's occupation of Ireland—he defected and formed the Saint Patrick's Battalion. I feel very proud to have him as our ancestor, and I know you do, too.

Do you remember dreaming about him when you were a little girl? You were visiting us, and I held you on my lap and told you the story of John Patrick Riley. I remember you being so moved by the fact that he'd been branded a deserter, a "D" burned into his cheek. It made you cry, and you asked me to draw a "D" on your cheek, too. I did, and on my own as well.

That night you dreamed of him as an angel—after his death, lingering in Mexico to protect the people who needed protecting. You said he looked after two little girls, and one of them was you. I've often wondered if that dream, and your knowledge of John Riley, influenced your decision to study anthropology, particularly because of your research trip to Mexico.

He died in Veracruz and his death certificate read "Juan Reley." He was forty-five, unmarried, and the curate who filled out the certificate said he died of drunkenness, without sacraments. You know very well that I am a lapsed Catholic, like yourself, and I believe John Riley died with abundant sacraments. He followed his heart and did what was right, and how many people can we say that about?

His Irish name is Seán Pádraic Ó Raghallaigh. If it weren't too late to have a son, that's what I would name him. Riley never left Mexico, although he could have. These are all discoveries I am making, and I wanted to share them with you, Julia.

No one escapes this life without suffering—not a person

on earth knows that better than you. Take heart in knowing
our ancestor fought against the unfair in life, and in spite of
what that Catholic curate wrote, I believe he died with more
sacraments than the damn church can count. And I believe he
has passed them on to you, dear child.

Take care, let the Malibu air soothe your soul, and any time
you want to join my research team (just me at the moment),
you are welcome. We could co-author the definitive biography
of John Riley. Graciela sends her love.

> *Love,*
> *Uncle John*

Julia closed her eyes to listen to the music and remember those dreams she'd had about John Riley. She did remember crying over his story—the combination of his family starving, and his having to leave beautiful Ireland, and then having to fight for what he had considered to be the wrong side. It had made her sad to think of soldiers burning a "D" into his face, and spitting on him and calling him a deserter.

Her food came, and she ate it slowly. It was good, but nothing like the dinner she'd had with Roberto. She read John's letter again, and wondered if he was right: had knowing that John Riley was their distant relative influenced and inspired her all along?

Those dreams had been so vivid. Whenever she was scared, his ghost would protect her. When she was eleven, a neighborhood boy bullied her on the way home from school—pulled her coat off in January and threw it up in a tree. It was snowing, and she'd had to walk the rest of the way, nearly a mile, in shirtsleeves.

That night John Riley had come to her dream. Instead of a snowy New England street, Julia and another girl walked down a jungle path. A monster appeared—it had blond hair and blue eyes like the neighborhood boy, but was ten feet tall with scaly skin and bloody fangs. He grabbed Julia's friend, and somehow that felt more terrible than if he'd attacked Julia.

Sometimes you can't scream in your dreams. That had always been true for Julia. She opened her mouth and no sound came out. But John Riley heard anyway, appeared out of nowhere. He grabbed Julia's friend from the monster's arms, set her down gently, and killed the monster so he'd never hurt anyone again.

Pulling her out of her reverie, the mariachis approached Julia's table and played a beautiful ballad. She thought of Roberto, wished he were sitting beside her. She could still feel his kiss, how it had felt to be standing in the orchard with him, their bodies pressed together. What would happen when she got back to the Casa?

She was falling in love with him. It had been building for weeks, maybe even from that first night they'd sat together on the steps. The way he looked at her made her blood tingle—her emotions had never run anything but high, but with Peter she'd kept herself in check. When she'd cried, he'd always said she was being dramatic. She'd gotten very good at sublimating her passions.

When the mariachis finished playing, she paid her check and went up to her room. She checked her phone. It had been on the whole time, but with the band playing she hadn't heard it ring. Jack Leary had left a message giving her his address in Yuma, Arizona, and telling her he would be expecting her when she got there. She lay down on the bed with its white roses coverlet and closed her eyes and thought of kissing Roberto under the lemon trees.

Jack Leary

Waiting for Julia Hughes to arrive, Jack straightened up the living room and remembered to open the curtains. Louella would have liked that. She always said there was nothing worse than a dark room on a sunny day. She'd have gone out to the garden, cut some of her desert grasses, and arranged them in a vase. Jack had let the yard go to hell. He'd wound up mowing the whole thing down to a stubby little field of dry brown whatever. At least he could see the snakes better.

He put a pot of coffee on and sat down at the kitchen table to wait. This house was so empty now. Louella's two old cats, Lee-lee and Nomar, slept all the time and barely gave him the time of day. Sugar, Louella's teacup Yorkshire terrier, was another story. She missed Louella as much as Jack did, and she sat at his feet while he read the paper.

The news was depressing, as usual. Here in Yuma it was all about the border. The drug cartels, the kidnappings, Mexico's new president and was he better or worse than the last one, another seven border crossers found dead in the back of a truck. It just went on and on. There was only one reason Jack stayed in Arizona instead of moving back to Boston, where he came from.

Louella. She had wanted to be buried next to her parents, out in the back corner of what used to be their old ranch and was now, except for the small cemetery, a mall with every store Yuma thought it couldn't live without.

Jack heard tires crunching on the driveway, and realized his guest had arrived.

Sugar ran to the screen door barking and guarding the property as if she were a German shepherd.

"Well, hello," the woman said, crouching down so she was eye level with Sugar. "Aren't you brave? Good dog . . ."

Jack opened the door, and Sugar ran out, flying in circles still barking, but finally letting the lady pet her on the head and then rolling onto her back so she could get her tummy rubbed.

"What kind of guard dog are you, Sugar?" he asked.

"Oh, she's a good one," the woman said. "I can tell. She just knows I'm friendly. I think she smells Bonnie on me."

"That your dog?"

"Yes, my old girl. She didn't make the trip with me, though." Standing, she shook Jack's hand. "I'm Julia Hughes. Thanks for seeing me."

"Jack Leary. Not sure how I can help, but come on in."

He gestured for Julia to sit at the table. She was small, about five-four, with a tiny frame but a nice figure. Big blue eyes and pale skin, silver-blond hair. She had some small freckles on her cheeks and arms, and she reminded him of his sister Eileen when she was young. He made Julia Hughes for Irish.

"So, you're retired," she said, after he served her a mug of coffee.

"Yep," he said. "Nearly two years now."

"That must feel good."

"Oh yeah," he said. "All the free time in the world. Now, what can I do for you, Ms. Hughes?"

"Julia," she said.

"Fine then. Julia."

"Well," she said. "It's like I said in the message. It has to do with a case you once worked."

"Uh-huh," he said. She'd described it well enough. "I remember. Some of them stand out. That was one of them that did."

"Can you tell me why?"

He stared at her across his coffee mug. She looked intelligent, but what kind of question was that? Jack steered clear of reporters, journalists, any kind of writer who might want to make a buck off the stories of the dead and despairing.

"Why?" he asked. "Because a little girl got lost. Now listen, you never did tell me what's your angle in this. What is it to you? You didn't mention being a reporter, and you're clearly not Mexican."

"I have to be Mexican to care?" she asked.

Well, what the hell? It was like he'd slapped her. Tears had sprung into her eyes so fast he hadn't seen them coming at all. She wiped them away and composed herself with head-snapping speed.

"Let's start over," he said. "What brings you here?"

"I want to find out what happened to Rosa Rodriguez."

He nodded. "Okay. How are you connected?"

"I know her father."

"From where?"

She didn't reply.

He peered at her, wondering how much she knew about the whole immigration mess, and figured she didn't want the dad getting in trouble for being illegal.

"I'm retired," he said. "I'm not turning him in."

"Still. What's the difference how I know him? He told me his story. Rosa's been missing five years. I checked with a friend at the Reunion Project, and he said no remains they have on file can be matched to her."

"Well, hell, what is he doing, looking at a computer screen? Coyotes could have dragged her far from that rock where her father left her."

"He didn't really *leave* her," she said.

She was quick to defend the father, Jack noted, but what did she really know? Passing through the desert was like a mirage. Facts shimmered and disappeared into the hot sun. But in this case, he had personal knowledge of the mistakes his squad had made that day.

"He told us about her," Jack said. "And by the time we were able to recon, she was gone. And I suspect he went back, too."

"He did," she said. "So what happened? It was only a matter of hours. He said she was so dehydrated and weak, she couldn't have walked away on her own. Could she?"

"Doubtful," he said.

"Did you look for footprints? She was wearing—"

"Bright green sneakers. I know. And yes, we did. Of course we did. We even brought out. . ." He stopped himself. No need for her to get into the politics of the agency or to know more than would be helpful about what happened next. There was a fine line between giving people information and false hope.

"Brought out what?" she asked.

"Now listen," he said, turning the tables. "What's your interest in this? You're not a family member; I'm not sure I have the right to give you any information at all."

"If I were a family member," she said, "would I *have* any right?"

"Huh," he said. "Undocumented Mexicans don't, it's true. But why do the Border Patrol and ICE always come off looking like the bad guys to people like you? You come down to the border—what, your first time here?"

She nodded.

"And you want to help, I get it. But we have a job, and you don't see what we do. We stop a truck, we don't know whether it's going to be full of families looking for a better life or meth couriers for the Sinaloa cartel armed with AKs. And the coyotes, they 'help' people cross. Lady, they want their money. They take them through ever more rural and dangerous passes to avoid us. And it's getting these people killed. Didn't the father tell you about that?"

"Yes," she said.

"Several members of that group died, as I recall."

"Before," she said, "you said 'we brought out . . .' Please tell me."

He tried to think back, get the details straight in his mind. He had reviewed the file before she came—when he retired he made copies of twenty or so cases that haunted him. This was definitely one, for reasons Julia Hughes might never want to know.

"You know, your best bet really is the place you already visited," he said. "The Reunion Project. Did you go to their office in Tucson?"

"San Diego," she said. "I met with the director, Juan Rios."

"How do you know him?"

"Through a friend, one of his colleagues. In a sense, we're in the same field—anthropology. Juan is on the forensic side of it, but eleven years ago my daughter and I spent a few months studying at a site in Mexico."

"How old is your daughter?"

"She was ten that summer," Julia said.

And just like that, Leary had his answer. The way she closed her eyes, her hesitation, the way she gave him the age her daughter had been eleven years ago. He knew why she was pursuing the case of Rosa Rodriguez.

"What was her name?" he asked.

"Jenny."

"What happened?"

"Car crash."

"I'm sorry," he said.

"How did you know?" she asked.

He smiled sadly. There were so many ways—how she'd answered him, the sorrow in her blue eyes. And this mission she was on—he had to admit it was unusual. The people who came to him were generally journalists after a story or naturalized Mexicans looking for their loved ones. Julia was searching her heart out for Rosa Rodriguez to try to staunch the pain of her own loss. So Leary decided to tell her.

"Shadow Wolves," he said.

"Excuse me?"

"Earlier you asked me who we brought out on Rosa's case. Shadow Wolves. They're an elite squad, expert trackers, Native Americans. We generally use them to catch drug smugglers, mules carrying cocaine and methamphetamine. But I requested that they look for Rosa."

"Why?" she asked.

He was quiet for a few minutes. He got up and refilled their coffee mugs, finally remembered to put the muffins he'd bought at the store that morning on the table. Louella would have wanted him to. He sat down again, looked Julia deeply in the eyes.

"The reason I wanted the Shadow Wolves on it is that there were parts of the story that didn't fit," he said.

"Roberto's story?"

He saw the blood drain from her face. "No," he said quickly. "We believed him. But shortly after we caught his group, some others came along the same route. We captured six, but the others, including the coyotes, got away."

"Could one of them have rescued Rosa?" Julia asked.

"We wanted to think so. That's why we called in the Wolves—to track that second group."

"What did they discover?"

"Nothing definitive enough to tell you. I could ask Latham Nez if he'd be willing to talk to you. He holds everything very close. But as a favor to me, he might do it. He's the head of the team that handled Rosa's case."

"Would you ask him?"

Leary glanced at the picture of him and Louella standing outside their teardrop camper, on a trip to Yellowstone four summers ago. He could feel her with him now, wanting him to help Jenny's mother.

They weren't going to find Rosa, but he had learned over the years that no search was ever futile. Finding the quarry wasn't always the point. In fact it rarely was.

He nodded, and made the call with Julia Hughes looking on.

"Latham Nez, it's been a long time. This is Jack Leary."

chapter seven

Julia

Latham Nez couldn't see her till the next day, so she checked into the Sonoran, a motel a few miles from Jack's house. Jack invited her for dinner, but she was exhausted and said she'd meet him in the morning.

The motel had a southwestern theme, cactus plants in the lobby and all the walls painted soothing adobe colors of brick, sunflower, and dusky blue. She turned up the air conditioner in her room and lay flat on the bed.

She stared at Roberto's number programmed into her phone. She wanted to call, but there was a lot to explain. There could be news about Rosa—should she tell him now or wait till she'd met with Latham Nez?

Her mind was flooded with thoughts and ideas about Rosa, but her heart was remembering the trip to Mexico she and Jenny had taken. They had stayed in motels just like this one. Jenny had loved the colors, the warm décor. In spite of her objections to leaving Black Hall that summer, she had taken this style back home, painted her room to resemble a pueblo, sunset colors, the stately elm framed in the big window in the middle of the ochre-colored wall.

Jenny called her father nearly every night. Julia would say hello at the end, but mainly the conversation was Jenny telling him about what she had seen, new foods she had eaten, how much she missed the beach. Julia's stomach would tighten when she took the receiver. Peter sounded indulgent, as if he were letting her spend time away from home, on an adventure vacation. It made her blood boil.

Jenny, always vigilant, picked up on it. She would watch Julia on the phone with Peter as if trying to figure out her parents' marriage.

"Alice's parents are getting divorced," Jenny said one night, in a motel room strikingly similar to this one. There were two double beds, and although they'd turned in for the night, neither of them could sleep.

"I know," Julia said.

"It's sad when parents get divorced," Jenny said, her voice thin.

"Very sad, I know," Julia said, understanding exactly what Jenny was getting at.

"I wish we were all together this summer."

"We will be soon."

"When are we going home?"

"In three more weeks," Julia said. "There'll be lots of summer left."

"We can all go to the beach together and do what we always do," Jenny said.

"Yes."

"This is not my favorite summer," Jenny said quietly.

"I know, Jen," Julia said.

In return she got an exasperated sigh, and the sound of Jenny tossing in her bed. That week Jenny began deciding what her own life would be like when she fell in love. On a piece of beige motel stationery, Julia found a list Jenny had made. The fact she'd left it on her bedside table instead of tucking it into her journal made Julia realize the list was intended for her benefit as well.

1. Love is everything.
2. No secrets from each other
3. If you say I love you, it can never be taken back.
4. Never spend the summer apart.
5. Never spend a night apart, unless one of you has to be in the hospital or something equally urgent.
6. Talk on the phone every day.
7. NOTHING is more important than taking your husband's (or wife's) phone call.
8. Eternal closeness
9. Meals together EVERY NIGHT

Now, eleven years later, Julia closed her eyes and thought of how thoroughly Jenny had followed her own plan. She had loved Timmy with everything she had, and for at least a year, he had loved her the same way. Maybe her passion and intensity had scared him off—just as Julia's had created its own distance between Peter and her.

Holding her phone, heart beating fast, she stared at Roberto's name. She pressed Dial, and after a few rings the call went to voicemail. She felt both relieved and disappointed.

"Hi, Roberto, it's Julia. I just wanted to thank you for taking care of Bonnie. Lion told me." She paused, overflowing with things to say, knowing she would say none of them. "Please pet Bonnie for me and tell her I'll be home soon, in a day or so. I miss her . . . and I miss you. Good night, Roberto."

Roberto

Roberto, staying at the Casa, didn't get Julia's call, because he was taking Bonnie for her evening walk. Cell reception was unreliable at best, and the farther he went from the Casa, the worse it was. When he returned to the house and gave Bonnie a fresh bowl of water, he listened to the message. Her voice was beautiful and gentle, and he listened to the message again, especially the part where she said she missed him.

He wanted to call her back, but she hadn't asked him to, and she clearly said "Good night." So perhaps, wherever she was, she had gone to bed. He didn't want to disturb her, but it moved him that she'd called.

He sat in the kitchen chair and petted the old dog between her ears for a long time. She rested her chin on his knee, looking up at him with her big two-colored eyes. He remembered seeing her that first day, thinking his grandmother would have called her a *bruja*. But after getting to know Bonnie, he knew there was nothing witch-like about her.

He walked through the house, leaving a few lights on for the dog and to make it look occupied. He didn't think anyone would dare break into the Casa with his staying on the property, but robberies in the hills and canyons of Malibu were not unknown.

When he got to the room Julia was staying in, he paused in the doorway, then entered. Her suitcases stood in the corner, but she'd unpacked the bag of books and arranged them on the desk. There was a framed photo beside them, and feeling like an intruder, he walked over to look at it.

There was Julia, her arms around a girl who had to be Jenny. They stood on the porch of a house, beaming at the camera. Roberto saw the mother-daughter similarity in their eyes, the shape of their faces, their smiles. He touched their faces. Then he couldn't help himself—he pulled out his wallet and removed a photo of Rosa. He couldn't have explained why he did this, but he tucked Rosa's photo into the corner of the picture frame—he wanted them to be close, Julia and their two daughters. He would remove it before Julia returned to the Casa, but for now he left it there.

Leaving the room, he paused by the bed. He gazed down at it and pressed his hand into the pillow. Although he wasn't religious, he wanted to bless Julia, and her travels, and her dreams, and he couldn't think of any other way to do it.

Then he walked away.

Jack

As Jack Leary drove Julia Hughes to meet Latham Nez, he gave her a little background on the elite group of trackers.

"Shadow Wolves are expert at cutting sign," he said. "They have to have at least one-quarter Native American blood, and they patrol the eighty-mile stretch of Tohono O'odham reservation along the border."

"Why are they so good?"

"Skills passed down through the generations. Some smugglers are almost equally good at disguising their routes. But a Shadow Wolf will notice one pebble out of place, no exaggeration, and ten miles later he'll capture his quarry."

"They work for the reservation?"

"No. They're ICE, U.S. Border Patrol agents—hey, there's Latham's Jeep up ahead."

Julia seemed wide-eyed, driving through the desert. Hearing about this place was one thing, but seeing it and feeling the heat on the truck windows, no matter how much air-conditioning was blasting inside, was a humbling experience. Jack pulled over behind Latham's vehicle, and called his radio to let him know they were there.

While they waited in the cool truck, Julia turned to him.

"Jack Leary," she said, and then, seemingly out of the blue, "Are you Irish?"

"Hell yes. Could there be any doubt with a name like Leary?"

"Before I was married, I was Julia Riley."

"Ha, I knew I liked you. What part of Ireland are your people from?"

"Connemara," she said. "My uncle's over there now, researching an ancestor. Have you ever heard of John Riley?"

Leary beamed, and went through his center console, came up with a CD and pushed it in. Tim O'Brien sang about John Riley coming from Galway to fight in the U.S. Army.

"That's him."

"Every Irishman who finds his way to the border learns about John Riley pretty fast."

Latham walked over to the truck. Stepping out into 103-degree heat, Leary made the introductions.

Latham wore traditional camo clothes and a wide-brimmed hat. His dark skin was sunburned, and his features were strong and proud. He was mainly Tohono O'odham, but Leary remembered hearing he was part Navajo, too. Shadow Wolves came from several tribes, including Sioux, Blackfoot, Lakota, and Yaqui.

"What can I do for you, miss?" he asked.

"I'm looking for information about a girl who was lost five years ago. Jack told me you might know something about her," Julia said.

"I told you," Leary prodded him. Latham was closemouthed, especially about agency matters, and he would be careful about what he gave up. "The six-year-old from Puebla, we took her father into custody, she was left by the boulder in Sector 34, May 12, 2007."

"Uh-huh," Latham said.

Leary glared at him. If he was going to be a dick and treat him like an outsider, Leary was going to be pissed.

"Rosa Rodriguez," Leary said. "We talked about this."

"What do you want to know, miss?" Latham asked.

"What happened to her?"

"We don't have that information."

"For chrissakes, Latham—tell her what you told me."

"It's hot out here," Latham said. "Especially if you're not used to desert heat."

"There's an Applebee's up the road. My treat," Leary said.

"We can talk there," Latham said.

chapter eight

Julia

They sat in a booth and ordered lunch and iced tea, and when her salad came she couldn't eat a bite. She listened intently to every word Latham spoke.

"That rock where Rosa's father left her," Latham began. "That was the source. Right away my colleagues and I determined she'd been taken, shortly after her father was picked up, by a different group."

"Group?" she asked.

"Border crossers," Latham said. "They most often travel in groups."

"But who would take Rosa and not report it? Maybe not right away, but once they got safely to where they were going?"

"People have different reasons for being in the desert," Latham said matter-of-factly. "The coyotes are smugglers. Yes, they help innocent people cross. But there are ugly stories, too."

"That's true," Jack said. "But there could be many reasons they didn't report Rosa. They might have tried, and not known who to contact. They are vulnerable themselves, here illegally, and they might not have wanted to get themselves—or Rosa's family—in trouble."

"Anyway," Latham continued. "We tracked this one group before the boulder, and again after. Footprints tell us everything: height, weight, sometimes nationality depending on the footgear, whether they're weighted down with backpacks or whatever they might be carrying."

"One of the walkers picked Rosa up?" Julia asked, unable to contain her excitement.

"Yes. From the footprints, we saw that a man traveling with a group of twelve others began carrying an additional forty-eight-pound weight. That's small for a six-year-old, but assuming she came from poverty in Roberto's town of Santa Cruz Tlaxcala, it fits."

"How far did you follow them?"

"A ways. They seem to have gotten lost before reaching the main road. They veered off into the foothills."

"But they made it?"

"Some may have," Latham said. "We found four bodies."

"Oh," she said, feeling her stomach knot.

"The terrain became rocky, more difficult to follow. Eventually the path intersected a road where some may have been picked up by their contacts."

"And Rosa?"

"We didn't find her body," Latham said. "But we found these."

He had carried a file with him, and opened it, and pushed two separate photos across the table to Julia. Each showed a single small dust-covered lime-green sneaker.

"They were half a mile apart. Neither was on the trail where we tracked the group. They were in rough mountain terrain. That's not a hopeful sign."

"She might have lost them," Julia said. "They could have come off while the man was carrying her. Or if she walked, she could have gotten them stuck in the rocks. That happened to Jenny, my daughter, when we were crabbing at low tide, all those rocks, and they just caught one of her sneakers in the wrong way and it came right off . . ."

"See that?" Latham asked, pointing to a brown patch covering the side of her right sneaker. "That's blood."

"It could be mud."

"We tested."

"Maybe she had a blister that got rubbed raw—or she fell down and scraped her ankle."

"It's more likely her body was dragged from the scene by animals," Latham said.

"When did you determine that?" Jack asked, sounding angry, offended that he hadn't been told.

"Look, you're retired—I looked up the file as a favor to you. And this case is five years old, Jack. I followed the trail, but the rest was done in the lab."

Jack spread the photos across the table, staring at them.

"It's a theory, Jack, that's all. But it's our best working theory. If we could spend one hundred percent of our time on Rosa Rodriguez, we'd know for sure. But you know how it is. How backed up we are. Those hills are full of coyotes and mountain lions. We think one of them dragged Rosa off, that her bones are scattered over the rocks."

"But you don't know for sure," Jack said. "Why don't you get your fellow Wolves and go find her remains?"

"'Remains'? You don't know that's what you'd be looking for. She might have made it," Julia said. "There's no proof of her death!"

"Julia, proof of death is rare in the desert. We do our best, but do you how many people we identify? A small percentage," Latham said.

"Needle in a haystack, Julia. Don't get your hopes up," Jack said.

"But without a body . . . even bones . . . If any had been collected, they would be in a morgue, and Juan would have found the data," she said.

"We consider the sneakers to be a strong indication that she is dead," Latham said.

"Did you find her doll? Maria?"

"No. But we matched the blood with her father's. We DNA-tested him when he was arrested."

"Then why didn't you tell him?"

"Where would we find him?" Jack asked. "He's undocumented. The last thing he wants is for his address to be known by ICE. Forget about this, Julia. It's very sad; I know it's not what you hoped for. Try to let it go."

"That is wise advice," Latham said. "As hard as it is to accept, she's just another border casualty."

"She's also someone's daughter," Julia said.

Roberto

Julia had left him that phone message, and he'd saved it and listened to it many times. The sound of her voice, speaking just to him, so soft and beautiful, saying his name. He wanted to save it forever.

She didn't come home until two nights later. He heard her car come up the cobblestoned driveway. The car door slammed, and she let herself into the house. He lay on his narrow bed, hypervigilant for any sound. He stared out the open door toward the barn because he knew when she turned off the house lights, he'd see their reflection on the weathered red boards disappear.

But the house lights stayed on. Soon the door opened again. He thought she must be walking Bonnie, and he considered joining her. But would it be an intrusion? She had left that phone message. Did that mean anything? He felt that she respected him, but he'd also heard something else in her voice, a closeness different from anything he had in his life.

Before he had the chance to walk out and meet her and Bonnie, her footsteps came down the hill toward his cabin. By the time she knocked on his door, his heart was racing.

"Roberto," she said. "I'm sorry it's so late."

"That's okay, Julia. Are you all right?"

She didn't reply. He stood there in his work jeans and T-shirt. There was a square table and two chairs in the corner. He held one out for her, and she sat down. He turned on a lamp and sat across from her. Maybe he should offer her coffee or tea, but he couldn't take his eyes off her.

She was right here, in his cabin. Her blue eyes were on fire, she seemed agitated, so he reached across the table to hold her hand.

"Hola, Julia," he said.

"Hola." Finally, a smile. But it was fleeting, here and gone.

"What's wrong?" he asked.

"I wanted to wait until tomorrow," she said. "Let you have a good night's sleep . . ."

"I don't need sleep." And holding her hand, he felt he didn't need anything—food, air, water, sleep, if he could just stay here like this.

"I took a trip to learn about Rosa," she said. "I should have told you before I left, but we had that talk, and I know you were very upset."

"I'm sorry for how I acted," he said. "My feelings—they weren't

because of you. They had to do with Rosa. I never talk about her
the way I do with you."

"I know that."

He couldn't breathe or speak. Now it was Julia squeezing his
hand, holding his gaze with hers, her blue eyes so bright and sad,
he felt a lump in his chest, as if his heart had seized.

"What did you do?" he asked.

"I followed some of the leads I told you about," she said. "I went
to La Jolla, to an organization called the Reunion Project."

"Bring people together?"

"Yes, sort of. Juan and his team focus on border crossers. They
have a database full of everyone who's been detained and arrested,
and every body that was ever found."

"Rosa's?" he asked, his bones and blood burning.

"No," she said quickly. "He has no record of anyone like Rosa.
But I tracked down Jack Leary—remember him?"

"Claro," Roberto said.

"I went to see him."

"He remembered us?"

"Absolutely. He's retired now, in Yuma. He told me some cases
stand out for him, and Rosa's is one of them. We met with Latham
Nez, a Shadow Wolf."

Shadow Wolf—what is that? he wondered but didn't ask. He felt
frozen.

"They're expert trackers. They work mostly on Tohono
O'odham land, but they're called out on special assignments. Jack
Leary brought them in to look for Rosa."

"We crossed just west of the reservation."

Julia nodded.

Roberto sat still as a stone, waiting.

"They traced her beyond the boulder where you last saw her.

Latham thinks another group of migrants came along and took her with them."

"Saved her?" Roberto asked, jumping up from the table.

Julia stayed seated. Her expression remained the same, composed. Then she looked down, and when she glanced up he saw tears glitter in her eyes.

"They don't think so," she said. "Apparently the group got lost, off track. They headed into foothills, rocky ground. Latham said four bodies were found—but not Rosa's. It seems some of them made it to the road and their pickup spot. But, Roberto, they found her sneakers."

"En serio?"

"Yes."

"They are sure they belonged to Rosa?"

Julia nodded.

"Then we have to go back and look! Get them to tell us where they found the shoes . . ."

Julia held his hand very tightly. "They don't think she survived."

"Mande?" he asked, his English deserting him.

"Roberto, they think she died. Her sneakers were found far apart from each other, and there was blood on one of them."

"They weren't Rosa's," he said. "They belonged to someone else!"

"They were hers. They tested the blood, and they were able to match it to her because of your DNA. When they picked you up . . ."

Roberto remembered. They had taken his fingerprints, then swabbed the inside of his mouth. He watched TV, cop shows, he knew they used DNA to catch criminals. But to determine that his daughter was dead? And the proof coming from him? It couldn't be.

"No," he said.

"That's what I told them," she said. "I didn't want to believe it."

Deep down, all these years, he had assumed that Rosa was dead.

He didn't feel it in his cells, in his skin, but what choice did he have? If she was anywhere in this world, they would find the way to each other. She was his *hija* flesh and blood, and he closed his eyes and felt her presence with him, as if she were standing in the room.

"What did they tell you that made you believe it?" he asked.

"They searched for her very hard," Julia said. "They wanted to find her. Latham Nez picked up the trail of a group, and he was sure one of the men had lifted Rosa up, to try to carry her to safety. But they got lost, Roberto."

He stared at Julia, but he was seeing the desert at night. How dark it was without the moon, how no trails were marked, and how the coyotes tried to keep everyone hidden, safe from La Migra. Maybe this Good Samaritan had walked through the night. Moonlight had led them through the desert, and darkness had sent them veering into the hills.

"No one from that group survived?"

"Some did," she said. "But they have no way of knowing who. Your group was the only one picked up by the Border Patrol in that area that night."

If those other crossers had gone first, maybe Roberto and Rosa would have made it safely together. He thought back to Altar, tried to picture all the faces he saw in that town, hundreds of people waiting for their coyote to call them into the trucks and vans.

He had dreamed of this, other travelers rescuing Rosa, wanting to bring her to his door. But those dreams ended in ways even worse than what the agents had told Julia. Rosa lost in the desert, walking with her saviors, being attacked by enormous black birds, Mexican jaguars, the most evil men on earth. Roberto would run or fly or jump to get to Rosa and rescue her before she was harmed, but she always disappeared before he arrived.

"Maria," he said out loud.

"Her doll?" Julia said, and he was touched she remembered.

"Did they find Maria?"

"No," she said. "Only her sneakers."

Silence fell between them. The window was open and he heard the sound of leaves rustling in the orchard.

"Gracias, Julia," he said after a minute.

He wanted to hug her. But he was trembling, ashamed that she would feel that and judge him for his weakness. A really strong man would never have lost his daughter, or sent this woman off to make sense of his terrible crossing.

She didn't give him the chance to protest. She stepped forward, held him in her arms. He was shaking, or maybe that was her. His mind raced with crazy thoughts. He felt her breath on his neck, and he wanted to tilt her head back and kiss her. The bed was right there. He wanted to lie with her, bodies pressed together, and hold each other all night, till the sun came up, and even after it rose.

"Julia," he whispered, "I would do anything for you."

Had she heard him? She stood so still, pressed against his body as if she wanted to become a part of it.

"You're my friend, aren't you?" she whispered. "My true friend?"

"Sí," he said. "Forever."

She kissed his neck, and his collarbone, and his shoulder. Then she stood on tiptoes and kissed him lightly on the lips. Now he wanted to lift her up, carry her to bed, feel life on a night of death, but she lowered herself down, put one hand on his chest, and backed away.

He watched her cross the property, through the trees and around the pool, and he saw her run up the front steps and into the big house. His nerves were screaming. Julia had given him more of Rosa's story than he'd known before, but it still led to the same place: her death in the desert.

chapter nine

Lion

He picked Julia up in the late morning and took her for a ride along the coast. The top was down, and they wore sunglasses against the brilliant sun. Her hair tossed in the wind, reminding him of rides with Graciela.

The day sparkled; the Pacific broke on Zuma Beach with waves full of diamonds. He zigzagged off the PCH to drive through Point Dume. The houses here were spectacular and private, hidden behind gates and hedges. Many were owned by movie stars, and Lion pointed out each one and recounted the parties he'd enjoyed there.

Julia turned away from the mansions and focused on what he called "the Hobbit cottage"—a house mostly hidden by archways and bowers of lush red and dark pink bougainvillea cascading over everything.

"I want to live there," she said.

"Oh, really?" he asked. "What about the Casa?"

"I mean after John and Graciela get back."

Lion glanced over. "You mean move to Malibu?"

"I don't know," she said, still staring at the flower-covered house. "Maybe."

They drove to the Point Dume overlook, where surfers generally snagged all six of the legal parking spots, and as usual there was no place to park. Lion contented himself with letting Julia enjoy the view across the fields of tall grass and wildflowers, to the ocean beyond.

"This is the best place to see migrating gray whales," she said. "I remember from when I was young, and John would take me here. We'd see mothers and babies hugging the coast, heading up to the Bering Sea. Wrong time of year now, though . . ."

"Speaking of John, we have so much to discuss over lunch," Lion said. "His letter, your mysterious trip . . . Did he mention Graciela?"

"Just to say she sent her love."

"Ah," he said.

They left Point Dume and headed down to Cross Creek and the Malibu Country Mart. The parking lot was full of Porsches and Bentleys, but Lion's vintage Jag always got a second look. He remembered when this shopping center had been comfortably downtrodden and local, and it was a point of contention that the stores on both sides of the street were now occupied by expensive boutiques—Ralph Lauren, Oliver Peoples, John Varvatos, Lanvin.

Malibu, for all its natural beauty and insular celebrity, loved to fight. No one ever agreed about anything, and the local papers were full of angry letters to the editor and scathing editorials on everything from these fancy stores to whether the high school football field should have lights. Lion was strongly in the no-light camp: he believed that light pollution was ruining America and that young people were better served by stargazing than Friday night football.

The hostess at Tra di Noi had his regular table ready—on the patio under an umbrella. Lion angled his chair to get into the full sun. He wore chinos and a faded red lisle shirt, a bit frayed around the collar. He'd bought it in Ravello on a long-ago visit to Gore Vidal's Villa La Rondinaia—Swallow's Nest. He'd been starring in a film with Sophia Loren, shot in Positano, and Gore had invited the cast to visit for the weekend. Now Gore was dead. Lion's friends were dropping like flies.

"Campari and soda," he ordered, and Julia did, too.

"The three woman just behind you are staring and pointing," Julia said.

"What can one expect?" he asked.

He loved coming here. People recognized him. Even if they didn't remember his name, they knew they'd seen him in "something." He was one of the Los Angeles film-world fixtures who gave visitors that little thrill they so loved, when they had a "sighting" and were able to return home and say they'd seen stars.

The waitress brought their Camparis and took their order: they would share a sliced-artichoke-and-parmesan salad and each have the *tonnarelli al filetto di pomodoro*—basically spaghetti marinara with the freshest tomatoes in California.

"You know, when I come here with Graciela, it's like magic," he said. "We're just a couple of old-timers, but people light up to see her. Or to see us together—they remember the film and . . ."

"Why do you keep doing it?" Julia asked.

"Doing what?"

"Chasing after her."

"That's not what I do! We're old friends. I admire her, of course, but . . ."

"You're in love with her," Julia said. "You've never been able to hide it."

"I don't even try."

"Lion," she said gently, "she's married to John, and she's not leaving him."

Lion took a large slug of his drink. It was most unbecoming to be lectured this way by Julia.

"Do you think I don't know that?" he asked. "It's quite obvious."

"I just keep thinking about what you said the other day. John dedicating his books to her. He has another one in the works."

"Lovely. And all I can give her is memories of film shoots and my old horses. How she used to love them. And me." He stared at Julia as if daring her. "She did, you know. And neither one of us thought it wrong."

"John might have disagreed."

"Oh, come on. He knew. He was buried in his research, married to the most passionate woman on earth. Did he really think we were just horseback riding? To quote Irene in that wonderful remake of *The Forsyte Saga*, 'I believe that misconduct can happen only where there's no love.'"

"You remember the line."

"I live by the line," he said. "So, speaking of love, how is yours? And what made you disappear?"

"My love?"

"Roberto. Let's not argue about it. Tell me about the trip—what were you up to?"

"He lost his daughter when he crossed the border. Five years ago, just like Jenny. I was trying to find out about her. But oh, Lion . . . there was nothing good."

"Good Lord," Lion said.

Lion sipped his Campari, filled with mixed feelings. Compassion for Roberto, of course; but was Julia serious about him? Lion had been thinking this was a fling—romance at the Casa. Julia had always been so caring, but did she know what she was getting into? Lion gazed at her with the affection of a man who'd adored her since her childhood. She had been through hell these last years.

"Not long ago you told me you were happy," he said. "Are you still?"

"I think I am," she said.

He laughed. The waitress delivered their salad and split it between two plates. "You're not sure?"

"I'm not used to it," she said. "Not like this."

"You like him?"

She nodded, picking at her salad. One of the three ladies at the next table approached and asked if Lion would mind having his picture taken with her. Lion obliged, and that made Julia smile. Then the friends wanted photos. It took a few minutes, and by the time he sat down the pasta had arrived.

"Is Roberto the reason you want to move to Malibu?"

"No!" she said too quickly.

"Part of the reason?"

"I just liked that little house, that's all."

"Hm," Lion said. But he could see it in her face. Her spirit had been resurrected since she'd arrived at the Casa, and her eyes looked alive again. She had something to look forward to, and how could he begrudge her that? The fact that Graciela was in Ireland, leaving no opportunity for a chance or planned meeting, weighed heavy on his heart. She'd sent him two postcards and had promised a love letter. But when he came right down to it, he had to admit the truth: she was with John. And that was her choice.

"I've always hated coming in second," he said. "I'm a terrible loser. When friends of mine were nominated for Academy Awards, I loathed them. I'd pretend to be happy, send them telegrams and air-kiss them all over the place, but deep inside my chest was a wizened-up tar ball of resentment."

"But you won!"

"Only once."

She laughed. "You're saying you feel that way about John?" she asked.

"How could I?" Lion asked, sighing. "He's practically my dearest friend and one of the best men on earth. So, what did his letter say?"

"He offered me a chance to help him on his book about our ancestor."

"The Irishman who fell in love with Mexico."

"Yes."

"Clearly you relate," Lion said.

"Clearly," she said softly.

They turned their attention to their meals. Julia pretended to be absorbed in swirling the strands of spaghetti. But Lion saw the worry lines in her forehead and knew, with all of his actor's instinct, that she was thinking about Roberto and his little girl and whatever she had learned on her trip that had taken away hope.

Jack

He went out to Louella's grave as he did every Wednesday morning, to clean off her headstone and her parents', and to tend the flowers he'd planted there. One thing this part of the country had was dust. The slightest wind would stir it up. He used a rag to wipe down her name and dates and the words the stone carver had chiseled: *Most beloved wife on earth and in heaven*. He'd written that himself because it was true.

Sometimes he brought Sugar along, but not today. He watered the flowers with a gallon jug and stayed crouched there, as if he could talk straight through the granite slab to Louella. He felt haunted by his visit with Julia Hughes. She was searching for a little girl she didn't even know.

He understood how loss, more terrible than you could believe possible, could come over you like a fever, turn you into a person you barely recognized. The day he learned Louella's lymphoma had come back and spread, he'd wanted to die himself. During the last week of her life, he had felt like a desert animal full of desperation and thirst, and one night he'd howled into his pillow like no coyote he'd ever heard.

Louella would have known what to say to Julia. The best Jack had been able to do was call in Lathan Nez, and a big help he'd been. Sure, he'd had a few more details to add, but nothing conclusive that would tell Julia what she wanted to know. Julia wanted to tell the father whether he could bury his daughter or not. People needed that. Even if there wasn't a grave to visit, they had to find a place in their minds to say goodbye.

That was the hell of the desert. So much uncertainty. When the border fence was built around the urban areas of California and Arizona, politicians thought it would stop illegal immigration by funneling migrants into "inhospitable"—deadly—terrain. Hell no, it didn't stop them—and if the muckety-mucks had spent any time on the border before building the wall, they'd have known. They'd have realized that the migrants who make this trip feel they have no choice. They know it is their last trip—either they're going to make it or die trying. They come to the States to provide for their families because their kids are starving.

Louella had always understood that. Married to a border agent, she'd volunteered with a group called Salvation who helped the migrants by placing water stations in the desert. They marked them with blue flags on tall masts so they could be seen from far away. It wasn't a church group, but she had been a religious woman, and she'd put her faith to work.

"Don't tell me about it," Jack used to say to her. "You're undermining what we're doing. You're encouraging them."

"We're keeping a few of them alive," she said. "Sweetheart, the fence, the wall, is inhumane. People are dying."

"That's their choice," he actually said. "They come here illegally, that's the chance they take."

"When did you get so hard?" she asked, holding his face between her hands. "They're human beings like us, looking for a better life for their families. You understand that, don't you? You did it for us."

And it was true—at the start of their marriage, jobs were scarce and Jack didn't have a college degree—just two years at Northeastern that didn't count for much. He'd wanted to join the FBI, like his grandfather Brendan Leary, but they wouldn't take him because of his lack of education. He'd given up his dream of working for the federal government, got a job selling copy machines.

God, had he hated that. It was the most soulless work imaginable, going into hermetically sealed office buildings and trying to sell pieces of crap designed to break down just so the businesses would be forced to buy the service contract as well. That job kept him and Louella afloat for a whole year, until he saw the posting for the Border Patrol position.

He could have called one of his granddad's old protégés at the Bureau, but he hadn't done that when he applied to the FBI and he wouldn't do it now. If he couldn't stand on his own feet, he didn't deserve the job.

But he got it. And he was good at it. At first he carried with him his grandfather's mission of public service, but right around the time the fence was built he changed. Seeing so much suffering, and chasing people through the desert just to keep them from dying and to deport them back to where they came from, dragged him down. And that's when he got hard.

Louella loved him anyway, even when he came home in a mean mood. She told him it was because he was losing his humanity.

"It's a humanitarian crisis," she said. "And you're part of the problem. That's why you can't sleep at night."

He hadn't even told her about the beatings his guys gave the migrants they caught, sometimes pushing their faces into cacti. They were supposed to carry water in their vehicles, and half the time they didn't, and the people they picked up would be delirious with dehydration, and they'd drop them off at the processing center, take away their medication—some of them diabetic, going into insulin shock. More than once Jack had himself used his blackjack to hit migrants trying to escape.

Louella dressed in white to go to her volunteer job. Long pants, a long-sleeved shirt, a white scarf around her neck, and a wide-brimmed white hat. Jack knew it was because white reflected the heat, and where she had to walk carrying water to refill the *agua* stations—sometimes a mile or so into the desert—it was hotter than blazes. He often thought of what the migrants must have thought, seeing her appear like an apparition, calling out in Spanish, "Hola, mis amigos! Tenemos agua, comida, y medicina para todos."

He plucked some dead blossoms off the flowers he had planted at her grave. She had been moved by the Rosa Rodriguez story. Of course he had told her, and by then she had helped him start meditating, relaxing, seeing his work as a way to help, not hurt others. She was his savior.

He remembered one of the last cases before he retired—Fernanda Cruz Castillo. Her group of thirty had been walking at night when they tripped a sensor. ICE sent helicopters to hover over the migrants, very specifically to churn up the desert sand and create a dust storm. It disoriented everyone, temporarily blinding some, made them disperse. Agents with night-vision goggles picked up most of them, but several evaded arrest. Fernanda was one—not because she was adept at hiding, but because she'd gotten blisters and could barely walk and had fallen behind.

Her husband, Diego, had been among those picked up. He kept telling people at the processing center about his wife, but they didn't respond. It was seventy-two hours later, when he was on the deportation line, that he caught Jack's attention. He told him about Fernanda. Louella had just died, and he swore her angel was sitting on his shoulder. She told him what to do. Jack pulled Diego out of the line, took him in his Explorer to the spot where he'd last seen Fernanda.

Diego had been sitting with her, trying to encourage her to keep going, just before the helicopters came. They had three children at home in Oaxaca, staying with her parents, so Diego and Fernanda could try to get seasonal work in the States, make enough money to feed the family for the year. "Do it for the *hijos*!" Diego had begged her. "One more step, another step . . ." But her feet were raw and bleeding, and she couldn't walk. She sat there crying, knowing she was letting everyone in the family down.

When the border agents came to capture the group, Diego ran to tell them about Fernanda. They shoved him into a prickly pear, the long spines going into his arms, hands, and face. They kept saying, "Show us your papers, your passport." And he just kept telling them about Fernanda.

Driving him back to the spot, Jack saw that he had not received medical treatment. The cactus spines were still embedded in his skin, crusted with blood and pus.

"She has beautiful long brown hair, and she's wearing an orange shirt," he said. "Jeans and a pair of Nike sneakers."

By the time they reached her, her shirt was no longer orange. Jack tried to get Diego to stay in the vehicle, but he ran ahead. The sight that awaited the two men remained burned in Jack's mind.

The sand was wet, as if water had been spilled. But in fact the moisture was all of Fernanda's bodily fluids and body fat, melted into the dirt. Carnivores and insects had devoured every part of her they could reach. Her long brown hair was a tangled nest above her bare skull, and her shirt had been torn off, and her body ravaged—her skin gone, and all her internal organs eaten—so that just her skull, spine, and rib cage remained. Her arms had been torn off and dragged away. Her legs and feet remained encased in the jeans and Nikes.

Diego tried to gather her bones into his arms, to hold her as he cried. Jack had to pry him away. He radioed for agents to come and retrieve the body. Then he drove Diego back to the deportation line. That was the last he saw of him.

Now, driving away from Louella's grave, he knew he had a mission. He put on Tim O'Brien's CD for inspiration. Julia Hughes had shown up at his door for a reason. The fact that she was Irish and connected to John Riley, that old ghost who connected the Mexicans and Irish and reminded them of their own hearts, was part of it. He knew fate had brought her into his life—Louella would have been the first to say that.

He headed to a dirt field by a long gap in the big border wall west of the Tohono O'odham Nation, near where Roberto and Rosa's group had crossed, and where Latham had tracked Rosa. It was also where Louella and her friends from Salvation gathered on Wednesday mornings with water to distribute to the water stations they had created in the desert. When he saw the cars and trucks, and people dressed in white, he knew he'd timed it well.

"Jack!" called Patricia Finnegan when she spotted him.

His arm shot up. Patricia was just who he wanted to see. She'd been Louella's best friend. She and her husband, Mike, had frequently gotten together with Jack and Louella for dinner and to play bridge, one week at the Learys' house, the next at the Finnegans'—before Mike had died of a heart attack a month after retiring—he'd been a border agent with Jack, a great guy.

"How are you, kid?" he asked, giving her a big hug.

"Good, Jack. And you?"

"Fine. I was just out to see Louella."

"I miss her every day."

"Me too."

"We miss her here, too," Patricia said.

"Well, she loved doing it. As much grief as I gave her for it."

"You came around," she said. "Mike did, too. Are you telling me you want to join us today? We could always use some extra muscle—that water is heavy."

"I can't," he said. "I'm on a job . . . sort of. But I wanted to ask you something, Patricia. While you're out there, you find things people leave behind, don't you?"

"Of course," she said. "You know. You've seen the jackets and backpacks and empty water jugs and photos . . ."

"Yeah, I remember. I wonder if you ever come across any dolls."

"Many," she said. "A lot of the children start out carrying their favorite toys, but leave them along the way when they get too tired and the toys get too heavy."

"It's been years since this one was lost," he began.

"It could still be there," she said. "The desert mummifies everything. Objects seem to last forever."

"Will you keep your eyes out for a doll with angel wings? They're homemade, sewn on by the child's great-grandmother."

"I will," Patricia said. She didn't ask for the child's story; out here one tragedy blended into another. "You know, you might check with Kathryn Martin. She's an artist from L.A. who collects things left behind by migrants and makes sculptures out of them."

"Sounds like a scavenger to me."

"Found objects," Patricia said. "That's what they're called. It might even be the name of her gallery."

"Huh. I'll check it out," he said, making a mental note to tell Julia about it. "Anyway, good to see you, Patricia."

"You too, Jack."

They hugged, and he left the parking lot determined to make Latham Nez tell him what he wanted to know.

chapter ten

Julia

The night was hot, so she swam in the pool. Jack had called, and she was touched by the way he was taking this on, pursuing a new lead, and telling her about the gallery of found objects. At the end of the conversation, he asked about Jenny and said he felt that Julia was dedicating her search for information about Rosa to her own daughter.

Now, swimming in the dark under the stars, Julia thought him very perceptive. She'd been tempted to tell him the whole truth of how Jenny had died, but couldn't bear to say the words out loud. As she stroked from one end of the pool to the other, over and over, she felt tension leaving her body. When she paused in the shallow end, catching her breath, she looked up and saw Roberto.

"Hi, she said.

"Hola," Roberto said. He was walking up the hill from his cabin and came over to crouch by the side of the pool.

"Is it nice in there?" he asked.

The underwater lights shimmered on his face, and she thought she saw him redden.

"It's beautiful and cool."

They stared at each other for a long moment. He seemed to want to say something, and she knew she did, too. She reached up, touched his chest. Then she bunched his T-shirt up in her fist.

"Come in," she said.

"I can't swim," he said.

"I'll teach you."

He paused as if considering, then stepped a few feet away to take off his T-shirt, jeans, and boots. She watched him fold his clothes, lay them neatly on the ground. He wore black boxer briefs. He crossed his arms across his chest as if he were cold—but he couldn't be. There was no breeze tonight, and the temperature hovered around eighty degrees.

The steps into the pool were wide and curved; she stood on the bottom one and gave him her hand, and he took a step toward her.

"It's only up to my waist here, see?" she asked. "You can stand."

He walked into the pool, and she could see him smiling.

"Feels good, right?"

"Sí," he said.

"Duck down and get your shoulders wet," she said, and he did, and his smile got bigger.

"Can you float?" she asked.

"I don't think so," he said.

"Ever tried?"

"No," he said. "I've never been in a pool before."

"A river, a pond?"

"No."

"Okay," she said. "It's easy. Just lie on your back in the water.

You know your feet can touch bottom. But just trust the water to hold you up."

He seemed hesitant, but she nodded encouragement. He leaned back the way she showed him and instantly sank. He came up in a panic, sputtering.

"Sorry," he said. "I guess I can't."

"Yes, you can," Julia said. They stood waist-deep facing each other. His brown eyes looked deep and warm, and were gazing intently into hers. "Do you trust me?"

"Claro que sí," he said.

"Okay. Then know I won't let you down. I'm going to support you while you float."

She put her hands on his shoulders, and began to ease him down. His tan skin felt so smooth under her fingers. He lay on his back, and she stood beside him and supported him with both arms. His body was rigid, fighting the water. If she weren't holding him, he would sink.

"Relax," she said. "Breathe . . . let me see you breathe."

He took a gulp of air.

"Not like that," she whispered. "All the way in, down to your belly, then all the way out."

She held him close, against her body, and as he began to breathe deeply, she felt him start to unwind. The night air was heavy, perfumed with lemon and coastal sage. Roberto closed his eyes. Gradually Julia held him less securely: first with her arms extended under his back and legs, then with both hands, finally with one finger under the small of his back.

He had stopped struggling, and she felt him giving up control. She knew he could do it; he'd given himself over to the water.

"You're almost there," she said. "I've still got you, but in a minute I'm going to let you go. I'm right here, and remember, you can touch bottom."

"Okay," he said.

"You ready?"

His smile was his reply.

She supported him a few more seconds, then stepped away. Roberto floated on the water, arms extended outward. She felt so happy. Swimming had given her a lifetime of pleasure; floating was a first step, but now that he'd learned to trust his own buoyancy, she knew he could do it.

"Wow," she said. "How does it feel?"

The question broke the spell—although he didn't panic like before. He just came out of the float and stood with his feet on the bottom. There were four inches of water between them. He put his hands on her shoulders, and she felt the shock of his touch. Then he pulled her body against his.

"Is okay?" he whispered.

She didn't answer, and he kissed her. She felt a tidal surge, nothing to do with the warm water surrounding them, his kiss soft at first, sending tremors through her body. His mouth warm on hers, parting her lips, making her want something she thought she'd lost or forgotten or never ever had before.

Now he took her hand, led her up the steps and out of the pool. He kissed her again on dry land, and she sensed him hesitating and wondering. His cabin was one way, the main house the other. She waited just as long as she could, and he decided. He picked her up and carried her toward his cabin.

It was small and rustic, one room, with a narrow bed. They stripped off their wet bathing things, and he pulled back the covers and laid her down on the mattress. The windows were open, but no breeze came through. The heat enveloped their bodies, and the way he touched her and the heavy lemon-scented air made Julia dizzy. She arched her back, pressing her body into his as he filled her, and she felt an ecstatic shiver electrify her skin, all the way into her bones.

They fell asleep in each other's arms. She awoke to the sound of his heartbeat, or maybe something else. A moth beat against the window screen above them, then flew away, leaving wing prints of white dust. Julia stared up at them, tiny images imprinted on the mesh, and she thought of angel wings in the desert and at the beach and in the midst of the lemon orchard.

Roberto

Driving home to Boyle Heights on the 10 freeway, he couldn't believe that he hadn't dreamed it. Holding Julia, waking up with her in bed, he had stared into her blue eyes. He felt in awe of her beauty and shocked by the way she was looking at him, as if she felt for him the way he did for her.

He had no idea where to hold Julia in his mind. She was his bosses' niece, American, a gringa, the occupant of the big house on the hill. He had pride, dignity, he knew how to act, but what did this mean? His feelings had been exploding almost since she'd arrived, that first time they'd talked about Rosa and Jenny.

Sometimes he'd imagined she had them too, strong emotions for him. But he'd always tell himself he was wrong. Even his father had warned him in very few words about hoping for something he had no right to hope for.

The traffic was bad at the exit to the 405; he slowed down and didn't care. He was in no hurry to put miles between himself and the Casa, between himself and Julia. She had given him an address, told him it was an art gallery, and asked him to meet her there that night. An art gallery! He had never been to one before. He didn't know what to wear, and he was embarrassed to ask her.

She seemed not to care that he was Mexican or poor. Being with Julia made him feel good about himself and think of his good teachers instead of the bad ones. He thought of Rigo, the teacher who cared the most. He encouraged the kids. Rigo saw that Roberto was intelligent, and he had him memorize *El Brindis del Bohemio* by Guillermo Aguirre y Fierro. The poem was long and complicated and emotional, and Roberto remembered it still.

And on Mother's Day when Roberto was fourteen, skinny, six feet tall and embarrassed by his height, Rigo had him stand in front of the whole assembly, all the students' parents and Roberto's grandmother, and sing Juan Gabriel's "Amor Eterno." At first he had felt his face turning red, feeling as if he would combust, but then he got comfortable, felt good, and he finished the song and at the end all the mothers and his grandmother were crying.

"Amor Eterno." He knew that song by heart now, but he never thought he would have the feeling. He'd been with women, but rarely had he felt the love described in the lyrics. He could honestly say that until now he'd felt true love only twice in his life, both times before he came to the States.

His first girlfriend, in seventh grade, Aracelia. He had held her hand and believed in that moment that he would die for her. After she moved away, there were girls he would see at school and dances, but no one special until Adriana, Rosa's mother. Their love had lasted only until she'd had the baby, and then she'd left them both.

The traffic was moving now, and he drove his truck fast to the Boyle Heights exit. Roberto parked in front of his father's house. He went into his apartment for a minute and glanced at his face in the mirror.

Everything looked the same, but inside he was changed. What he had felt before was not love, not compared to this. He smelled his forearm and wrist; they had brushed across Julia's skin and hair, and he closed his eyes and held on to her scent.

He wanted to have that smell with him forever; he wanted everything with her, the love of her and their love of their daughters; and having sung that Juan Gabriel song about eternal love so many times, he wondered if this was how it felt to know its meaning in his bones.

"Hey, hijo!" his father called from outside.

"Hola, Papá," he said, and went out to join him. His father was fixing the bricks around Esperanza's garden today. Roberto had time to help, so he dug right in.

They mixed concrete and hauled a bale of red bricks from the back of his father's truck. The sun beat down—at least one hundred degrees, much hotter than Malibu—and Roberto thought about the pool, learning to float with Julia's arms holding him up. He must have been smiling like a fool, because his father noticed.

"What?" his father asked.

"Nothing."

"You've got a good joke? Tell me."

"Not a joke. Just a memory."

"Of what?"

Roberto wanted to tell him. He was bursting, but he knew to keep it inside. His father would warn or belittle him, tell him to stay away from Julia, did he want to lose his job, what if something went wrong and she told her uncle? Roberto knew his father well. He didn't like to lie, but he knew the truth would cause a fight.

"Just thinking of Rigo, my old teacher," he said.

"Ai ai ai," his father said. "My mother still talks about that, you standing in front of everyone as if you were Juan Gabriel."

"No, I didn't think that," Roberto said. Better to concentrate on the bricks. He had sketched out a better plan: a small wall, perfectly round, four bricks high. It would look pretty for Esperanza, and not be too high for her to lean over.

"Juan Gabriel is good," his father said, making peace. "'Amor Eterno' is one of his best songs. I wish I had been there when you sang."

"I know," Roberto said. His father hadn't even had to say that. Roberto knew how much his father regretted missing so much time, the years of Roberto's childhood. He was jealous of teachers like Rigo, who'd had the chance to influence Roberto and teach him good things.

"You were my best teacher," Roberto said. "I learned the important things from you."

He glanced at his father and saw his eyes wet and his moustache drooping with sadness. There was so much about Mexico to make a person cry. The fact they loved it so much and had to leave it, and the reality of all they had left behind. Roberto thought of Rosa and, for the first time since leaving Julia that morning, felt his insides clench.

The two men worked side by side in the afternoon heat until the wall was built. They talked a little about work—Roberto in the orchard, his father doing a job for Feng. Roberto had often helped his father work for Feng, a Chinese businessman who specialized in the demolition of swimming pools. Feng had customers who bought houses in the Valley, and the first thing they wanted was to demo the pool—smash the concrete, fill the hole with soil, plant grass.

Less maintenance, fewer expenses. Water cost a lot in Southern California, and heating the pool was for rich people. But after last night, Roberto would never understand demolishing a pool again.

They finally finished the wall. Roberto took a quick shower and trimmed his beard and moustache. He put on clothes he thought would be right—dark jeans and a black T-shirt. He didn't have much choice, but these were what he would wear to a Mexican party and he hoped Julia wouldn't be disappointed. The wall between his apartment and his father's was so thin, his father smelled the Polo cologne he patted on.

"Where are you going?" his father called through the wall.

"Nowhere special," Roberto answered as he walked into the room.

"You look nice!" Esperanza said, smiling so wide her gold tooth showed.

"You seeing a woman?" his father asked.

"Maybe," Roberto said.

Now his father smiled, too. He nodded approvingly. "Good, son," he said. "Find a wife."

Roberto laughed and shook his head. His father said the same thing every time Roberto went out on the town. Walking onto the street, he realized he should have washed his truck. The black finish was covered with road dust and tree pollen, and he felt a jolt of shame realizing he'd be pulling up in front of an art gallery with a dirty truck. But there was no time to clean it—he had told Julia he would see her there at five—so he just got on the road.

The art gallery was called Found Objects, and it was located downtown, in the shadows of the tall buildings, next to El Pueblo de Los Angeles and La Iglesia de Nuestra Señora Reina de Los Angeles—Our Lady Queen of the Angels Church. He found a parking place in front of Union Station and was glad he didn't have to pull up right in front of the gallery. He approached La Placita Olvera and located Found Objects.

The building looked historic, built from adobe bricks. Julia stood just outside the door waiting for him and waved when she saw him coming.

He could barely breathe. She looked incredible. She wore a short black dress, black boots, and red lipstick. Her long hair was swept up, held in place with a jeweled clip.

"Hi, Roberto," she said.

"Julia," he said. "You're the most beautiful woman in the world."

She laughed, embarrassed, but he meant it.

He wished they were back at his cabin. Seeing her dressed up this way, all he could think of was taking off her clothes and making love to her. Other people walked past, and he barely noticed.

"Ready to go in?" she asked.

"Sure."

They paused in the doorway. He hardly knew what to think—she cared about how he felt about something as minor as seeing trash from the desert. In his world nothing was easy, and there was pain in life. You just went through it the best you could. The look in her eyes was so full of love, as if she had just laid a hand on his heart.

"Gracias, Julia. It's fine," he said.

So they walked in. The air-conditioning hit him, and it felt good. Mexican music was playing, but slow and sad, like something from church. A few people were in the large room. No one spoke. The light was dim, and he smelled candle smoke. Votive candles were burning in small alcoves throughout the space. This was an art gallery, he thought. But it felt like a shrine.

Everything here was from the desert. Jackets faded from the sun, shirts stained from sweat, a hat brown from blood. Many shoes, some in pairs, all beaten-looking except for one almost brand-new pair of Pumas.

There were wallets and Mexican and Guatemalan ID cards. Fake U.S. papers. A coloring book of the Disney characters Roberto

and then Rosa used to love. A child's notebook with a pink cover.
Jeans and belts and hair ties and a toothbrush. Men's underwear,
a razor, some knives.

Roberto and Julia walked slowly, taking everything in. Roberto's skin felt clammy, and he no longer smelled the candles—his
senses were full of the desert. He smelled dust, dirt, sweat, fear, and
death. Everything here made him remember the crossing.

"Are you okay?" she asked, as if she'd seen right through him.

"Bien, gracias," he said.

This wasn't art. It was people's lives. Were they alive or dead?
Had they made it or not? He glanced around. A Mexican couple
stood across the room, and the woman was crying quietly. What
were they looking at? It didn't matter. Roberto knew that they were
remembering their journey, just as he was.

The woman who had collected these things had arranged them
in piles, but with no apparent order at all. But then he noticed a sign
on the wall, in both English and Spanish. He and Julia stopped to
read it.

> Everything here was collected on trips I made to the
> Sonoran Desert with Salvation, a group that maintains
> water stations for migrants crossing the border.
>
> Although the objects were spread out over many miles,
> I have placed them in roughly the same patterns in
> which I found them.
>
> If you recognize anything, or know who it belongs to,
> please speak to the person at the desk and sign the
> register. I wish to return everything possible to the
> families who lost them.

"Wow," he said. "That's nice."

"I wonder how many times it's happened," Julia said. "How

often someone will come here and find something they left behind."

"No one," Roberto said.

They walked into the next room. Roberto stared at everything. Crushed plastic water jugs, just like the kind he had carried. Maybe he and Rosa had drunk from one of them. Rosary beads carved from black wood, like the kind his grandmother had given him and he had given Julia. She squeezed his hand when she saw them. Bracelets woven from once-colorful thread, now bleached by time and the sun. White socks discolored with blood and dirt, holes where toes had poked through.

A yellow skirt, a New York Yankees sweatshirt with the number 2 and the name JETER on the back. A teddy bear. Mickey Mouse sunglasses. Aviator sunglasses. A woman's purse woven from fine black thread and decorated with pop-tops from soda cans. A pink baby carrier.

Roberto could barely breathe. He thought of the parent carrying that baby girl. Had the carrier broken and had the father carried the infant in his arms? Had they made it to wherever they were going together? Or had the baby been lost along with the carrier? He wanted to touch it, to feel the pink floral fabric, as if it could tell him the story of the family it belonged to.

He felt afraid yet excited, as if he would look in the next pile of items and find Rosa herself. Her beautiful thick black hair, her twinkling eyes, and her thin brown arms reaching up to grab his neck. He would carry her right out of here, and he would love her and never let her go. His head swam, the way it had in the desert, when the heat had knocked him down, when it had made his little girl so sick she couldn't go on. He felt confused, a little crazy.

"Roberto!" Julia said.

And then he saw what Julia saw—and Rosa *was* there, and

Roberto was reaching for her, clutching her to his chest, the smell of her filling his nose, and he buried his face in her shoulder whispering her name. Only it wasn't Rosa, it was her doll, Maria, and the gossamer wings his grandmother had sewn on were still there, tickling his neck, and he was saying his daughter's name, "Rosa, Rosa, Rosa," over and over.

chapter eleven

Julia

They had driven separately, and he followed in his truck back to the Casa. Entering the kitchen, Julia saw that Roberto had brought Maria inside; she lay on the table. Whatever color the doll had once been, she had faded to dun, the same shade as desert sand. She had long black yarn hair, most of which had been lost. Her eyes were black knots, her mouth a smile stitched with red thread. She wore a flowing dress, and had sheer wings.

"My grandmother told Rosa that Maria could fly," Roberto said, holding the doll. "I think Rosa believed it. She kept saying so in the truck, and when we were walking. I think she thought Maria would fly us away."

Had Rosa thought that in the desert after her father was gone? Julia wondered. She took Roberto's hand and led him through the house, toward the wide staircase. The thick walls held the cool air inside, and when they got upstairs the breeze through the windows fluttered the curtains.

This room had always felt magical to her. In spite of the heavy, carved wooden Mexican furniture, it seemed to float on air above the coastline. The view took in the canyon and surrounding peaks, and the blue ocean spreading west, interrupted only by the dark and mysterious Channel Islands, and passing ships whose running lights looked like stars fallen into the sea.

Roberto walked up behind her. He put his arms around her, kissed her bare neck. Outside the window a vine of night-blooming jasmine climbed the wall. The sun had not quite set, so the white flowers were closed tight. Bees twined around the blossoms, legs coated with golden pollen. Julia watched them, hypnotized by their dance and the feeling of Roberto's lips on her skin.

"I can't believe we found her there," she said without turning around.

"Rosa's doll?"

"Yes. The exhibit sounded powerful to me, but I never would have thought . . . I'm sorry."

"For what?"

"The shock. What you must feel to have found her. What does it mean?"

"No se," he said. "But I feel glad, Julia. This is the closest I've felt to Rosa in five years. I held Maria just the way she did, and I feel Rosa with me again."

Julia turned. "You do?"

"Yes. So much." He stopped talking, tried to hold the emotion inside. "Rosa held this doll, and carried her and loved her. My grandmother made it for her."

"It's how I feel about Bonnie," Julia whispered. "Jenny touched her."

"I know. And now I have Rosa's doll, and you brought me to her." His voice broke, and he couldn't hold back the tears. He turned his face away, but she leaned close, kissed his cheeks, crying quietly herself.

Outside, the bees were gone. The sun went down behind the western mountains and the sky turned red and gold. The wave crests were amber, and the ocean darkened to deep purple. The jasmine began to open, releasing its seductive fragrance.

Roberto and Julia walked to the bed. She wasn't sure who was leading whom. They undressed each other and slid under the covers. Her aunt's Anichini sheets seemed obscenely decadent in light of where they'd just been. She wanted to apologize for everything, and realized that that was her default mode—she'd been saying she was sorry for five years.

For so long Julia had felt she'd fallen from grace, but here she felt forgiven. Roberto's feelings for her washed it all away. His hand gently stroked her shoulder, moving softly down the curve of her back, pulling her body against his.

There was eloquence in their silence, the way he entered her with silken heat, his eyes never leaving hers. He hovered over her, thrusting faster and faster, and she lost herself somewhere between his skin and hers. They were beyond time, everything but sensation obliterated, no past and no future, just this feeling of being lifted into heaven.

They slept together that night. The bed, the house, this life, was theirs. She woke around three and watched him sleeping beside her. Her skin looked so pale next to his in the cool blue dark. The night had turned chilly, so she reached down for the peach satin comforter, pulled it over them. He didn't stir. He slept with abandon, just giving himself over to unconsciousness.

She wished she could do that. Most nights she paced. She sometimes wondered what it would look like if her sleep was filmed, the way they did in sleep studies, with the images sped up. Tossing and turning, then out of bed, around the house, back to bed, lights on, lights off, TV on, TV off, go to the kitchen, look in the refrigerator, drink water, pee, back to bed, try to sleep, out of bed, around the house.

Roberto was breathing deeply and steadily, the way she'd wanted him to in the pool, when he was learning to let go and float. Lying beside him, she tried to imitate his breath. Their legs were touching, so reassuring. Her breath deepened and she began to relax. They were floating together, in this big warm bed, and she closed her eyes and went back to sleep.

They woke up the next morning to a roar in the canyon. All the trees were tossing, palms dropping fronds, lemons shaking loose, the windows rattling. The Santa Ana winds had started.

chapter twelve

Jack

He loaded Sugar into the Explorer, picked up half a dozen donuts and two large coffees from Bess's Bakery, and drove out to the same parking lot where he'd run into Patricia last week. He'd persuaded Latham to meet him, but it had taken awhile. Being on active duty, Latham didn't have much time for old cases.

Still, he respected Jack for the work they had done together. They had busted a drug mule transporting nine hundred pounds of marijuana and found the safe house where the cartel had hidden many bales more as well as bricks of meth and cocaine. There'd been a shootout, and Jack had drawn on a guy who had Latham in his sights. Jack had taken him out with one shot to the forehead. Latham didn't like to be beholden to anyone, but Jack knew he had thanked the Great Spirit for Jack's steady hand and good aim.

He saw the white and green Border Patrol truck from a distance, flashed his lights to let Latham know he was almost there. Jack pulled into the dirt lot next to him, rolled down the window, and got blasted in the face by the scalding desert air.

"I got donuts," he said.

"Bring 'em," Latham said.

Jack left the Explorer running, AC on, so Sugar wouldn't get too hot. Then he carried the bag and coffees into Latham's truck, handed him a large coffee, and bit hungrily into a cruller while Latham chose a honey-dipped.

"So," Jack said. "Talk to me, and I'll be on my way."

"Not much to tell you," Latham said.

"I didn't think there would be," Jack said. "Obviously there's no hard evidence."

"I didn't say that," Latham said. "When I track someone, I produce evidence. You're looking for the identity of the group moving north with Rosa Rodriguez, at least until the crossers split up and she wound up in the western sector."

"Well, we don't know *where* she wound up," Jack said. "All we know is where her sneakers were found."

"Fine. You know my theory."

"I do, and consider it a possibility," Jack said. "So, what evidence did you produce that could help me?"

"Three things came from the second group, the one that continued with Rosa after her father was picked up. One: a degraded print of a rope-soled shoe with the word 'Marcie's' woven into the sole. Another: on the body of a deceased twenty-year-old male, we found an Arizona Diamondbacks tattoo."

"What's 'Marcie's'?" Jack asked. "It sounds familiar."

"A chain of stores in Mexico. According to the report, these crossers might have come from Veracruz. The male had a one-way plane ticket in his pocket—from Tucson down there."

Jack wrote "Marcie's—Veracruz" and "Diamondbacks" in his

notebook. "Rope-soled women's shoes, definitely Mexican-style," he said. "But the tattoo and the plane ticket on the guy—what do they mean? If he flew down, why didn't he fly back? What nationality was he?"

"His dental work was American," Latham said. "That's as much as we know."

"Okay, thanks, Latham."

"No problem, Jack."

The two men shook hands and said goodbye.

Jack climbed into his Explorer, then sat back while Sugar launched herself at him, barking with mad joy at being reunited. Louella probably wouldn't have approved, but Jack broke off a piece of donut and fed it to the tiny terrier.

He glanced around the lot for Patricia's Lexus. It wasn't there; today must not be a water station day. Pulling onto the road, he drove toward home thinking of Veracruz. He, Louella, Patricia, and her husband, Mike, had vacationed there in the past. It was a port city, and he liked the waterfront—he needed salt water once in a while to remind him of Boston.

Three clues—the tattoo, the shoe, and the ticket to Veracruz. He put in a CD by Ry Cooder and the Chieftains and felt it pump him up in a way he didn't fully understand. He was pretty sure Patricia would look after Sugar. All he had to do was pack a bag, and he'd be on his way.

Julia

The first week of December, the Santa Ana winds tore through the canyon with a freight train roar. Julia heard it from the moment she woke up each morning, and it kept her tossing and turning through each night. Even Bonnie seemed unsettled, not wanting to take her usual walks or stray far from the house. Lion told Julia the Santa Anas always filled him with a sense of doom, so he was taking off to visit friends on Martha's Vineyard till it was safe to return.

Downed power lines had sparked fire in the western Santa Monica Mountains, consuming two hundred acres so far. Although it was miles away, Julia smelled the smoke and watched National Guard aircraft flying west to drop flame retardant in the wooded mountains. Roberto had called Serapio and the others to come to work, and they patrolled the orchard and kept the irrigation going, vigilant about the threat of wildfires.

He had told Julia not to worry. She sat at a writing desk in her bedroom, facing the ocean, away from the fires. Back in Connecticut, most of the heavy winds had come from the sea, swirling off the Atlantic into Long Island Sound. Their house had been a quarter mile from the beach, separated from the sand by a salt pond, right at sea level.

"Hola, Julia!"

She walked out the French doors and onto her terrace, looked down at the yard sloping toward the Pacific, and saw Roberto standing there.

"Hi," she called. "Everything okay?"

"Sí," he said. "For now, but the fire is getting closer. The fire department came to give us an update."

"Is the Casa in danger? Should I call John?"

"Yes, I think it would be good, but we are still safe," Roberto said. "They'll come back and tell us if we have to leave."

"How are you doing?"

"Good," he said. "I won't let anything happen."

"You against the fire," she said.

"Sí, amor."

"I'm coming down to help," Julia said.

"You don't have to."

She smiled at him, saw his deep brown eyes red from the smoke, worry lines across his forehead, and felt a flood of emotion. She didn't speak, but thought, *Yes, I do.*

chapter thirteen

Jack

The busy port of Veracruz was a riot of contrasts. Oil rigs sat just outside the harbor and huge container ships filled the wharves. High-rises towered over mom-and-pop *tiendas*. Tourists flocked to Fort San Juan de Ulúa, built by the Spanish in 1582 to protect the gold-rich city from pirates. Now the waterfront was patrolled by the military.

At nine in the morning, Jack walked along *el malecón*, the harbor boardwalk. The walkway was lined with shops and stalls, very few of them open yet. He knew from Patricia that this was the general area where Marcie's sold shoes, but he hadn't found the shop yet.

He'd flown in the night before, checked into the Hotel Candile-jas, which overlooked the commercial port, *malecón,* and old light-houses. After checking in, he had walked around town, getting his bearings.

The city looked the same as when he'd come here with Louella and the Finnegans, but the atmosphere had turned tense. The Zetas drug cartel had taken hold, and last spring several crime reporters and photographers had been killed throughout Veracruz State. Believing the police had been infiltrated by the Zetas, Mexico's last president had replaced the eight-hundred-officer police force with naval infantry and marines, and they were in evidence everywhere.

Walking through the city's main square—the Zocalo—Jack saw heavily uniformed men wearing Kevlar vests and was tempted to stop and talk shop with them—*hey, guys, how's the drug war going?* But he was hungry, and he no longer had a badge, and even if he had, they wouldn't have talked to him. Music played while under tall palm trees crowds of people danced, as they had last time he was here, lending the scene an uneasy sense of normalcy.

He passed the Municipal Palace, a baroque wedding cake of a building, and the Catedral Virgen de la Ascunción. He paused outside the large church. The doors inside the arched entry were open, and a Mass was being said. He smelled incense and heard the priest saying the Consecration in Spanish. His Irish Catholicism flared up, but he couldn't make himself go inside.

He knew all the expensive tourist restaurants were on the harbor, so he wandered to the marketplace, Mercado Hidalgo, and ate a plate of *arroz de tumbada*—rice and the freshest seafood possible. It tasted so good he ordered a second plate. *Jarochos*—as the locals referred to themselves—sat around him, eating and talking, and Jack felt good that he'd found this place on his own, off the beaten path.

This was his first time back to any of the Mexican seaside towns he'd visited on vacation with Louella. Jack had avoided checking into the hotel where they'd stayed, or eating at the portside *palapa* that had been her favorite. At home, missing her had dulled to an ache, but here the sense of her was fresh—every sight reminded him of the delight she'd taken.

Now, walking along the waterfront, he saw the vast and ornate Faro Carranza and remembered taking pictures of Louella with it in the background. He'd never seen a lighthouse like it—it seemed more like a residence for royalty, white and imposing, with two floors of arched windows, decorative pediments at either end, and rising dead-center, a tall square clock tower topped by the domed enclosure that held the lighthouse lens.

"It's so beautiful," she'd said. "Looks like a fairy-tale castle."

"It's gaudy," he'd said.

"How can you say that?"

"I'm from New England. I know how lighthouses are supposed to look—plain white towers. Brick or stone if necessary."

"This is Mexico, not Boston."

"That's for sure.

"Well, this lighthouse is romantic."

"Romance is your department, kid. It doesn't even function as a lighthouse anymore."

"So what?"

"Things should work."

"It's probably too expensive to run, but the guidebook says it has naval offices on the first floor. Does that meet your standards?"

"Plain and functioning, Louella," he'd said. "Aids to navigation. That's how I like my lighthouses."

She had laughed at him as usual, and he had walked along loving the salt air and seeing her happy. Later they'd met up with Mike and Patricia, and he and Mike had bought Cuban cigars from some guy on the dock and walked along looking at tankers, freighters, oil derricks, and fishing boats while Louella and Patricia had gone off on their own. It must have been on that walk that they'd stopped at Marcie's and bought the shoes.

He had passed the area where most of the shops were located

and wondered if he'd missed it. Some of the establishments had hand-lettered signs; others had awnings professionally printed with the store or restaurant names. Walking back the way he'd come, he stared at each storefront more carefully.

José's Mariscos stood between the El Malecón café and Delfi4Ever, a shop that sold beaded jewelry. Jack looked at the fresh seafood on display at José's—crabs, spiny lobster, octopus, shrimp, tiny clams the size of his thumbnail, all glistening on ice. Raising his gaze to the row of awnings, he walked another hundred feet, and there he saw the sign: MARCIE'S.

The awning's lettering had faded, but the shop's display was vibrant. A woman stood outside, watering pots of geraniums. She looked about Louella's age, quite a bit heavier, and with curly black hair. She wore a red dress and a pair of rope-soled shoes. Jack's heart quickened, and he cleared his throat. She turned around, smiling.

"Marcie?" he asked.

She laughed. "No, there isn't a real Marcie anymore, but I do run the shop. I'm Maya."

"I won't take much of your time. I'm Jack Leary, a retired U.S. border agent, and I'm trying to identify two Mexican migrants who crossed the border. One died in the desert."

"Sí?" she asked and frowned.

"Sí. Is this the only Marcie's in Veracruz?"

She nodded. "Why?"

"We found footprints, rope-soled shoes that said 'Marcie's.'"

"I sell so many pairs," she said. "And there are other Marcie franchises all over Mexico. I'm sorry, but I don't think I can help you."

"We think the woman who was wearing them was with a man who died. He had a sports team tattoo—the Arizona Diamondbacks. And he had a plane ticket from Tucson in his pocket."

Maya looked stunned and Jack's heart began to race.

She sat heavily on the bench outside her shop and stared out into the harbor. "It can't be," she said.

"Tell me what you know."

"Five years ago," she began, and trailed off. "That's when they left."

Jack took a deep breath. Five years—this was it. "Who left?" he asked.

"There was a girl who worked for me, Felicia," Maya said. "She had a boyfriend who'd come down from the States on one of the boats that tend the oil wells. A sweet boy, Eduardo. He was always around the docks while the boat was in port, you see. He fell in love with her and stayed here when the boat pulled out."

"He had a Diamondbacks tattoo?"

She nodded. "He was from from Tucson, but worked for an oil company, servicing the rigs. He was a mechanic—it was a good job."

"What happened to them?"

"He was a U.S. citizen, and they married so she could have a green card. But the wait—she would have had to stay in Mexico for months, maybe a year, till her papers came through. He couldn't stand to be away from her that long, and he had to work."

"So they went north?" Jack asked. "He wanted to take her back to Tucson?"

"Yes." Her eyes filled. "You know, they were so young and very foolish. Because he was from Arizona, he thought he would have an easier time in the desert, that he would be able to find his way. Poor Eduardo."

"We don't know if Felicia made it or not," Jack said. "We found the shoe print, but nothing more."

"Oh, she made it," Maya said. "She called her mother as soon as she reached Tucson. We thought she would come back home right away, because Eduardo had died, but she decided to stay with his family and raise their child."

"Their child?"

"Yes," Maya said. "She was pregnant even before they left Veracruz—she just didn't know it."

"Do you have her address?" Jack asked.

Maya's face closed off. She tightened her lips and looked away.

"Look," Jack said. "I swear I won't turn Felicia in. I'm trying to find a little girl and get her back to her father. This man lost his daughter on the crossing, and we think Felicia and her group might have found her."

Maya looked at him again. "Felicia would have helped if she could."

"I believe that," Jack said.

"How old was the little girl?"

"Six. Do you have Felicia's phone number?"

Maya shook her head. "No, but she sent me a card for my birthday. It had an address."

"Could you look for it?" Jack asked.

Maya disappeared into her store. Jack looked out to sea, facing east, the way he'd do as a boy in South Boston. The light glinted on the harbor and the Caribbean beyond. Jack heard the metal shutters of the shops clanging up as they opened for business. Mariachis had started playing at the far end of the walkway. The music sounded happy and sad at the same time.

"I found it," Maya said. "But you have to swear to me you won't do anything to hurt her. You won't turn her in."

"I swear."

"On something that matters to you—more than anything in this world."

"Louella," he said without thinking. "My wife."

She nodded and handed him the envelope. Jack copied down the address. He recognized it as being in rural West Tuscon, out beyond I-10, past the Tucson Mountains.

"Thank you very much," he said.

"You're welcome," she said.

People strolled around him. Families, couples linked arm in arm, young people on cell phones. He listened to them speaking. He loved Spanish spoken by Mexicans. It had a softness and kindness to it, and when he heard it spoken he could always hear the love.

That's what Louella had seen in him. He'd been a hard-ass in a uniform for a long time, but that was his job. After a while the job wore him down. He got tired of arresting people trying to be with their families. His wife had loved him enough to see the best in him—he knew she was the reason he wanted so badly to find Rosa, to give Roberto some peace.

chapter fourteen

Roberto

The Rileys' orchard was the most tranquil place Roberto had ever been on earth, but today he felt restless and full of dread as they waited to see which way the fire would move. It was still far off, but the wind roared and shook the trees, and dense clouds of smoke darkened the mountains. In the near distance the sky glowed red; that meant the fire was just a ridge or two away.

Roberto was usually good at waiting. He always had been. Maybe it came from growing up in the country, knowing that there are some things you can't rush, stop, or control. He waited by working, doing the best he could. But Malibu fires were fast and unpredictable. This one could zigzag into another canyon or march straight to the orchard.

Right now he and Serapio were using the backhoe and shovels to dig a fire line, a wide trench that ran along the orchard's northern border. Two water tank trucks stood by, and Roberto had set up a tender, hoses, and a 350-gallons-per-minute pump to soak the vulnerable north side.

Until dawn, they'd had ten additional workers. Day laborers whom Roberto had found standing in the usual spot, hoping for a job. They had worked all night. When the sun came up, the fire marshal and sheriff arrived to give Roberto a report on the fire. As soon as their cars drove away, the men started leaving.

"Hey," Roberto had called to Geraldo, a Oaxacan he had used many times before—very reliable and hardworking. "Where are you going?"

"Lo siento, amigo. Too dangerous," Geraldo said.

Roberto knew he didn't mean the fire—he was worried about the officials.

"They're not going to be checking papers," Roberto said. "All they care about is saving the property."

"Too dangerous," Geraldo repeated.

Roberto could only watch him leave with the others. They crammed into two old vehicles, both without inspection stickers, and drove away. Cops couldn't just ask for papers, but if they got you on motor vehicle violations or saw something about you they didn't like, they could search you for probable cause. If you didn't have a driver's license, which none of them did, they impounded your vehicle, no questions asked.

So now it was just Roberto and Serapio.

"Tell me what do to," Julia said, striding over from the house.

"Julia, no," he said. "The smoke will burn your eyes."

She smiled and shook her head.

He tried again. "Julia, it might not be safe. They told us this fire is moving quickly. Feel the wind?"

"Yes," she said. "It's strong."

"Sixty miles an hour."

He had promised her everything would be okay, but now, seeing the red sky, he wasn't so sure. The fire had been declared Level 2, maximum emergency, and if it cleared the next peak, Casa Riley and surrounding properties would be evacuated.

"Did you talk to your uncle?" Roberto asked.

"Yes. He told me to leave—all of us."

"I think that is a good idea. The fire department might evacuate us soon. You go now just in case, and I'll stay until they come."

"I'm staying with you," she said. She looked back and forth along the gully they had dug. The backhoe had scored the earth, left bare dirt where before had been rosebushes and morning glories. One area was confined by boulders and too narrow for the heavy machine, so Serapio was attacking it with a pickax.

She grabbed a shovel from the pile the workers had left. He hesitated. She was the owner's niece, she didn't have to do this. He watched her pull yellow garden gloves from the back pocket of her jeans. He had seen Señora Riley wear them to clip roses.

Julia carried the shovel over to where Serapio was digging, and went to work on the trench. Serapio beamed at her—his face was black with soot, just like Roberto's probably was. Roberto took off his red bandanna and soaked it in the water tender, then went to Julia and tied it around her neck.

"Pull it up over your face," he said. "Around your mouth and nose. It will help you breathe."

She did. Reluctantly, he left her there, climbed onto the backhoe, and went back to extending the fire line. Every time he turned to look over his shoulder, he saw her digging as hard as any worker, casting the dirt in a pile behind her, moving with an insistent rhythm.

Sirens sounded down the mountain, and the tanker planes flew back and forth overhead. They swept up water from the Pacific, dumped it on the fire. A sheriff's car from the Lost Hills station came up the hill, parked in the turnaround. The officer got out and started waving his arms.

Roberto shut down the backhoe, climbed down to see what he wanted. Julia was already there, talking to him.

"Man, you can't use that equipment right now," the sheriff told Roberto. His nametag said *Hernandez*. "You want a spark to set off the orchard?"

"Okay," Roberto said, feeling embarrassed, chastised in front of Julia. But she seemed not to notice.

"What about the fire?" Julia asked. "How bad is it?"

"Over twenty homes lost so far. I came to tell you to get ready to evacuate," the sheriff said. "We're starting to contain the fire in the next canyon, but you are smack in its path." His radio crackled and he silenced it.

"We really have to leave?" Julia asked.

"It's the best idea, ma'am."

Roberto felt chills run down his spine. They'd had fires in Mexico, set off by dry lightning strikes. He'd seen what a wildfire could do to acres of farmland, and that was without the special conditions set up by the Santa Monica Mountains. Señor Riley had told him the day he'd offered him the job.

"The winds come in the fall," he'd said. "They blow through the canyons to the sea, and after a hot summer, the chaparral is pure dry tinder. If a fire starts, the Santa Anas will push it all the way to the sea. It follows established wildlife trails—like the ones we have crisscrossing the orchard. And the fire won't stop until the winds stop blowing."

"We had fires in Mexico," Roberto had said.

"So you know what to do."

"Sí. Dig fire lines, put out the flames the best we can."

Riley had laughed. "Yes to the first part, no to the second. The local fire station will deal with the actual fire. Your job is to prepare for the worst, then get out safe before the fire comes. See those trees?"

He'd pointed to the tall, broad, ancient live oaks, their branches curving and curling all the way down to the ground, their trunks scarred black.

"Those trees caught fire in both '70 and '78. We've been lucky with the house, but we lost the orchard once. The main thing, Roberto, is we don't want to lose you or anyone here. That's rule number one."

"Gracias, señor," Roberto had said.

Now helicopters were flying overhead and the sky was darkening with smoke.

"Time to go," the cop said.

"But the orchard," Julia said.

"Julia, we have to get out," Roberto said, taking her arm.

"Hey," Officer Hernandez said, "don't panic, we have seventy engine companies on the fire and it's partly contained. Just get in your vehicles and go." Roberto caught him eyeing the black Tundra. It had barely passed inspection the last time, and his tailpipe was held on with baling wire.

"What is it?" Julia asked Roberto.

"Nothing," he said. "Let's get Bonnie. Serapio!"

Serapio also had his eye on the sheriff, who was walking around the two trucks. Roberto's was at least registered and insured. Serapio could be in real trouble because his was neither.

"Don't worry, man," Hernandez said. He was stocky and broad with a moustache, probably a Mexican lucky enough to have gotten papers. Or maybe he'd been born here. "I'm not giving you shit on a day like this. Just get out of here safe, okay?"

Julia had registered Roberto's alarm and was running toward the house to find Bonnie and the car keys. Roberto took off after her, not wanting to let her out of his sight for a second.

The canyon let out a howl, as if monsters had come alive. Roberto turned to see flames leap a thousand feet into the sky. The line of fire advanced like a lit fuse, across the nearby ridge, moving so fast Roberto could feel the heat.

"Go!" he yelled to Serapio. His friend ran to his truck—Hernandez was in his patrol car, on the radio, calling for help, but sirens were already sounding nearby.

If he didn't get Julia out of here right away, the fire would block their driveway. He tore into the house, up the stairs to her bedroom. There she was, on her knees, halfway under the bed. He didn't ask, just knelt beside her and looked.

Bonnie was huddled as far back along the wall as she could get. She was panting hard, her whole body trembling.

"I can't get her to come out," Julia said.

Roberto stood, walked around to the other side of the bed, nearest to where Bonnie was lying. He picked the heavy wood bed up with one arm and reached for Bonnie with the other. Scooping her against his chest, he felt her shivering uncontrollably.

"Move fast, amor," he said to Julia.

She nodded and he nudged her to run, and he followed her down the stairs. Sirens screamed up the hill, and Bonnie whimpered in terror and squirmed to get out of his arms.

"Shh," he whispered to calm her. "Estas tranquila, niña . . ."

They exited the house into billows of smoke. Flames licked the rock cliff just north of the fire line, fifty yards from the first row of lemon trees. Fire engines came from two directions: the driveway, and the unpaved fire road to the northwest.

Helicopters hovered just overhead, and Roberto felt the rush from the rotors and blinked against all the dust and dirt stirred into the air. The smoke was thick, black as night. He adjusted Bonnie and tried to put his arm around Julia, to keep her close.

Bonnie yelped, scrambled from his grasp, and took off.

"Bonnie!" Julia yelled. "Come here!"

Firefighters swarmed through the orchard, wearing heavy coats, helmets, and breathing equipment. Roberto saw Hernandez and pushed Julia straight at him. But she tore free of both of them and ran straight into the smoke, after Bonnie. Roberto was right behind her.

He sat beside Julia and tried to catch his breath. He had thought both she and Bonnie were lost. Running through the black smoke was a nightmare—he could hear her voice but couldn't tell exactly where it was coming from. He knew every inch of the orchard; he'd walked through it on the darkest nights. So he trusted his own compass, and the feel of his feet on the ground, and made sure he got between Julia and the cliff.

Bonnie had such good instincts. Moisture from the sea below swept up the hillside from the beach and provided a narrow strip of clear air along the cliff path. The old dog was panting, pacing back and forth right along the edge. Out over the ocean, the air was clean, except for one thick plume of smoke. Behind them was a wall of it. Roberto was ready to take off his shirt, cover her eyes and run her back to the truck when they heard Julia calling.

At the sound of her voice, Bonnie barked. She didn't even hesitate, but bolted back into the orchard toward Julia. Roberto caught Bonnie and stood with her in the clearing along the cliff. They waited for Julia, but she didn't come. Roberto felt frozen with fear. Had she fallen, passed out?

He picked up Bonnie and held her tight, willing her not to fight him. Walked back into the smoke, getting his bearings, calling Julia's name.

"Man, get the hell out of here," a firefighter said.

"I have to find Julia."

"Give me the damn dog," the firefighter said. "And get your friend and get going."

The animal part of Roberto's brain took over. He heard Julia keening, and although the noise and smoke threw her voice in a million directions, he went straight for her. She had stumbled into the middle of the orchard, surrounded by wind-rattled trees. Water from the fire hoses dripped from thick green leaves as if they'd just had a heavy rain.

She fought him so hard, he wasn't sure she knew who he was, or where they were. He couldn't remember what he said to her, but he picked her up and walked her toward the emergency vehicles.

Julia

Bonnie was in a panic. She knew what people couldn't know and felt what humans couldn't feel. The day Jenny died, Bonnie had done the same thing: hidden under Jenny's bed, to get away from the sirens and sorrow and death of the girl she'd loved most in the world. Back then Bonnie was a young dog, and Julia was too lost in her own grief to worry. She'd just set food and water at Jenny's bedside, then sat leaning against the wall, a few feet away from where the dog was hiding.

Julia wasn't thinking now, just running blindly after Bonnie. Bonnie was her only living link to Jenny. For five years Julia had thought that if she lost Bonnie, she'd want to die herself.

The land felt uneven beneath her feet. She tripped on a furrow, caught herself just before crashing into a lemon tree. She heard water spraying, the crank of the firefighters' hoses.

"Bonnie!" she called, choking and coughing in the smoke.

She stopped to listen for Bonnie's barking, but heard nothing but the terrifying noise of the wind, fire, and emergency crews. An animal rustled through the rosebushes, off to her left near the coast path.

"Bonnie!" she cried, and then she felt arms around her waist, pulling her away from the sound. She smelled scorched hair and skin.

"Julia," Roberto said. "Come with me."

"I don't want to! Not without her."

"She's fine," he said.

"No, she ran . . ."

"We have her," Roberto said.

Julia shook her head, not believing him, straining to run toward the path.

Roberto picked her up, and she began sobbing into his shoulder. He moved fast, as if his feet knew the way, because she knew he couldn't see a foot in front of them. He held her head so her face pressed against his neck, to keep her from breathing soot and ash.

"*Te amo*, Julia," he said roughly, his voice almost too hoarse to speak. They got to the driveway, packed with emergency vehicles. An EMT rushed to them, put an oxygen mask over Julia's face. The pure oxygen made her light-headed; she turned to look at Roberto and saw him standing right beside her. Bonnie was tethered to a fire truck with a rope.

"I love you, I love you," Julia said, but she wasn't sure who she was saying it to.

Roberto crouched down, held her hand. He'd saved their lives. He gazed at her so gently they might have been alone in the orchard, not surrounded by emergency crews. She smiled at him, and her eyelids began to flutter. She had wanted to die, and now she didn't, but she couldn't stay awake.

Now, lying on a gurney in the driveway, Julia opened her eyes and saw Roberto still watching her.

"Hola," he said.

"Hola," she said. "Thank you."

"You're my heart."

"You're mine."

She raised her head to make sure Bonnie was still there, and she saw her lying right next to the gurney where Julia could almost touch her. But something was different—it was quiet, almost hushed. Some of the emergency personnel were gone, and the air was free of smoke. She glanced around. The house was intact, the lemon trees still standing, the entire scene coated with fine white ash. The lawn, the trees, the rocks, the lemons, the stone walls, and the tile fountain: everything looked as if it were covered with snow.

Julia looked up and saw blue sky.

"What happened?" she asked.

"You sleep for a long time, amor."

"How long?"

"Twenty minutes, maybe."

"What about the fire?"

"The wind stopped blowing," he said. "The canyon and our fire line kept it away from the orchard just long enough for the wind to die."

"The fire's out?"

"They've contained it, but with the wind gone, it'll die much faster."

The police and firefighters were starting to depart. Their cars and trucks maneuvered out of tight spots on the narrow, hilly driveway, beep-beep-beeping as they went in reverse. Julia sat up. She gave Roberto her hand and he helped her to her feet. She wobbled slightly, then steadied herself.

Sheriff Hernandez walked over to them.

"Well, that was a miracle," he said.

"Close, right?" Roberto asked.

"Whew," Hernandez said, exhaling and pointing toward the north ledge. "Look—you can see the rocks are black where the fire cleared the top. We all saw it coming, thought this place was done for sure."

"And the wind stopped," Julia said. Her throat ached; her voice was hoarse. The sheriff nodded.

"Yeah," he said. "Casa Riley was the last stop on the way to the ocean. You were spared. You still might want to leave."

"Do you know about Lion Cushing's house?" she asked.

"He's on Turenne Road off Topanga Canyon, right?" Hernandez asked. "The fire missed them completely."

"Oh, good. He always leaves when there's a fire in the area. I'll let him know."

"He knows," Hernandez said, laughing. "He has the direct line to my boss. The L.A. sheriff is a big fan of his."

Julia smiled—that was Lion. "Thanks for everything you and everyone did," she said.

Julia, Roberto, and Bonnie walked back into the house. The thick walls and leaded casement windows had kept the smoke out, just as they had in previous Malibu fires. Julia put down a fresh bowl of water for Bonnie. She lapped it up while Roberto wet a towel and rubbed the soot off her fur.

"She could use a bath," he said.

They gave her one in the downstairs bathroom, filling the tub with warm water, lifting her in, and giving her a shampoo. Roberto seemed completely at ease, lathering up Bonnie's fur, rinsing her with a pitcher from the kitchen. The bathwater turned black, so they let it out and filled the tub again.

Bonnie kept shaking herself off, getting them wet, making them laugh. Julia was used to it, and she loved seeing Roberto's reaction. Bonnie had always loved her baths. When her coat smelled clean, they rinsed her one more time and let her out of the tub and used every towel in the bathroom to dry her.

"She feels better," Roberto said.

"She does," Julia said. They watched her go to her bed in the corner of the kitchen, circle once, and lie down. She rested her head on her paws.

"This is how I know the fire is really out," Roberto said, nodding toward Bonnie. "Because she can relax. She senses everything."

"Like when she was so scared, under the bed?"

"Sí. But also when she made her way to the cliff—the only place she could breathe."

"She did?'" Julia asked.

Roberto held her face in his hands, looked into her eyes. "Yes. But when she heard your voice, she ran straight back into the smoke to find you."

"You saved us, Roberto," she said.

"I love this dog," he said. "When she ran, it helped me get to you. I knew you needed me."

You needed me. Julia felt those words on her skin. She hadn't let herself need anyone, or even want someone, in such a long time. Roberto held her close, kissed her. They headed for the stairs, walked up together, side by side, to take a shower and wash the fire off of them.

When they got upstairs, walked into her bedroom, Julia heard her cell phone beep. She glanced at the screen, saw that John, Lion, and Jack Leary had called. Everyone but John could wait.

"Roberto," she said.

"Sí?"

She handed him her phone. "Will you please call John?"

"I'm sure he wants to hear from you and know that you are okay," Roberto said.

"You can tell him that," Julia said. "You're the orchard manager, and you should call."

Roberto looked proud as he took the phone. Julia showed which number to dial, then went into the bathroom to turn on the shower. While the water was getting hot, she stepped toward the bedroom door so she could listen.

"Señor Riley," she heard Roberto say. "We had a bad fire, but the house and orchard were saved. Most of all, Julia is safe . . ."

chapter fifteen

Roberto

He had never done this before, taken a shower with a woman. The Rileys' bathroom was large, and this was the biggest shower he had ever seen. He felt shy at first, but as soon as he stepped under the hot water with Julia, his inhibitions disappeared.

Kissing her while hot water flowed over them made him crazy in a way he'd never felt before. Every part of his body was alive, and she felt so warm and slippery in his arms—it was as if they were merging through each other's skin. She rubbed his body with soap, and that showed him to do the same to hers. They washed each other's hair.

Soot swirled down the drain. He had never felt this clean in his life. They stayed there long after all the black smoke had been washed from their hair and skin, just kissing and loving each other.

He felt Julia's hands sliding down his back, her breasts against his chest, and when she reached down to touch him he realized what she wanted.

"Here?" he asked.

"Yes," she said. "If you want."

"I do," he said.

Julia was so soft, and he wrapped her in his arms to protect her warm skin from touching the tile walls. As he entered her he lifted her up, and she wrapped her legs around his waist.

She felt light, and he held her with one arm while bracing them against the cool wall with his other. They were eye level, and he looked into her blue eyes, still so exotic to him. She barely blinked, hot water running down her face, and having her watch him that way brought them ever closer, beyond what he believed possible.

His body quivered with intense sensation, the water making their skin slippery, and driving him crazy. He cupped his hands around her ass, and her legs closed around his waist. She leaned her head against his, bit his shoulder and moaned. He heard her ecstasy and felt his own overtaking him.

He moved faster and faster. She held on, and that excited him even more; he heard the Spanish pouring out, his mouth against her ear.

When he finished, his legs were weak. He eased Julia down, and they smiled at each other.

"Julia," he said, "I never did that."

"In the shower?"

He nodded. Maybe he shouldn't have told her. Not because she'd think he was naïve, but because he didn't think it polite to talk about the past with women, and he hoped she wouldn't tell him hers with men. But she must have felt the same way, because she didn't reply. Just wrapped him in a soft, thick towel and led him to the bed.

They dried off, then climbed under the sheets. The sheets were softer than any fabric he'd ever felt, as if they were spun from clouds. Julia lay close to him, her head on the same pillow. Out the arched doors that led to the balcony were blue sky and the Pacific Ocean.

"Thank you for today," she said.

"La, Julia . . ."

"Two hours ago we thought we were going to lose Bonnie, the house, everything. And here we are."

"Este es mi cielo," he said.

"How do you say 'What?' in Spanish?"

"Mexicans say, '*Mande?*'"

"Okay, then. *Mande?*"

"This is my heaven," he said.

"The orchard?"

"No. In this bed, with you."

"Me too," she said.

As impossible as it was, he believed her. They lay together under the light sheet and she fell asleep first. He listened to her breathing, so quiet and steady, until it became part of his heartbeat. The blue sky began to fade, and sunset colors of orange, purple, and gold filled the doorway. He didn't want this day to end. The sun set so early at this time of year, but exhaustion from the day's events overtook them. He held Julia and knew this couldn't last. But for now it was real, so he stayed awake as long as he could to feel what was honest and truly happening between them, and then he fell asleep.

The next morning, Julia made breakfast: eggs, bacon, lemon muffins, fresh orange juice, the best coffee Roberto had ever drunk. They sat on the ocean-side terrace, where sun poured down and warmed them, as if this were normal, as if they were a couple. He kissed her goodbye and went to work.

Now that the fire was out, Roberto and Serapio started cleaning up the orchard. They had to wash and sweep ash off all the plants and trees and grass. Firefighters had dragged their hoses over flower beds, knocked low branches off some of the lemon trees. The smell of smoke was gone, replaced by a terrible odor from the trees that had burned up the canyon. Today the wind blew off the ocean, clean and salty, pushing the fire smell eastward.

"So," Serapio said, when they were on the far side of the orchard, the Casa blocked from view. "You and the lady."

"Mande?"

"Come on—you slept in the big house last night. I got here early and you weren't in your cabin."

Roberto didn't reply. He stood on a ladder, attacking a broken limb with a long saw, and he pretended it required more concentration than it actually did.

"Tell me, did you console her? She was upset about the fire?"

Guys talked, Roberto, too. He was so proud of being with Julia, bursting to tell Serapio—his friend and co-worker for three years now. But he honored Julia too much. Maybe she wouldn't want people knowing.

"You're crazy," he said.

"Come on, you can tell me. Was she good?"

Roberto ignored him. Many Mexicans talked of what it would be like to be with a gringa. How different, how the same, so many questions. Roberto had only known Spanish girls before. He could tell Serapio that being with this gringa was totally different—but not because of the sex, or the startling difference between her white and his brown skin, or even what it was like to hold her close and look into her blue eyes. But because he was in love with her.

"Fine, be like that," Serapio said. "But be careful, amigo."

"Why?"

"You sleeping with the boss's niece, you could lose your job. Screw it up for everyone. He'll fire all the Mexicans."

"He's not like that."

"So you did have sex with her!"

Roberto smiled, but only because Serapio was standing on the ground and could not see. He just kept working on the branch, and when it was about to fall he told Serapio to step away. The limb cracked and dropped hard to the ground.

On to the next tree, and the next. This was how Roberto managed to stay in his skin, and it always had been. He did his work, one small job after another, they all added up and filled the minutes and hours, and he kept himself as sane as a man who had fallen into an impossible love could be.

chapter sixteen

Lion

He felt like an old potentate returning to his homeland to survey the damage. Fortunately his house had been completely spared, but driving through nearby canyons, he was filled with horror. Only the most foolish people lived in Malibu. You had to be capable of denial, to imagine that after centuries of Santa Ana winds and the fires they fanned, your house would be spared. Time was on the side of the devil winds.

The ridge behind Casa Riley was now a blackened, smoldering wasteland. He held his breath taking the hill up to the driveway. In spite of what law enforcement had told him, he was certain there was no way the Casa could have survived intact. He approached it the way he would have an old friend who had been attacked by a shark, expecting to see scars, gaping wounds, and a leg missing.

But no—pulling into the turnaround, he surveyed the scene and saw it as sparkling as ever. The fine film of white ash looked like crystallized sugar, making the property remind him of a *Nut-cracker* stage set. He half expected the tile fountain and flower gardens to be made of marzipan.

Julia and Bonnie came to the kitchen door and ran out to meet him. Julia hugged him as if he were her long-lost uncle returning from war, even though she'd been the one who'd battled the fire.

"Thank God," he said. "That's all I can say."

"I know," Julia said.

"You didn't call me back. I left you a message, and I got worried."

"Oh, I'm so sorry—I just got off the phone with John. Lion, I can't believe what happened. We came so close, but then the wind just stopped."

"Just like *that*?"

"Pretty much," Julia said. "The sheriff said it was a miracle."

"Well, obviously," Lion said. "That smell, though."

"I know," she said.

"They say fire keeps the mountains healthy," Lion said. "But it's hard to believe when you see what the canyon looks like right now."

"I haven't left the property, so I haven't seen," Julia said.

"Shall we take a tour?"

"Well, I could use a trip to the grocery store," she said.

"My God, you're so practical. Must be the New Englander in you. I was thinking more about brunch at Shutters."

"Lion, I just had a big breakfast."

"You little blink of a thing? Well, come with me anyway. You can have a mimosa while I have lemon ricotta pancakes."

She hesitated. He saw her gaze off in the direction of the sound of a chain saw. The workers were hidden by glistening white foliage, but Lion knew who she was looking for.

"He's a big boy," he said. "He's done a fine job of running this property for some time now."

"I'm not doubting his abilities," she said.

"Oh. Sits the wind in *that* quarter," he said. "We're at the point where you can't bear to be apart for an hour?"

"Stop," she said. "Let me tell him I'm going out."

Lion watched her run through the lemon grove, just as she had a thousand times when she was a girl. She had that aspect again—carefree and lighthearted. He would have breathed deeply with profound happiness if it weren't for the chokingly dreadful burning smell.

She returned, smiling. After leading Bonnie back into the house, she emerged with her purse, wearing sunglasses. Lion regarded her carefully. Although she came from John's blood, not Graciela's, she had elegance and grace that reminded him of her aunt. She didn't have Graciela's glamour—even with the dark glasses—but who did?

Roberto had brought her back to life. Under Malibu's magical spell, in this enchanted orchard, Julia's feelings for him had caused her to bloom.

But Lion was old. He had seen so much, had experienced even more, when it came to star-crossed love. Over time he had discovered there was a formula to what worked and what didn't. Passion was one thing, but a lasting relationship required so much more. It bored him, and he wished more than anything that unconventional loves could last—they would make this world a better and more interesting place. But they always ended.

He dreaded the heartbreak that he knew lay ahead for Julia. She wasn't a woman who would give her heart lightly—she had had it under lock and key these last five years, and even before that, when her marriage to Peter had been falling to pieces.

Lion wanted Julia and Roberto to be happy in their Casa love nest, but unions between educated women and the help never lasted. He knew their love had an expiration date.

She did seem to love Malibu. Perhaps she would do what she'd said on their last car ride, and buy a little house nearby. If that happened, Lion knew she would gravitate to the academics and intellectuals. People always thought Los Angeles was a mere playground where people cared only about looking good on the outside—and they were absolutely right. But there was also a healthy enclave of writers, professors, and philosophical types, at UCLA, USC, and Pepperdine. He was sure there were anthropologists somewhere in the Los Angeles basin.

They drove along the ocean into Santa Monica, to the very end of Pico Boulevard and Lion's favorite hotel in the world: Shutters on the Beach.

Built of pale gray shingles with white trim and shutters, directly on the sand, it was a Nantucket fantasy beach hotel. The circular drive was full of valets, all of whom knew Lion by name.

"Hello, Mr. Cushing," Arturo said, taking the Jaguar.

"Hello, Arturo."

Lion squired Julia inside and enjoyed her pleasure at seeing the lobby again—she'd been here before with John and Graciela. It was a favorite spot for family dinners and celebrations. The room was long—a perfect ocean view at one end, but dim coziness throughout, fires blazing in two fireplaces, chic sofas facing each other for intimate conversations, original art and lithographs on the walls.

Jonathan, the concierge, greeted them and said their table was waiting. They went downstairs to Coast Restaurant, sat in the corner banquette with its striped cushions and windows directly on the beach. The waiters wore sorbet-colored shirts and Vineyard Vines ties patterned with tiny bicycles, surfboards, starfish. Luis brought coffee and fresh-squeezed grapefruit juice right away.

"We love it here, don't we?" Lion asked.

"We do," Julia said.

True to her word, she stuck to coffee and juice while Lion gobbled down the lemon ricotta pancakes he'd been craving. It pleased him greatly when she asked for a bite—he fixed her one with a bit of pancake, a raspberry, and real maple syrup and butter. He felt like a doting uncle, with an entire day to devote to his favorite nonbiological niece. They read the *Los Angeles Times* and *New York Times,* drank more coffee, and spent a leisurely hour.

"Now what shall we do?" Lion asked.

"I don't know," she said.

"Something different," he said. "Not the same old thing."

She thought for a minute, and the light in her eyes changed. "I wanted Roberto to show it to me, but maybe we could go first—Mariachi Square," she said.

"What a fascinating idea," he said. "East Los Angeles—I must admit I don't know it well, but they just renovated the old Boyle Hotel, where all the mariachis live, and who wouldn't want to see that?"

When they got into his car, he pulled up to Ocean Drive and looked at Julia. "Let's take the long way, shall we? It helps me digest."

Although it was out of the way, he took a winding route to leafy, twisty, hilly Sunset—his favorite way into town. He loved the great stands of eucalyptus trees shading the road, tall and straight with fragrant silver green leaves. Nearly every street he passed contained bits of his history: locations where he'd filmed, houses where he'd played.

"Look!" she said, watching a hawk take off from its perch in a sycamore, lift into the blue sky to disappear over the treetops.

"Nature everywhere," he said. "Aren't you tired of it after fighting the fire?"

"No," she said, laughing as if he'd made a joke.

"The thing about Malibu, darling," he said, "is balance. Nature kicks our asses out there, so we need to go into town now and then. This is a great idea of yours."

"Thank you."

The Rolling Stones played from his speakers. Lion had known Mick and, particularly, Keith from Topanga Canyon. The music made him nostalgic, reminded him of the days of working with Vanessa Redgrave, Catherine Deneuve, and Jane Fonda. The most beautiful, intelligent actresses on earth. He glanced at Julia.

He passed the main gate to Bel Air, then the Pink Palace—the Beverly Hills Hotel—where for two years the studio had kept a bungalow just for him. Graciela had loved it so. On to the Sunset Strip with all the towering billboards advertising movies and movie stars, past the building where his manager had offices and atop which sat Soho House, a club to which he belonged but never used.

They passed the Chateau Marmont, another hotel he knew far too well, and Laurel Canyon, and drove through Hollywood. As they approached the Los Angeles River, he knew they were close to East L.A.

"So," he said. "You want to see where Roberto comes from?"

"Yes," she said.

"You're good together, you know."

"Thank you."

"Has marriage been mentioned?" he asked.

"God, Lion! Give us a chance," she said, laughing.

"Darling, he's illegal! Marriage to you would get him a green card. Has he brought that up?"

"No, and he wouldn't," Julia said.

"I'm sorry, don't be offended. I'm sure that's not what he's after."

"I know that, too," she said. "I've been alone for years now; so has he. He's amazing, but I don't know what will happen. We'd have to know it was real . . ."

"Isn't it real?"

"Lion, why are you pushing me?"

Why was he? He knew why he was asking her these questions—they had more to do with him than with her.

"You know, a marriage of convenience is not unheard of."

"It is for me."

"Not really," Lion said. He struggled to keep his voice steady. He rarely spoke about it. "One took place in your own family."

"What are you talking about?"

"Graciela married John so she wouldn't be deported after the picture finished shooting."

"I've never heard that before," she said.

"She needed an American citizen, and he was it."

"But aren't you an American citizen, Lion?" she asked gently.

"Well, yes," he said.

Under the circumstances it was very kind of her not to ask the next question: *Then why didn't she marry you?* He had never been able to answer in any way that didn't crush his heart into pieces.

"She loves you," Julia said.

"How do you know?"

"I grew up seeing it," she said. "Maybe she needed John because he's so steady, and he's not an actor."

"Actors can't be reliable?" Lion asked, knowing that "steady" was never a word that would be applied to him.

"I'm sure they—you—can. But your profession is so incredible. You're both stars, and maybe she was afraid you'd compete with each other. Or maybe she thought if one won an award, the other would be jealous. And weren't there romances on the set when you were shooting different movies?"

Lion pondered her question. Yes, there had been many romances. As much as he loved Graciela, he hadn't been faithful to her. He'd excused that by telling himself she was married to another man. But in truth, he doubted that he would have resisted all those leading ladies, makeup artists, that Australian director and her irresistible accent.

"The point is, whether you're married to her or not, you love each other," Julia said.

"Well, yes, we do," he said. "Or I do, anyway."

"She loves you, too. You're part of the family, Lion."

Lion stared straight ahead at the river so she wouldn't see his eyes glittering and know that her words, however loving, could never make up for the fact Graciela had married John instead of him.

Julia

She felt intensely aware of Lion's emotion, and fell silent so he could be alone with his thoughts. They passed train tracks and warehouses, then crossed the Los Angeles River and drove up bustling tree-lined Cesar E. Chavez Avenue, alive with shops and restaurants. There were street murals, elaborate and colorful, depicting Zapata, Pancho Villa, and the Mexican flag.

Julia felt entranced by the murals. One showed a school in cross section, with students studying, teachers at the blackboard, the library full of books, angels hovering over the school roof. Another was an homage to Diego Rivera—a Mexican pueblo and workers painted in his strong style, thick and foreshortened, with a portrait of Diego and his love Frida Kahlo in the corner.

"Can we park and walk around?" Julia asked.

"Just tell me where."

They circled around, drove past White Memorial Medical Center, onto East First Street. The buildings of downtown Los Angeles shimmered in the heat, like a mirage, across the river. Julia heard music, and turned her head to see the domed kiosk marking Mariachi Plaza.

"Here!" she said.

"And just look at that hotel!" Lion said, his voice animated again as he pointed out the newly renovated Boyle Hotel—a four-story red brick Victorian and Romanesque Revival building with a turret, a graceful domed cupola, and a bronze sign at the corner with the original date, 1889.

Lion had to drive around looking for a spot. The area was busy. There were several vans with band names and phone numbers hand-scrawled on the sides. Julia and Lion paused at the Spanish colonial bandstand, where many mariachis had gathered in their charro clothing and sombreros.

Cars circled the square, and Julia watched the freelance mariachis smile at the drivers, hoping to be chosen for Friday night celebrations. One driver rolled down his window, spoke to a man wearing a dark green charro suit. The mariachi gestured to his band. Six men carrying instruments hurried to their van and followed the car away. Meanwhile, another band played Mexican folk music.

A mural of the Virgin of Guadalupe dominated one wall, bouquets of flowers and votive candles laid at her feet. Other paintings showed mariachis playing guitars, both on earth and in the clouds of heaven above. Julia's skin tingled as she thought of Rosa, of how Roberto had told her this had been their destination. Had Rosa remembered? What if she really had made her way to Mariachi Square?

Even as she and Lion strolled around, Julia knew she was dreaming. And the truth was, she wouldn't even want Rosa here—the plaza was grittily romantic, but nowhere for an eleven-year-old girl to be alone. People hurried all around, in and out of the Gold Line subway station.

Julia remembered a Saturday when, at thirteen, Jenny had told her she was spending all day at her friend Martha's, but instead they'd taken Amtrak into the city. They had gone to the Plaza Hotel, wanting to see the portrait of Eloise. Jenny had led Martha northwest across Central Park—the same route she'd taken with Julia a month earlier—to the American Museum of Natural History to see the panorama of the Yaquis and other Sonoran Desert people.

Washing Jenny's jeans, Julia had found her train ticket and museum admission receipt. She'd had to wait all day for Jenny to get home from school, feeling more and more upset as the hours passed. She could hear her own mother's voice: "You could have been raped/kidnapped/murdered!"

By the time Jenny got home, Julia had calmed down enough to ask, "Why didn't you just tell me?"

"I wanted to do it on my own," Jenny had said.

"Well, I would have let you go, but I would have preferred knowing where you were instead of your lying to me."

"Mom, you're just saying that," Jenny said. "Think about it. There's no way you'd have let me go to New York alone with Martha."

Julia had thought about it, and had known Jenny was right. There were so many dangers in the world—if she had had her way, she'd never have let Jenny out of her sight. Julia had wished she could wrap Jenny in safety forever, and she had believed that meant keeping her home, in tiny bucolic seaside Black Hall.

Yet now, standing in Mariachi Plaza, Julia knew that safe Black Hall, where nothing bad could ever happen, was where Jenny had died. Maybe life was too capricious for even the best parents to manage. Roberto had done his best as a father, with the most disastrous results possible.

"Are you okay?" Lion asked.

"Yes," she said. "Enjoying the music."

"I once had a majordomo who arranged a party at my house. We had a taco truck and a mariachi band. What a hit that was. We'll have to do it again."

"That would be fun," Julia said. The heat had tired her out, and she was still feeling the aftereffects of the fire and everything else that had happened yesterday. They found a bench in the shade, and Lion spotted a coffee and fruit ice cart. He went to check it out, and Julia pulled out her phone. She had been meaning to call Jack back.

"Finally," he said when he answered.

"What did you mean?" Julia asked.

"I'm on the trail, Julia. I tracked down the Marcie footprint, and it turns out it belonged to a woman named Felicia traveling with the Diamondback tattoo guy."

"The man who died?"

"Yes—but Felicia is alive. I'm in my car now, heading to her house. I'll let you know what I learn as soon as I see her."

"Could Rosa be with her?" Julia asked, standing up.

"I don't think so. She's been in touch with her mother and friends in Mexico, and she didn't mention her. But I'll find out what happened in the desert. We'll at least know that much."

Lion walked toward her with two cups of pomegranate ice, and she met him halfway.

"I thought this would refresh us," he said.

"Thank you," she said. "But we have to get back to the Casa right away."

"Why, is there a problem?"

"No. Jack Leary is about to find out what happened to Rosa, and I want to be with Roberto when he calls."

"Let's go then," Lion said, and they hurried to his car.

chapter seventeen

Jack

He drove east from Yuma toward the address Maya had given him. This rural area had been part of his sector, and he knew it well. The road took him through swaths of desert, sun-bleached rock formations, and purple mountains in the distance. Saguaro cactus grew everywhere, tall and mysterious. If Louella had been with him, she'd have had her binoculars out—watching for pygmy owls and elf owls piping out from the nests they'd built in cactus cavities.

The houses along this stretch were poor, and far between. When he came to the address Maya had given him, he took a deep breath. It was a trailer, the roof caving in, a satellite dish on the corner. But attempts had been made to make it look nice: a cactus garden along the side, a shrine to Our Lady of Guadalupe, an American flag next to the door. A child's toys were in the yard: a doll, a baby carriage, and miniature garden tools. Jack's throat felt dry.

He knocked on the door.

No answer, but he saw a curtain move.

"Felicia?" he called. "You have a daughter? I see her doll. I'm not here to give you any trouble. I'm just looking for another little girl, Rosa. I think you knew her."

He stood silently for a full minute as the front door opened. A woman stood inside, her hand on the shoulder of a little girl who looked to be about four years old. Behind them he saw shadows of other people, four or five, trying to stay out of sight.

"Hello, Felicia. I'm Jack Leary," he said. "Your mother's friend Maya told me where I could find you."

"I know. She found my number and called," Felicia said.

"You have a beautiful daughter," he said, crouching down until he was eye level with the child. "What's your name?"

"Mamá?" the girl asked, looking up for guidance.

"Se llama Eduarda," Felicia said.

"Named for her father who died in the desert," Jack said.

Felicia's eyes filled with tears. "Sí," she said. Then she clutched her daughter and asked him, "Migra? Policia?"

"No, not at all," Jack said in Spanish. "I just want to ask you about what happened in the desert."

"Eduardo murió."

"I know. I'm sorry," Jack said.

"Gracias," she said.

"You were with other people, right?"

"Yes, we got lost."

"But you made it here safely."

"Thank God," she said, touching the top of Eduarda's head.

"You helped a girl," Jack said. "You found her along the way, while you were walking."

"Sí," Felicia said. "She was alone."

"Is she here?" Jack asked.

"Of course not," she said. "This is Eduardo's family's house. Too many people already."

"I understand. Do you know where she is?" Jack asked. "Did she make it to the States with you?"

"Yes, but she was very sick. Unconscious. She went to the hospital."

"Which hospital?" Julia asked.

"Pais Grande Medical Center," Felicia said. "We left her at night, at the door."

"You were on foot?" Jack asked.

"No. By then we were in a car. We had met our friends."

"Pais Grande isn't so far from here. Did you ever find out what happened to her next?" Jack asked.

"I don't know. Once I called to inquire. I asked about la niña from the desert. They asked if I was her family, and I couldn't lie, so they wouldn't give me information. *Lo siento*," Felicia said.

"No, don't be sorry," Jack said, looking into Felicia's eyes. "You saved her life. She was alive when you left her at the hospital in Pais Grande, and that is because of you. Her family will be very grateful for the information."

He left her trailer with a plan of what to do next. It felt good to be on the case again, and this time he wouldn't have to turn anyone in. He would learn if Rosa had survived. If she had, he doubted that she was still in the area, but anything was possible. Somebody at the clinic would have seen her, treated her. And somewhere out there was the answer.

chapter eighteen

Julia

That night Julia dreamed of Jenny. She had always been such a good rider, and she was riding a big bay horse. Julia stood outside a white fence, cheering her on. It seemed to be a horse show, a hunt seat competition. Jenny looked beautiful in her black jacket and hunt cap, buff breeches and tall black leather boots.

Timmy was watching too, from across the ring. He was standing there with his new girlfriend, and Julia felt panicked that Jenny would see them. If Julia could just keep Jenny from seeing, she could save her life, and everything would go on as it was supposed to.

Jenny rode over to Julia and stopped. She sat high on the beautiful dark horse, looking at her mother with sadness in her eyes.

"Jen," Julia said, reaching for her hand.

"It's okay, Mom, I saw them. You can't protect me."

"Stay with me, sweetheart. I don't want you to die."

Jenny cast a glance over her shoulder, looking straight at Timmy.

"Hearts are made to be broken," Jenny said.

"What do you mean?"

"I love with everything I have. I wouldn't change that, even if it killed me. You wouldn't want me to."

"Jenny!"

Then Jenny urged her horse into a full gallop, and they jumped the fence. In dream magic, Julia went soaring after them. She followed Jenny and the horse flying through the sky. Jenny's English riding clothes became a faded, tattered dress, and the horse changed color from dark brown to pale gold.

They landed in the desert, and Julia recognized the place where she and Jenny had spent that summer working. Only instead of anthropologists, there was a long stream of people walking north. She searched the group for Jenny, and found her near the head of the line.

Jenny was standing with a young girl: Rosa.

"I love you, Mom," Jenny said, looking up at Julia. "I didn't leave because of you, I left because of me."

Julia couldn't hold back tears. She stepped forward and hugged her daughter. Jenny's neck smelled the way it always had. Julia didn't want to let go, but when she did, Jenny was gone. The line of people had disappeared, and Rosa stood there alone. Julia picked her up.

Her arms were heavy with the weight of Rosa, but when she woke up she was in bed with Roberto. The dream had felt so real, she slid out from under the covers and walked to the open doorway onto the balcony, expecting to see horses and the two girls in the yard. Dawn was an hour away, but the eastern sky was starting to lighten through mist rising from the sea.

"Julia?" Roberto said, waking up, lifting onto his elbow.

"I just had a dream," she said, looking at him.

"Sí?"

"About the girls."

"It was just a dream, amor," he said.

"Jenny and Rosa were together," she said. "I don't *want* it to be just a dream."

Julia felt his eyes on her as she turned back toward the sea and felt guilty for the thoughts coursing through her mind. As horrible as Roberto's last five years had been, at least he had the chance of finding his daughter—while Jenny was gone forever.

"I heard her voice," she said.

"Jenny's?"

"Yes. In the dream; it was exactly the way she always sounded, but she was older. Twenty-one, the age she would be now. And Rosa was eleven."

"Jenny is helping Rosa," he said.

"Do you really believe that?"

"Sí, amor," he said.

"I wish Jack would call," Julia said.

She stood in the doorway scanning the yard. Two coyotes skulked along the coast path. As if sensing her, they turned to look, and she saw their eyes glowing red-gold in the first light. They rustled into the brush and disappeared. Maybe she'd dreamed them, too.

"I want to go to Arizona," Roberto said.

"Jack didn't tell me enough details to know where," Julia said. "We have to wait until he calls." She paused as something else occurred to her. "Roberto, will it be safe for you to go down there, so close to the border?"

"You mean ICE?"

"Yes. What if they pick you up?"

"Julia, it could happen. That's the truth: it's bad down there for illegals. But I have to go anyway, to be where Rosa was . . ."

The prospect scared her, but she understood. Roberto started to get out of bed, but she put her hand on his chest and climbed back in. She could only imagine how torturous it was, waiting to hear anything, even a tidbit, about what had happened to Rosa.

The morning air was damp and cool, and his body felt hot under the comforter. They held each other, legs entwined. Her mouth found his, kissed him long and gently. Their hands ran down each other's sides, and she felt his smooth skin under her hand, callused from digging the fire trench, and felt herself melting into him.

He kissed her neck, shoulders, and lips, holding her and whispering words in Spanish. She felt emotion beyond desire, looking into his velvet brown eyes. He held her hips as she shifted on top of him. She wanted no space between them, needed to feel him inside so she could forget where she ended and he began. Deep inside she felt very still, while sweat ran down her back and their bodies began to shudder.

They slept in each other's arms for a few minutes, then woke for good. Roberto got up to take a shower, and Julia pulled on an oversized shirt and went downstairs to feed Bonnie and make coffee.

Bonnie stood at the kitchen door, anxious to get out. Julia walked into the yard with her, barefoot and feeling the cool dew on her toes. Bonnie started around the house, toward the seaward side, but Julia stopped her. The sun hadn't risen high enough yet. The mountains belonged to the coyotes and other wild things until after dawn.

Roberto met them in the courtyard holding two mugs of coffee. He and Julia sat on the fountain's edge and Bonnie lay contentedly on the front step. The sun rose and struck the lemon trees. Yellow fruit glowed in the bright sun breaking through the sea mist. Hummingbirds darted in and out of the bougainvillea. And remnants of Julia's dream drifted around her head like fragments of morning fog.

chapter nineteen

Jack

It was Saturday, and his original plan had been to wait until Monday, when the administrator would be working at the clinic. But the Pais Grande Medical Center was small, with barely any staff at all, and he was counting on the fact that somebody there would remember Rosa. He had been there countless times while he was working. Plenty of illegal immigrants, too dehydrated and dispirited to continue, went to the clinic and gave themselves up. But he believed that an unconscious child abandoned on their doorstep would stand out.

The sun was up and already hot. Shadows from giant saguaro cacti fell across the pavement when he turned off the interstate and headed south for Pais Grande. Heat quivered above the ground, making the road look as if it were lifting up, rising toward the cloudless sky.

He'd given Julia Hughes just enough information so that Roberto was probably climbing the walls to hear the latest, so he dialed the number.

"Hello?" Julia's voice answered.

"Hi," he said. "I wanted to fill you in."

"Tell me!"

"I don't know much yet," he said. "I did speak to the woman who found Rosa in the desert. She was very helpful."

"Hold on," Julia said. Jack heard her calling Roberto.

"Look, don't get your hopes up yet," Jack said. "The woman told me Rosa was very sick. They dropped her off at a medical clinic in Pais Grande. I'm on my way there now."

"But she was alive?" Julia said.

"Yes, at the time they left her at the clinic, but that's all I know. Maybe I should have waited and called you after I found out."

"No, no! You did the right thing." She couldn't keep the excitement out of her voice. "Just stay in touch, okay?"

"Yep," Jack said. "I'll call you right away."

They hung up, and he kept driving. He slung his arm across the seat beside him, as if Louella was sitting right there and he was resting his right hand on her shoulder.

Entering town he saw the sign: PAIS GRANDE, POPULATION 3100. He saw lots of trailers and stucco houses and a cheap strip mall with a taco restaurant, pharmacy, and offices for an immigration lawyer, one gas station, and there at the end of Main Street, the one-story medical center.

Jack parked in the small parking lot and walked to the front door. The sign said PAIS GRANDE–SONORA MEDICAL CENTER: SERVING RURAL ARIZONA SINCE 1975. He tried the door and he walked into a blast of air-conditioning. The waiting room was full, as if everyone had waited until Saturday to get sick.

"May I help you?" a woman asked, sitting at a central desk. She was middle-aged with brown skin and friendly eyes, graying black hair pulled back in a long ponytail. The plaque on her desk said *Veronica Gonzalez, RN*. He glanced up and down the two short hallways radiating to her left and right, saw that they were lined with exam rooms. Patients waited in chairs and on gurneys.

"How are you doing?" he asked.

"Just fine," she said. "Haven't seen you here lately."

"I retired," he said.

"No way!" she said. "You're an institution."

He laughed. "I've been gone two years. Guess I'm not that much of an institution."

"Well, we miss you. What can I do for you?"

"I'm looking for someone," he said.

She stared at him, impassive. They had always been on opposite sides—though her legal obligation was to report migrants, he knew her sympathy lay with them. He had been the enemy.

"I know you've worked here a long time, Ronnie," he said.

"Twelve years," she said.

"Well, this goes back a few years—five. A migrant group passing by left a six-year-old girl at your door. She was very sick, unconscious. Does that ring a bell?"

"There are so many cases, Jack," she said.

"The girl was Mexican; if she came to, she'd have been crying for her father."

"Still doesn't tell me much."

"She would have had bare feet—we found her sneakers in the desert, covered in blood. So she'd have had injuries, cuts. You probably called her Jane Doe—the woman who left her didn't stick around long enough to give any information."

"I assure you that if the child was undocumented, we followed procedure and contacted ICE."

"Look, I'm sure you did. I'm retired now, I'm not interested in getting you or anyone in trouble, least of all the girl."

Ronnie's lips were tight—she didn't trust him. She probably

thought once a border agent, always a border agent. He took a deep breath to break the tension.

He spotted a wall covered with children's drawings and paintings. A surprising number of them had the desert as their subject: families holding hands walking down a path, scary red eyes in the darkness, saguaro and prickly-pear cacti, dead bodies.

"Wow, kids did those?" he asked.

"Yes," she said. "We get many children sick making the crossing. They are dehydrated, sunburned, covered with bug bites. Some have seen their parents die. All need treatment for trauma—and of course there's no funding for such care. Regardless, once we fill out the proper paperwork, we transfer the children to a hospital that can better help them."

"I know the procedure, but which hospital would you have used for her?"

"Depends," Ronnie said.

"On what?"

"The severity of the case; more commonly, which hospital has a bed available. Things like that. May I ask why you're involved?"

"It's an old case of mine," he said. "I know you think we're a bunch of heartless bastards, and sometimes we are. But I want to make this one right."

"How would you make it right?"

"Learning the truth of what happened to her, telling her father. He's lived with not knowing for five years. Will you check your records for May 2007?"

Ronnie nodded. A line had formed behind Jack, and she seemed impatient. Her fingers clicked on the keyboard, and she came up with a file.

"Jane Doe, May 2007," she said. "Six-year-old female, dehydrated, multiple injuries—including infected cuts on both feet. She drifted in and out, but never became fully conscious—she called for her father, but couldn't tell us his name, or even hers."

"You mean she's alive?"

"She survived long enough for us to transfer her to Tucson." Ronnie's brow furrowed as she scrolled through the file.

Jack studied her face, seeing the worry there. This was a nurse who cared.

"Here it is," Ronnie said, handwriting the information on a notepad. "Jane Doe, case number 4134. We sent her to San Jacinto Hospital."

"Thank you," he said.

"I hope it helps," she said.

On the way out of Pais Grande, he picked up two *carne asada* tacos from the place in the strip mall and ate them as he drove. The sauce was homemade and extra spicy, and he liked the way it made his mouth burn. He drove fast, up the rural road to Route 8, and turned the music up nice and loud.

San Jacinto was a good hospital, but it seemed a strange choice to him. He couldn't remember ever taking someone to San Jacinto.

Tucson rose from the desert, silver and tall. His chest tightened, and he felt the blood rush to his head. He got off the highway an exit too soon and had to waste fifteen minutes finding the hospital. The city reminded him of work and of losing Louella. He hadn't been back in a long time, and if it weren't for Rosa Rodriguez, he wouldn't be returning now.

Roberto

Julia's car was loaded up for the trip, Bonnie in the back seat. It made sense for her to drive—they would be many hours on the road, lots of speed traps, and Roberto didn't have a license.

From the minute they heard that Rosa had last been seen in Pais Grande, Arizona, Roberto had to get there as soon as possible. He had arranged for Serapio to run the orchard for a few days. Lion was going to check on the house every day.

First, before they headed south, he wanted to see his father. Once they got close, Roberto directed her to North Boyle Avenue.

Julia found a space on the street, and she parked the car.

"Should Bonnie and I wait here?" she asked.

"No," he said. "Of course not. I want to introduce you."

"Bonnie too?"

"Sí." Roberto smiled, but inside he felt nervous. He glanced at the house, saw his father and Esperanza crowded at the window, looking out from behind the curtain.

As they all got out of the car, Roberto put his arm around Julia's waist and unlatched the gate on the chain link fence and walked her up the front steps. Pink roses and bright blue morning glories were blooming, and the tomato plants were heavy with red fruit— he saw Julia smile as she checked them out. His father opened the door before he had the chance to knock.

"Hola, Papá," Roberto said. "This is Julia Hughes."

"I'm so glad to meet you," Julia said, shaking his hand.

"Glad to meet you, too," his father said. He was very shy about his English, but after many years here he understood everything and spoke very well. "This is my wife, Esperanza."

The two women hugged. Roberto felt happy to see Esperanza's genuine delight at meeting Julia. She beamed, gesturing for Julia to come in, checking out Julia's hair, clothes, shoes—all very modest, nothing like what Esperanza would assume the Malibu lady would wear.

"What about Bonnie?" Julia asked. "Would you rather we left her in the yard?"

"No, of course not," his father said. "Bring her in."

Esperanza hurried to the kitchen. They heard water running, and she returned with a bowl for Bonnie, who instantly began to lap it up.

The whole house was so small, the living room just large enough to hold two short couches facing each other, a table in the middle, and the TV. Roberto tried to see it through Julia's eyes. He was sure she'd never entered a house like this before. But she seemed happy, settling down on the couch, accepting the glass of Dr Pepper that Esperanza set on a lace doily on the table before her, her gaze taking in all the photos on the wall and Esperanza's shrine to the Virgin of Guadalupe in the corner.

"I'm so happy to be here and meet you both," she said.

"Gracias," Esperanza said. She sat beside Roberto's father on the opposite couch, and Roberto sat beside Julia. They all faced one another. Roberto's father's eyes burned into his, and he cleared his throat, knowing he had to start talking.

"Papá," he said.

He saw his father steeling himself for news. Roberto was holding Julia's hand. Maybe his father thought they had come to say they were getting married. Roberto glanced at Julia, her calm blue eyes and elegant profile.

"Oh, there she is!" Julia said, turning to look at the framed photo of Rosa. "What a beautiful picture."

"It was taken at her school," Roberto said.

"Papá," Roberto said, "we have news about her."

"News—how?" he asked.

"Julia," Roberto said. "She's done research, *investigación,* and she found a trail that leads to Rosa."

"Rosa! She is alive?" his father asked, jumping to his feet.

"Papa, slow down."

"We don't know yet, Señor Rodriguez," Julia said. "The border agent who picked up Roberto found out that five years ago Rosa was seen at a hospital in Pais Grande, Arizona. She was sick, but alive."

"Dios mío," he said, pacing.

"I came to tell you that we are going there now," Roberto said.

"Going where?"

"To Pais Grande."

"No! Are you crazy?"

"What else would I do?" Roberto asked. "My daughter was there, I will go look for her."

"It's near the border, no?"

"Sí," Roberto said.

"So you want to go back to Mexico? Because that's what will happen. ICE will catch you. Or your 'friend' the border agent will arrest you. Pais Grande is where many get caught."

Roberto and his father stared at each other. They both knew that what he was saying was true. Roberto swallowed, not wanting to look at Julia. This was the real reason he'd wanted to see his father today—because if he did get caught, and sent back, he might not see him for a long time.

"I trust Jack Leary—the agent," Julia said.

"Uh-huh," his father said, too polite to speak against her. But Roberto and his father and Esperanza knew the border, and knew that trust had a different meaning down there.

"What would you do, Papá?" Roberto asked.

His father squinted, the expression making his face look angry. But Roberto knew he was trying to hide his feelings. He was shorter, thicker than Roberto, and paced around the room. Finally he sat down heavily.

At last he spoke. "I would do what you are doing," he said. "If you were lost, and I had the chance to find you, I would go."

Roberto nodded. He felt better, knowing that his father understood. "Gracias, Papá," Roberto said.

His father just stared. Bonnie had finished drinking water and now lay stretched out on the rug, relaxing. His father reached down to pet her, and she licked his hand.

"She is old?" he asked.

"Twelve," Julia said.

"The desert heat will not be good for her," he said. "Even in the car."

"She likes car rides," Julia said.

"Leave her with us," his father said. Roberto listened carefully, heard his father's voice crack.

Julia felt torn. She wanted Bonnie to be with her, but she also wanted her to be safe. "That's very nice of you," Julia said after a moment. "Are you sure?"

"Yes," his father said. "But I have a question."

"Okay," she said.

"Why are you taking this trip, Julia?" his father asked simply.

"Because I love your son," she said. "And I lost my daughter, too," she added softly.

It was time to go. Esperanza had been busy preparing a bag of food for the road. Julia programmed the family's number into her mobile phone, and Roberto glanced into the bag: cans of Dr Pepper, two burritos wrapped in waxed paper, and a box of small round cookies, covered in powdered sugar—Mexican wedding cookies. Roberto glanced up at Esperanza, and she winked.

They walked outside, and everyone hugged. Roberto felt joy and surprise at his father's reaction to meeting Julia. It nearly overwhelmed the sorrow he felt simmering just beneath the surface, to think that this could be the last time he saw his father for a while. Looking at Julia, standing beside his father, he felt strong—she was his luck, his angel, and he believed what she'd said—that they would all come home safely.

Esperanza asked Roberto and Julia to stand with Bonnie in front of the car, and she took their picture. Then Julia handed Esperanza her iPhone and asked her to take one for her, too.

When Julia started up the car, she rolled down the windows. Making a U-turn in the wide street, she drove very slowly so they could all wave. Both she and Esperanza waved their arms wildly, but Roberto and his father were given to smaller gestures. They each raised one hand. But then Roberto saw his father put his hand over his heart. He closed his eyes, to keep that image in his mind forever.

Once the house and his family were out of sight, Julia sped up, and they were on the freeway, on their way.

chapter twenty

Jack

Tucson on a Saturday was marginally better than Tucson on a weekday. Most offices were closed, so the streets weren't so busy. Jack had never been made for the city, and his already thin tolerance for crowds and traffic had only diminished as he'd gotten older.

He parked in San Jacinto Hospital's garage, and took the elevator to the lobby level. The hospital felt old, but—if such a thing was possible—kind of cozy. It wasn't all gleaming white like the other medical centers: the floor was terracotta tile, the walls were somewhere between tan and brown, there were statues of Saint Jacinto and the Virgin Mary everywhere, and crucifixes on each corridor.

There were nuns walking the halls—though only a few wore habits. "Good morning, Sister," Jack said, approaching a nun pushing a library cart. "Can you tell me where Medical Records is located?"

"In the basement," she said, "but they're closed today. You'll have to come back Monday."

"Okay, thanks. Now, where can I find the pediatrics floor?"

"Take the elevator and push four."

"Thank you," he said, glad she didn't ask whom he was visiting. She probably pegged him as a Catholic schoolboy from way back. Nuns, in their own way, were good at profiling.

He rode up to the fourth floor, and stepped into familiar territory. Medical floors, no matter the hospital, were set up the same way, with the nurses' desk in the center and patient rooms on hallways radiating out. He passed a young male doctor speaking to worried-looking parents and went straight to the desk. An older nun was on the computer.

"Excuse me, Sister," he said.

"Just a minute," she said.

He waited. A white-haired doctor, a real Dr. Spock type—carried a file behind the desk and placed it in a tray. The nun didn't even look up.

"Sister," the doctor said, "I need the number for—"

"Just a minute," she said sharply.

"I need it now."

"There's the phone book."

Jack hid a smile—she was just like the nuns he'd grown up with. They were focused and strict, and they didn't let anyone give them guff, even the monsignor. The doctor walked away. Jack killed time by wandering over to an alcove where a bronze statue of a nun in an old-school floor-length habit stood. He read the sign:

> Catherine McAuley
> opened the first House of Mercy
> on Lower Baggot Street in Dublin, Ireland,
> on September 24, 1827,
> as a place to shelter, feed, and educate women and girls.
> On December 12, 1831,
> Catherine and two companions took their vows
> and became the first Sisters of Mercy.

"Now," the old nun said, "how may I help you?"

"You're Sisters of Mercy?"

"That's right. Are you here to visit a patient?"

"Not a current patient," he said.

"Well, isn't that a smart answer?" she said. She had pale blue eyes and a glare that could put the fear of God in anyone. She reminded him of Sister Michael Joanne, his high school principal.

"Have you been on this floor long?" he asked.

"What does that have to do with the price of tea in China?"

He laughed, feeling more at home by the minute. "You're from Boston, aren't you?"

"Yes, and don't think I don't hear Dorchester in your own voice."

"The nuns at my school were Sisters of Notre Dame."

"A fine order."

"The reason I'm asking if you've been here long—"

"Your charms might work on the good Sisters of Notre Dame," she said. "But Sisters of Mercy are a little tougher. I've been here thirty-five years, long enough to know that whatever you're selling we're not buying."

"I'm not selling anything. I'm retired U.S. Border Patrol, and I'm following up on an old case. Trying to find a missing girl. She was transferred to this hospital from the Pais Grande clinic in May 2007."

"And you think I'm just going to look her up in the computer for you? Are you her father? No. Are you a family member? No. You do your job down at the border, and let us do ours here on the fourth floor."

"Here's her picture," Jack said, placing the photo of Rosa and her family on the desk.

The nun leaned over to look, but didn't pick it up. Her lips thinned.

"And here's the case number. She came in as a Jane Doe," he said.

The old nun slid both the picture and the slip of paper back to Jack. "You could be anyone," she said. "I should call security right now. You have no business on the pediatrics floor."

"Sister, her family needs to know what happened to her."

"Then have them contact Medical Records. Unless they have proof she is their daughter, and that can be tough with a Jane Doe, they will need a court order and a DNA test."

"The father is undocumented. He and Rosa crossed from Mexico, and she got sick and lost in the desert. He can't get a court order."

At that the nun paused. She reached for the photo again, and Jack saw her studying Rosa.

"I just read about Catherine McAuley," Jack said, pointing at the statue. "Your order was founded to help the poor. I see the map of Ireland on your face—just like you see it on mine. Our people knew poverty, just like the Mexicans know it now. Catherine McAuley tried to do something about it."

"Don't go telling me about my own order," she said. "And what's a retired border agent doing trying to help undocumented Mexicans? You don't hear that every day. Am I supposed to trust you just because you've got some Irish blood and went to Catholic school?"

"No," he said. "You're supposed to trust me because you know the truth when you hear it."

She drew the case number closer and her fingers began clicking on the keypad. "No matter what I find, I can't give out any information about the child without written permission from whoever is caring for her now."

"Understood," he said.

The sister frowned. She checked the number on the paper, and then reentered the sequence into her computer again.

"What's the problem?" Jack asked.

"She doesn't exist," the nun said. "As far as our records go, we never had a Jane Doe with that case number sent to us by the medical center in Pais Grande."

"Your files go back to 2007?

"They go back much further than that," she said.

Jack checked his watch: 3:15 p.m. It would take him an hour and a half to get back to Pais Grande, and no matter how late the clinic stayed open, he was pretty sure the shift would change at five. He thanked the nun and headed for the elevator and his car.

Luckily, traffic was light. With temperatures above one hundred, people didn't seem in a rush to head for the desert. He floored it to Route 8, took a left off the interstate at Gila Bend and headed south.

Passing through the Barry M. Goldwater Air Force Range, he hoped they weren't doing bombing exercises today. He crossed the line from Maricopa into Pima County. The Mexican border was less than twenty miles south. He couldn't help scanning, knowing that migrants were walking nearby, and if he stopped to cut sign he'd probably find a group within minutes.

He had seen Dodge Chargers on Route 8, known that the unmarked cars belonged to the Border Patrol. Now he passed a white and green SUV, same make and model as his, and raised a hand in greeting—the driver was Ralph Landers, a guy Jack had trained. It felt jarring but familiar to be back in his old territory, now on a completely different mission.

The desert around him glowed in late-day light. The sand seemed to be a thousand different colors instead of the relentless brown it always appeared under the noon sun. The saguaros were casting long shadows again, just as they had at daybreak this morning, only now the sun was in the west.

Narrowing, the road split and Jack took the fork heading for Pais Grande. He checked his watch—4:35. He gunned the engine and thought about going off road. He would save five minutes, but he heard a Predator B—an MQ-9 Reaper drone—overhead, and he didn't need to show up on camera in his old command station. So he stayed the course.

Barely ten minutes later he pulled into the parking lot beside the Pais Grande Medical Center. There were fewer cars than before, but an ambulance had backed into the emergency room bay. He hurried inside, found the waiting room full but no one at the desk. He'd missed Ronnie for the day; her nameplate had been replaced with one that said *Delfina Guerra, RN*.

He stood still, then walked back outside, his heart racing. Ronnie had said everyone pitched in; whatever the emergency, Delfina must have been helping. He paced the entryway, waiting to ask Delfina about the mix-up. All he could figure was that the clinic had sent the records to another Tucson hospital.

Glancing toward the parking lot, he saw a group of clinic staff heading toward their cars. Ronnie was among them. She spotted him right away but just kept walking—he couldn't blame her. It was Saturday night, and she was probably in a hurry to get home.

"Hey, Ronnie," he said, approaching her just as she reached her Toyota Camry. The white car was old, covered with dust, typical of any vehicle that drove through the desert every day.

"Oh, hi," she said.

"I have a couple of questions for you."

"I'm in a bit of a hurry," she said, unlocking her car, throwing her purse inside. She climbed behind the wheel, clearly not in the mood to talk.

"It won't take long. My trip to Tucson didn't go so well," he said.

"No?" she asked, starting the engine.

"No, not at all."

"Delfina can help you," she said. "A car crash victim just came in, and she's busy with that, but . . ."

"Hey, you live in Mexico," Jack said, noticing the SENTRI sticker on her windshield. It meant she had undergone a detailed background check and been preapproved as a low-risk traveler who could cross the border easily without inspection. The passes were given to workers who made daily, or at least frequent, trips from their homes in Mexico to work in the United States.

"Yes," she said. "Nurses are scarce everywhere, especially at a clinic like this. No one wants to work here."

"So you cross the border every day," he said. "Well, you're doing the work of the angels, that's for sure."

"Gracias," she said, giving a slight smile.

"You cross at Nogales?"

"Yes."

"Wow. I used to work that sector—I know a lot of the guys."

"I'd better go, my husband is waiting for his dinner."

"Okay," Jack said. "Just one thing—that Jane Doe case file didn't match up with the records at San Jacinto. Any chance you got the hospital wrong?"

"We don't make those kinds of mistakes," she said. "Have Delfina check for you."

"Or maybe transposed the digits on the case number?"

She tried to laugh. He picked up fear coming off her.

"I'm not blaming you," he said quickly. "It happens. I just—"

He heard tires on gravel and saw Ralph's SUV pulling into the lot. Ralph grinned, pointed, and rolled down his window.

"You old dog," he called. "I couldn't let you sneak by without tracking you down to say hello. How the hell you doing, Jack?"

Jack waved to let him know he'd be right there, then turned back to Ronnie. "Look, sorry to trouble you. I'll go check with Delfina. Have a good night." He started toward Ralph's SUV.

"Thank you," she said sounding relieved. She snapped on her

seat belt. "She'll help you. When you find Rosa, let us know how she's doing, okay?"

The hair on the back of Jack's neck stood up. He stopped walking and turned slowly toward Ronnie.

"How do you know her name is Rosa?"

"You must have said it," she said. "This morning."

He stared at the worry lines in her forehead, at the sweat breaking out along her brow.

"No, Ronnie," he said. "I didn't. I never said her name."

"You must have," she said, keeping her voice calm. "Otherwise, how would I know?"

"Good question: how *do* you know?" Jack asked.

Ronnie seemed to think about it. She looked up at the sky, hands gripping the steering wheel. She drew a deep breath. "I took her," she said.

Julia

The ride had been long and hot, and she was glad she'd left Bonnie with Roberto's father. As they passed Yuma and drove through the desert, he stared out the window around as if seeing it for the first time. Glancing over, she saw a shocked, numb look in his eyes. The brown landscape seemed endless. Raptors wheeled high overhead, hunting for prey.

She had programmed Pais Grande into her GPS, and they were getting close to the exit. She had a nervous feeling in her stomach, and she wasn't sure whether she was afraid of Border Patrol checkpoints or what they would or would not find at the clinic.

She reached across the gearshift and held his hand. It was hot and sweaty; he wiped it on his jeans, then took her hand again.

"Are you okay?" she asked.

"Yes," he said. "But it feels strange."

"I can imagine."

"We walked very near here." He gestured south. "The rock is over there."

He didn't have to say which rock.

"Now I am in a car with you, moving fast," he said. "It seems like a different life."

"It is," she said.

She kept her eyes on the road, but she felt him watching her. Why couldn't it be a different life for both of them? She felt as if they were walking a fine edge, steeper than the coast path. The sky had been so blue, but the colors had changed to gold and lavender, and oncoming traffic had their headlights on. Some of the vehicles could be Border Patrol, but she knew they wouldn't stop an old Volvo station wagon with Connecticut plates.

"I won't let anything happen to you," she said.

He squeezed her hand but said nothing.

Lion's words had been haunting her. She glanced over at him. "Have you ever tried to get papers?" she asked.

"Be legal?" he asked.

"Yes, get a green card."

"Of course that's what I want," he said. "But it's very hard."

"There's a way," she said.

"What is that way?"

How strange it felt to be having this conversation as they sped along a road through the Sonoran Desert. Purple shadows fell across the road, and the sky glowed a gorgeous, unearthly rose.

"We could get married," she said.

The silence was electric, and she felt blood rush to her face. He touched her arm, gestured for her to pull off the road. The tires bumped onto gravel as she drove onto the shoulder.

"Amor," he said. She could hear the smile in his voice. "You don't know me very long."

"But I know you well."

"Julia," he said, "no one in my life has ever loved me like this. My family, yes, but that is different. Sometimes it's too much to believe."

"Why?"

"Because you could have anyone. You are beautiful, educated. I'm . . . not. Why do you want me?"

"Because I love you."

He leaned across to put his arms around her, kiss her. He stroked her cheek and hair.

"Te amo, Julia," he said. "But I would never marry you for a green card. When we know it is right, I will be the one to ask you. I don't want you to marry to 'help' me. Only to love me."

"I do," she said.

"Estas es mi vida," he said. "My life and my heart."

She stared into his eyes for a long time, and then started driving again. She didn't want the police to find them pulled over, think they had car trouble. He reached across to hold her hand, and she wanted him never to let go.

Jack

"She was in terrible shape." Ronnie said. "She needed fluids, supervision, treatment of her wounds. And she'd been through major trauma—she'd never have gotten the right kind of care if I'd turned her in."

Jack had Ronnie sitting in the front seat of his SUV, and they were driving toward Nogales. It had been a challenge, getting Ralph to drive away without a good long jaw about the politics in Tuscon Sector and life after retirement.

"Keep talking," he said. "Tell me why you took her."

"Because I know what would have happened to her. I was the nurse assigned to her when she was admitted. If I had sent her to a Tucson hospital, she would have received critical care and then been released to a shelter to await deportation."

"Not always," Jack said. "She might have been considered for a foster care program."

"How often does that happen? And even if it did, what kind of attention would she really get? She was so fragile."

"So you kept her out of the system."

"The system," she said, shaking her head. "She was out of her mind, worried about her father. A little Mexican girl, not a word of English, traumatized beyond belief."

"I thought you said she was unconscious."

Sweat beaded on Ronnie's forehead, and she wiped it away with her sleeve. She tried to catch her breath, but couldn't. "You're trying to trip me up!" she said. "You're going to turn me in, and I'll lose my job and my license."

"No, I'm not, Ronnie. This is just between us."

Her face was bright red—he was afraid she'd have a heart attack, and he was feeling pretty anxious himself. He exhaled deeply, waiting for her to calm down.

"Trust me, okay?" he asked. "I told you—I'm here because of her father. That's all."

"Her father," Ronnie said. "My God, she loves him."

"Tell me."

"Well, that day—yes, she was unconscious. But she would come to, and cry for him. She begged us to look for him, but how could we?"

"Exactly," Jack said.

"She was very sick, with such a high fever I wasn't sure she'd live through the night."

"But she did."

"Yes."

"And then what?"

"My middle sister, Bernarda, is a nurse in Ciudad Juárez. The hospital there is excellent. They know how to deal with desert injuries, but also, especially, psychological damage in children."

"That city is a war zone."

"That's why they know how to treat children. I didn't intend Rosa to live there—only stay there until she was well enough to be released."

"So you sent me on a wild-goose chase to San Jacinto."

"Yes," Ronnie said. "I'm sorry, but I had to think, and make a plan. Rosa is very sensitive, and I didn't want you to just . . ."

"Rosa lives with you? She's okay?"

Now Ronnie smiled, ear to ear. "She's wonderful. She lives with my youngest sister and her family, right around the corner. Marisol is a nurse too, and she has loved Rosa as if she were her own. We all have."

"Can I meet her?" Jack said.

"I'll take you to her right now," Ronnie said.

chapter twenty-one

Rosa

Outside, dogs ran in the street and barked. She was in fifth grade and got straight As. She shared a room with Lita, her sister who wasn't really her sister. Their brothers Oscar and Gustavo, who weren't really her brothers, had bunk beds in the room next door, and sometimes Rosa wished she and Lita had bunk beds too, instead of having to share a mattress.

Lita was a teenager, a senior in high school determined to go to college, and it was bad enough she had to share her room with an eleven-year-old, much less share a mattress on the floor. Rosa thought Lita would like her better if they had a little space between them.

Their parents who weren't really Rosa's parents were Marisol and Emilio Garcia. Marisol was a nurse at the Red Cross medical clinic, and Emilio drove a garbage truck. They cared a lot about their children doing well in school, so Emilio had gotten each child his or her own desk—old junked tables from stops he made along his route, repaired and repainted for the kids.

Rosa kept hers very neat, while Lita's was a complete mess. Lita was into politics and was always demonstrating against the police for not really investigating "femicides"—the killing of women—in Ciudad Juárez, where their aunt Bernarda worked, so her desk was always covered with flyers, which she would clear away to do her homework.

Rosa's desk was the opposite. She had made herself a blotter out of construction paper and cardboard. The family shared a computer in the kitchen, so Rosa sometimes did her homework there, leaving her blotter free for a notebook and a tray to hold pens and pencils.

She had made the tray from a branch she found on the street. Emilio had helped her, using his knife to carve a smooth hollow. The only other thing on her desk was a small picture frame with her most treasured possession inside: a picture of herself, her father, and her great-grandmother, taken before she left Mexico.

Rosa had lived with the Garcias for almost half her life. She kept track. She got lost in the desert when she was six, and by the time she turned twelve in just a few months she would have spent as much time with the Garcias as she had with her papá.

When she got sent back to Mexico from the desert, she was very sick and spent a long time in hospitals—she had made it to the States, a little medical clinic, but her *tías* Ronnie and Bernarda had her transferred to Children's Hospital in Ciudad Juárez.

At first she did nothing but sleep, with tubes in her arms, bandages all over, and gauze on her eyes because the bright sun had burned her all over, even her eyes, and she was lucky she didn't go blind. They told her that a long time later. When she woke up, she didn't know where she was.

That seemed so strange to her because even now she remembered dreaming in the hospital, seeing the shadows of doctors and nurses moving behind her bandages. Her dreams were vivid, and in them her father was with her.

They were home, or sometimes they were walking in the desert, but always she could hear her name, Rosa, coming straight from her papá's lips. Telling her he loved her, he was taking her to a better place. She dreamed of her abuela, her great-grandmother rocking her in her lap, singing a song about the little burro.

In every dream she held Maria, the doll her abuela made for her before they left on the long journey, and sometimes in the dream she lost her father and Maria and she would cry in her sleep.

The *tías*—Ronnie and Marisol—would come to see her in the hospital where Bernarda worked. They told her she never had to worry, that they would be her family until they could find her own. They were all nurses, and even though Rosa was Bernarda's patient, the others would help change her dressings, read her stories, braid her hair.

Each of them had a husband and children, and Rosa would hear the sisters bicker about whose family Rosa should live with. They all wanted to take care of her. Bernarda lived and worked in Ciudad Juárez, where the drug war made life dangerous. Ronnie worked at the medical center in Pais Grande in Arizona, and she had taken a big chance by spiriting Rosa across the border, and they didn't want her to risk getting caught and being in trouble. By the time Rosa was well enough to leave the hospital, weeks later, Marisol took her home.

She knew she was lucky. They treated her well. Sometimes Emilio talked about wanting to cross, to go live in the States, saying anything there would be better than trying to raise a family in Altar, where it was so hard to make enough to support his family.

Rosa got scared when she heard that. She would have nightmares and scream in her sleep on the nights he talked about it.

He said he wouldn't care if they were all illegals, at least he wouldn't have to worry about the *cholos* in the town square, the coyotes who could take his kids and sell them and they'd never be seen again.

Lita got angry and snapped at him when she heard him say "illegals," and told him the better phrase was "undocumented immigrants." She was applying to colleges, and was trying to get a visa to study in the States at the best school she could get into.

She knew she'd probably end up going to Universidad Nacional Autonoma de Mexico in Mexico City. It was the country's best, and she had the grades to get in. She wanted to study political science and then become a lawyer. She said her family lived surrounded by suffering and she was sick of it and wanted to help people.

Rosa wanted to help people too, the way Susana had helped her. When she first woke up in Children's Hospital, she was too sick and weak to talk, and she still couldn't remember her name. That's when she had first met Susana, her therapist. Even though Rosa couldn't speak, Susana had sat by her side and "listened." Without words, Rosa and Susana had started to communicate.

During those weeks in the hospital, Rosa had needles in her body, tubes delivering fluids because without them she would have died. Her fever had been very high, and her heart stopped more than once. She had lost oxygen to her brain. It's a miracle . . . she heard that many times: that she didn't die, that she didn't lose brain function, that she was "normal."

But Rosa wasn't normal. She might look it on the outside, but even there she had doubts—she sometimes felt any stranger on the street could look right through her, see her broken heart and know her story.

She told Rosa she was in a special hospital; the rooms were full of children who had been through experiences so awful they couldn't bear to remember them. The hospital was known for helping children heal from wounds inside as well as outside.

Susana had helped Rosa remember things she had forgotten: first name, last name, where she had lived in Mexico, the sights and smells of her everyday life, anything that might help the authorities and the *tías*—Bernarda, Ronnie, and Marisol—find her real family.

Those days, even though the *tías* were so kind, and said she would always have a home with them, Susana became her most important person. She came to the hospital every day and helped her think about her father.

Rosa was small for her age, the skinniest girl in her class, and she wore glasses with a special tint because the desert sun had burned her eyes and made them sensitive. When she looked at the picture of her family, she saw that her hair was the same as before: long, brown, and wavy. In fact, except for the glasses, she looked almost the same as she had in the photo.

Yes, the girl in that photo was "normal," even special. "*Preciosa,*" her father had called her. Precious girl. She held the picture close to her face and kissed her father and great-grandmother. They were not alive, Rosa thought during her worst moments. If they were, they would have found her. But her heart told her that somewhere they *were* alive. She felt they missed her as much as she ached for them.

She'd had those feelings all along, even in the hospital. Closing her eyes, she went back there now: the bed with rails on the sides, tubes in her body, the constant taste of medicine on the back of her throat, the feeling she had to throw up. She had bandages all over: her feet, legs, hands, arms, and head. She had cracked ribs, sun poisoning, infected insect bites, and sores on nearly every part of her body.

They had bandaged her eyes with cool gauze pads, and changed them every hour. After a while they put on a bandage that allowed a tiny bit of light in, just so she could see enough to not be so scared. With that bandage people looked like shadows.

Susana had sat in a chair by the side of her bed. Her voice was warm and calm. *"Dime* . . . Tell me . . . ," Susana always began. "Tell me about your house at home."

"It was beautiful," Rosa would say. "I slept next to my great-grandmother. She prayed for us and I could hear her rosary beads clicking. My father slept in the other room, but he always told me a story before I fell asleep."

"What could you see when you looked out the window?"

"Other houses like ours. And Popo."

"Popo?"

"With the snowy hair, always protecting the girl mountain."

"Popo is a mountain?"

"Sí. Sometimes smoke comes out his head."

Susana and Rosa laughed at that, and Rosa heard Susana making scratching noises on her pad with her pen.

"What could you smell?"

That was easy and made Rosa smile—until she realized how much she missed it and then she started to cry.

"Tell me," Susana said softly.

But at that time, Rosa could not. The memory was too beautiful to say out loud. It was her treasure, and she had to hold on to it, to let herself dream that she would smell the lemons again, stand at the foot of her father's ladder while they talked and sang and he picked fruit from the tree.

"What else?" Susana would say. "What did you eat?"

"Beans and corn. Tamales for Navidad. Sometimes . . ." She stopped herself. She didn't like to tell this part because she knew it would shame her father and abuela. "Sometimes they didn't eat."

"Why?"

"If it was too dry and there was a drought, there wouldn't be any corn. And the orchard would not provide fruit to sell. At those times there wasn't enough work for my father to make money."

"So you had nothing to eat?"

"I always did," Rosa said. Her eyes filled with tears, stinging behind the bandage. "But sometimes they didn't. I tried to share my food but they wouldn't take it."

"They loved you," Susana said. Those words were the happiest words Rosa had heard since waking up in the hospital. She sobbed to hear them. "I love them, I love them, I want them . . ."

"I know," Susana said.

Susana didn't make empty promises about finding her father. She helped by listening and visiting every day, by slowly and surely helping Rosa get stronger. Soon she would be discharged, and go to live with Marisol and her family. Bernarda and Ronnie would visit all the time, and they promised her that if she needed Susana, they would take her to see her.

Yes, Rosa wanted to do well in school and someday be like Susana. Help little girls remember the things that would help them, and not be so scared of the things too terrible to keep in their minds.

She sat at her desk, listening to the family in another room. The boys were playing video games, Marisol was cooking dinner, and Emilio had just gotten home from work and was showing Marisol some things he found in the trash. They were a good family and she loved them, but they weren't hers. She had only one papá.

Some days after school she went to the square. It looked the same as it had the day she'd arrived in Altar with her papá. People bustled around, buses and vans pulling in and out, the same vendors selling backpacks, food, and water. Marisol said Rosa could only go to the plaza with Lita, and only if they stayed close to the Red Cross clinic.

But sometimes Rosa slipped away and walked to the church. She would sit on the steps, scanning the crowd for a tall man with short dark hair and a neat moustache. She looked for Miguel, her father's cousin, but he wasn't there. The old coyotes sat in the same place, but Rosa wouldn't go near them, not even to ask about her father. Then Lita would come running, grab her by the arm and shake her, ask if she *really* wanted to be abducted and sold for sex and never see the family again, because that's what happened to her friend Monica.

Rosa had homework and was supposed to write a story. It could be about anything. She knew it would be about her childhood, when she had lived with her real family and been happy. Because when she wrote stories about it, she could live in the world where she used to be her father's *preciosa,* where the lemon trees were beautiful, and all the goodness of life was right there.

chapter twenty-two

Roberto

At night the parking lot of the medical center at Pais Grande was nearly empty. When he and Julia pulled in, he stayed in the car while she went inside to talk to someone. He looked around for Leary's SUV, but it wasn't there. The night was pitch black, the way he remembered it being when he crossed. But when he looked up at the sky, even with the medical center lights, he saw stars burning— white swaths of stars, the constellations standing out so bright, reminding him of the myths his grandmother had taught him, and that he had passed on to Rosa.

He glanced at the door. It killed him not to be inside, but he didn't have long to wait. Julia walked out as soon as she'd gone in.

"What did they say about Rosa?" he asked.

"The woman at the desk said they have no record of her being here."

"And Leary?"

"She said they had a big emergency here today—if he stopped by, she didn't see him."

Roberto closed his eyes for a moment, trying to hold himself together.

Julia dialed Leary's number and put the call on the speaker.

"I was about to call you," Leary said.

"We're in Pais Grande."

"I thought you and Roberto were waiting in Malibu until I had real news."

"Roberto had other ideas. Where are you?"

"In Mexico," he said.

"Why?" Julia asked.

"Because that's where Rosa is."

"Rosa?" Roberto asked.

"She's alive, Roberto. And she's asking for you."

Roberto's heart seized, and he started to cry.

"Can you bring her here?" Julia asked, glancing at Roberto. She knew what he knew—their lives were about to change forever.

"You know I can't do that," Leary said. "She's Mexican, Julia. If he wants her, he has to cross the border and come back."

"But . . . ," Julia began.

Roberto took her hand. He held it as gently and lovingly as he could. He wanted all the love in his heart to flow into hers, so she would know and understand everything he was feeling for her as he said out loud, so both she and Leary would hear, "Yes. I am coming for her. Where is she?"

"Have Julia drive to the checkpoint in Nogales. We'll be waiting on the other side."

Julia

This was everything she had wanted, to see Roberto and Rosa together again, but it felt like the end of her world. Driving to

Nogales, she felt Roberto's hand on her back, her shoulders, stroking her hair. His eyes glistened with tears that wouldn't stop.

"Are you okay?" he asked.

"I'm so happy for you," she said.

"Gracias, amor."

"Oh God, she'll be so overjoyed to see you."

"This is all happening because of you," he said.

"Shh," she said, because she couldn't bear to hear it. Her bones ached inside, as if they might just give out. When they'd first met, Julia and Roberto both believed they would never see their daughters alive again. Being so close to finding Rosa made Julia ache for Jenny even more.

To find Rosa, she had to lose Roberto. Why had she not known that? The road through the desert was pitch black.

Signs for the Mexican border were everywhere. TEN MILES AHEAD. FIVE MILES AHEAD. LAST EXIT BEFORE LEAVING THE UNITED STATES. She saw a roadblock on the opposite side of the highway, stopping cars and vans to check for migrants hiding in the back or in the trunk. Her heart was breaking because they were about to say goodbye.

"It's happening so fast," she said.

"Yes," he said.

"We really found her."

Roberto didn't answer. Traffic stopped because they were approaching the border. The area was crowded with motels and businesses, and a freight line ran just alongside the highway. A moment later Julia saw the wall—a massive fence really, with thick steel bars twenty-five feet high. She could look through them, even from inside the car, and see Mexico. It was like looking into a jail cell.

Surveillance towers equipped with cameras and a guard shack

rose at intervals along the fence. She saw a sign advertising SECURE PARKING $5.00 and pulled into the lot.

"Roberto, if you stay here . . ."

"I can't," he said.

"But if you cross, they won't let you back. Let me go, talk to Jack, and see if I can bring her to you."

"Amor, you know I have to go to her now," he said.

Julia nodded. She and Roberto got out of the car with Rosa's doll and started walking toward a gate in the wall. A U.S. border guard stood there, checking documents.

Julia showed him her passport, and he stared from her to Roberto. He held out his hand for Roberto's papers.

"What is your purpose for crossing?" he asked.

"To see . . . ," Julia began, sweat breaking out because she noticed the guard watching Roberto carefully. He had one hand on his gun, and still holding Julia's passport, he clicked a button on the radio hanging from his belt loop and spoke into a mouthpiece.

"Victor, get over here," the guard said, not taking his eyes off Roberto. "We have a situation."

"Hey, Dan," came Jack's voice through the fence.

The border guard turned quickly and smiled. "Jack Leary! Holy shit—what are you doing on that side?"

"Family business," Jack said. "Let them through."

"We're waiting for Tonk here to show us some documentation."

Tonk? Julia wondered.

"I'll take care of it," Jack said. "They're with me."

"Man, you're putting me in a fucking bad position. I just called Vic."

"I trained you both," Jack said. "Glad to know you're so thorough. This one's mine, okay? One of my old cases."

"Okay, but if there's any blowback . . ."

"There won't be," Jack said.

Julia and Roberto pushed through the turnstile, then walked through the gate in the fence, and they were in Mexico.

Jack

"Tonk." That word had made Louella sick, and hearing it turned his stomach now. It had been coined long ago to describe illegal border crossers and referred to the sound made by a sap hitting a skull. He put it out of his mind as he turned to see Julia and Roberto, clutching each other's hands, coming toward him.

"Welcome back," he said to Roberto. He wasn't sure whether he meant it ironically or not. Roberto had kept one arm tightly around Julia and was craning his neck to look for Rosa.

"Is she here?" Julia asked.

"Yeah," Jack said.

They began to walk toward the street where Jack had left his SUV. The town was lively as usual on a Saturday night, hopping with locals and Americans who'd crossed for the evening.

Small, flat-roofed, brightly painted houses rose on the hillside—local officials supplied free colorful paint to residents who wanted to spiff up their homes. Jack knew they wanted to make a good impression on people looking through the wall from the U.S. side.

He walked ahead of Julia and Roberto, feeling more emotional than he had expected. Louella would have loved this: bringing a family together. The SUV was parked two blocks away under a streetlamp—he'd wanted to keep the occupants completely safe, and you never knew what might happen in a border town on a Saturday night or any night.

Ronnie, Marisol, and Rosa had followed in their car, but he felt it would be safer to have the three of them wait in his. He slowed down as they walked toward the SUV.

"I'm sure," Roberto said. He still hadn't spotted the SUV. "How far is she from here?"

"We're close," Jack said.

"But where?" he asked, craning his neck. "I need to see her."

"Where has she been living?" Julia asked.

"She got very lucky," Jack said. "Three guardian angels found her—three sisters, all of them nurses. She's been living in Altar with Marisol, the youngest, and her family. They've made sure Rosa's had excellent care."

"Altar," Roberto said, his voice cracking. "Where we started from."

"That's what Rosa says," Jack said.

The street was dim, but as they approached the streetlight, he could see his SUV—Ronnie in the front seat, Marisol and Rosa in the back. He waved, and saw Ronnie give a half turn. The back door flew open and Rosa jumped out. Jack looked at Roberto, saw the look in his eyes.

"Papá!" Rosa shouted.

"Rosa!"

They ran to each other and Roberto fell to his knees, holding Rosa in his arms, rocking her back and forth. The sisters remained in the SUV, and Jack and Julia stood where they were. He heard Julia sobbing quietly, and he did what Louella would have—slipped his arm around her as if she were his own daughter, and let her tears soak his shoulder.

chapter twenty-three

Julia

She met Ronnie and Marisol, and heard about Bernarda. Marisol wiped away tears, saying how hard it would be to live without Rosa, she'd become part of the family, she wanted Roberto to know that she and her sisters and husband and children were now *his* family too, that they would help however they could.

She listened to Jack reassure Ronnie that he would keep this whole scenario under the radar, maybe she'd gone against regulations, but sometimes rules were made to be broken, just look at how beautifully this story was turning out.

After a few minutes, Roberto turned and gestured to Julia. Julia had been holding Maria since they left their car on the other side, and she started to hand the doll to Roberto now.

"You, amor," he said. "You give it to her . . ."

Julia beamed to see the little girl she felt she already knew so well.

"Hola, Rosa," she said, crouching down.

"Rosa, this is Julia," Roberto said in Spanish. "She helped me find you."

"Gracias, Julia," Rosa said, barely able to tear her gaze from her father.

Rosa had grown at least six inches since the picture had been taken. Julia couldn't resist comparing her to Jenny at eleven—they were about the same height, both skinny, with a vivid intelligence in their bright eyes.

"Your father never stopped looking for you," Julia said. She held out the doll.

"Maria!" Rosa said, hugging and kissing her. "How, Papá? I lost her!"

"When your father was searching for you, he found Maria along the way."

"I knew he would come for me," Rosa said.

"You speak English!"

"You too, Papá. We learn in school."

Nearly six years without each other, Julia thought. Rosa held Maria as if she were a baby. She wore glasses. She stole shy glances at Julia but had wide-open eyes for her father, staring at him with such love and intensity it made Julia cry. She walked a few feet away and turned her head, to hide it from all of them.

Roberto's arms came around her. She pressed her face into his chest, felt Rosa glued to his leg. It made her smile in spite of herself.

"I'm so happy for you," she said.

"Julia, without you . . ."

"Roberto, it was always meant to be."

He shook his head. "Fate is different for Mexicans," he said. "If you were not in my life, Rosa wouldn't be either."

"I've loved being in your life," she said.

He held her face between his hands, looked deeply into her eyes. "*Siempre, amor.* You are in my life forever."

"But you can't come back with me," she said. "You're here now."

"I know. Rosa and I will return to my town."

"You'll see your grandmother."

"Sí," he said. "And I'll work in the lemon orchard, but I'll be thinking of ours."

"Ours?" she asked.

"Our lemon orchard," he said. "On the mountain by the sea, with Bonnie and Jenny. The place we fell in love."

Julia nodded, hugged him for a long time, until she heard the others approaching. The plan was for Roberto and Rosa to return to Marisol's house for the night, and tomorrow the family would drive them home—to their small farm town south of Puebla.

"Julia," Marisol said, "would you and Jack like to come over, have something to eat with us? We are not far away."

Julia glanced at Jack. He nodded, about to accept.

"No, thank you," she said. "I should be getting back."

"Amor," Roberto said, "it's a long drive for you alone. Please . . ."

She shook her head. She felt her throat burning, and she wasn't even sure she could speak. Goodbyes hurt so terribly. For years she had rewritten what she would say to Jenny, how she wished she could have held on to her forever. Right now, just as then, her heart was breaking and she knew another hour or two would not change anything.

She put her arms around his neck, stood on tiptoes so their eyes were level. "*Siempre.* Just as you said before," she whispered so the others couldn't hear.

"*Siempre,*" he whispered back.

His arms felt so strong and familiar. She closed her eyes for a moment, so she'd always remember the feeling of them around her shoulders. Rosa was waiting for him. She bent down, kissed the top of Rosa's head. Then she kissed the doll and said, "Maria, take good care of Rosa and Roberto."

"She will," Rosa said.

Julia and Roberto held hands but Julia backed away until there was space between them and then she looked at him for the last time and turned away. She heard the sisters speaking Spanish, and car doors closing, and an engine starting.

Jack held open the passenger door of the SUV and she got in.

"You might want to wave," he said. "Roberto's standing on the street watching you."

"Just drive," she said.

And Jack did. As they pulled away, she stole a quick glance behind her and saw Roberto standing beside the sisters' car, not waving, not moving, just watching. Jack stopped the SUV, as if to give her one last chance to run back. She didn't. In the side-view mirror, she saw Roberto finally climb into the car. Ronnie flashed her lights and beeped her horn, and Jack returned the signal.

Julia looked back and watched the car drive down the street, turn the corner, and disappear.

"You okay?" Jack asked.

"No," she said.

"You will be," he said.

He dropped her off at the parking lot, made sure she got into her car okay, and followed her out of Nogales. As she headed west, she knew he was behind her, and he stayed there the whole way to Yuma, where he turned off at his exit. He motioned her to do the same.

She felt reluctant, but did as he asked.

At the bottom of the exit ramp, he lowered his window and had her pull alongside. He handed her the Tim O'Brien CD.

"You need this," he said.

"No, you love it."

"Your ancestor would want you to have it," he said. "And my wife would, too. She was a great romantic, Julia. Maybe she and John Riley will even inspire you to head down to old Mexico. I'm sure Roberto will be waiting."

"Thanks, Jack," she said, and drove away.

The car smelled of Roberto—a combination of sweat, dirt, Polo, and lemons. She wanted the scent to cling to her skin; she never wanted to let it go. She glanced into the rearview mirror, to the back seat where Maria had been. This old Volvo had once driven Jenny around. She was with her still, every minute, and now their family car was filled with love for Roberto and Rosa, too.

Siempre, Roberto had said.

Julia wasn't tired at all. She knew she'd drive straight back to L.A., stop at Roberto's father's house to tell him what had happened, and pick up Bonnie. She couldn't wait to see her.

Maybe she would take her straight to Lion's house. No matter the time, he wouldn't mind being awakened. Julia would tell him the amazing, miraculous story of how they had found Rosa. She knew he would be overjoyed.

But oh, how it hurt to know the seat beside her where Roberto had been was empty. She kept her eyes on the road so she wouldn't have to see it. She put the CD in the player and as she listened she thought about Louella's belief in romance, and she let herself dream of Mexico.

A PENGUIN READERS GUIDE TO

THE
LEMON ORCHARD

Luanne Rice

An Introduction to
The Lemon Orchard

*"They sat in the kitchen, Julia so lost in the tale that
when he said the word* suerte, *'luck,' she could almost believe
that he'd had it, called it forth, that they were five years in
the past and their daughters both still with them."*

Five years ago, Julia's life was shattered when her husband, Peter,
and their only child, Jenny, died in a car crash not far from their
Connecticut home. Julia's grief is compounded by the fact that
the police believe that Jenny—who was only sixteen and nursing
her first broken heart—intentionally drove into a wall. After the
initial shock, Julia took what solace she could in her work as a
cultural anthropologist. "It had been her passion, to keep the
dead alive through learning how they had behaved, where they
had trekked in search of food, water, love" (p. 15). And now that
Jenny is gone, Julia continually replays the memories of their time
together, wondering if there was something she could have done
to prevent the crash.

When her aunt and uncle take an extended trip to Ireland,
Julia goes to stay at their beautiful Malibu home with her dog
Bonnie. She has been a regular visitor to Casa Riley and its
adjacent lemon orchard since childhood, but this is her first
visit following the accident. Walking on the cliffs high above the
beach, Julia experiences a fleeting moment when she thinks about
how easy it would be to just let go and escape into the sea.

Although the Rileys are away, someone else notices how close Julia walks to the precipice. Roberto is the latest in a long line of orchard managers, all of whom had come from Mexico seeking a better life. At first, Julia is uncomfortable with Roberto's concern until she recognizes that he's burdened by a sorrow of his own. She tells him about Jenny, and learns that Roberto, too, has lost a daughter. Since he is in the United States illegally, Roberto only reluctantly reveals more. Human traffickers called coyotes took Roberto, six–year–old Rosa, and a group of others from Mexico to Arizona through the Sonoran Desert. Roberto and Rosa were briefly separated just before he was picked up by the Border Patrol. When he was finally able to return to look for her, Rosa was gone.

Without resources, in constant fear of deportation, in desperation, Roberto gave her up for lost. But Julia feels there is reason for hope—and looking for Rosa makes Julia feel closer to Jenny. Soon, her burgeoning romance with Roberto awakens feelings she thought were gone forever. As Julia combs the Southwest for conclusive evidence of any sort, she discovers help in a most unexpected place. Meanwhile, Lion Cushing, the Rileys' movie star neighbor and old family friend, watches the pair warily. "Lion wanted Julia and Roberto to be happy in their Casa love nest, but unions between educated women and the help never lasted" (p. 229).

A captivating tale of unexpected love as well as a nuanced and profoundly moving examination of one of our nation's most controversial issues, *The Lemon Orchard* is one of bestselling author Luanne Rice's most powerful and compelling novels.

A Conversation with Luanne Rice

Julia has always felt close to the Mexican people, in part, because of her Irish ancestor John Riley, who fought for Mexican independence. Was there a real John Riley?

John Riley was born in Galway, Ireland, and immigrated to America through Mackinac, Michigan, in 1843. He and other Irish immigrants, fleeing famine and oppression at home, took jobs as soldiers in the U.S. Army. He defected to Mexico to form the San Patricio Battalion with other Irish-born soldiers. He was young, idealistic, charismatic, and saw Mexico as being the "side of right."

You write very empathetically about Julia's desire to be an anthropologist. Is this a field you ever considered going into yourself?

I studied anthropology with Professor June Macklin at Connecticut College. She was a wonderful teacher and ignited my lifelong interest in the subject. I've remained fascinated with migration, the movements of people in search of, always, a better life: more food, less hardship, opportunity.

The novel powerfully evokes the tensions of life along the Mexico–United States border and the horrors faced by Mexicans trying to cross the desert illegally. Did you spend a lot of time there while researching and writing the book?

I visited the border several times but did most of my research in Los Angeles, getting to know a family who crossed the desert much the way Roberto and Rosa did.

4

Are there organizations like The Reunion Project and the Found Objects gallery that are working to help undocumented immigrants who are separated from loved ones during their journey across the border?

There are forensic anthropologists who study human remains found in the Sonoran desert, and there are many people working to help immigrants during and after their crossings.

While Roberto and Rosa's story ends well, you share the stories of others that did not. Did you feel hesitant about including some of the more graphic details?

I wanted to tell the story in the truest possible way. I spoke to people who nearly died on the journey. Others saw death along the way. These stories affected me deeply. They are a part of our national history, shocking and real, happening right now.

Malibu and Boyle Heights may only be a short distance apart in terms of miles, but they couldn't be more different. What inspired you to bring these two disparate worlds together?

Living in Los Angeles has shown me how these worlds merge. You see workers waiting along the roadside, hoping to be chosen for a day's work. How can we not look beneath the surface and see them as people? Oscar Mondragon has done that. He runs the Malibu Labor Exchange out of a trailer near the Malibu City Hall and the public library. It's a place where workers are matched with employers, treated with dignity and respect.

5

Handsome, charming, and delightfully self-centered, Lion Cushing is a character straight out of Hollywood's Golden Era. What movie star or stars did you base him on?

Lion is inspired by the same friend upon whom I based Harrison Thaxter in *The Silver Boat*. But I also think of him as Peter O'Toole meets Albert Finney and fast-forwards to George Clooney.

Immigration reform is one of today's most hotly debated issues. Where do you see The Lemon Orchard *fitting into the discussion?*

I hope that readers will see immigration as a human story.

Whichever side of the issue one might be on, your novel humanizes both the would-be immigrants and the law-enforcement officials charged with patrolling the border. Was this your intention?

My intention was to write a good story with real characters. Black and white thinking—all good versus all bad—makes me uncomfortable. It's easy to blame one side or one group, but how realistic is that? I try to take a gentle approach, with compassion, not automatically shut down to ideas that make me feel uneasy. Everyone has a point of view, everyone has a story.

QUESTIONS FOR DISCUSSION

1. Julia and Peter's marriage was strained long before Jenny's death, but Julia felt guilty about the impending divorce because Jenny wanted them to stay together. Is staying in a marriage for the sake of your children ever a good idea?

2. Do you think Jenny's death was a suicide? If so, why might she have decided to take her father's life as well as her own?

3. How do Lion's feelings for Graciela change the way you feel about him?

4. Roberto chose to take Rosa with him on the difficult desert crossing rather than leave her behind to grow up without him. In hindsight, he realized that he had underestimated the dangers they would face. Do you sympathize with his decision? What would you have done in his place?

5. Julia loves her dog, Bonnie, all the more because Jenny loved her, too. And Roberto is overjoyed to find Rosa's beloved doll at Found Objects because she belonged to Rosa. Is there an object that you cherish because it belonged to a lost loved one?

6. Jack Leary decides to help Julia because he understands that it's her way of staying close to Jenny, but he comes to feel that his late wife, Louella, would approve of his mission. How might Roberto and Julia's story have turned out if Jack hadn't become involved?

7. Ronnie sends Jack on a wild-goose chase to Tucson, hoping that he won't come back and learn the truth about Rosa. Is she right to mistrust him? Do you condone Ronnie's decision to make Rosa "disappear" from the system?

8. *The Lemon Orchard* ends on an ambiguous note with Roberto and Rosa reunited and Julia returning to California alone. Do you think that Roberto and Julia's story will end here, too?

9. There are many Cinderella stories about women who are "rescued" from their less privileged lives by wealthier men. And—even in the twenty first century—relationships like Julia and Roberto's give many people pause. Why is it more socially acceptable for the man in a given couple to have a better education and more money than the woman?

10. Have you ever been involved with someone who came from a radically different socio-economic background than your own? How conscious were you of your differences?

11. America is the land of immigrants. Did Roberto's experience resonate with what you know about your family's journey to America?

12. What is your opinion on the United States' current immigration policies? Do you think that most would–be immigrants have a clear picture of what life in the States is really like?

To access Penguin Readers Guides online,
visit the Penguin Group (USA) Web site at www.penguin.com.

AVAILABLE FROM PENGUIN

Little Night

Clare Burke's life took a devastating turn when she defended her sister, Anne, from an abusive husband and ended up serving prison time for assault. Twenty years later, Anne's daughter shows up at Clare's doorstep, with Anne following after her. A poignant and affecting read, *Little Night* is a riveting story about women and the primal, tangled family ties that bind them together.

ISBN 978-0-14-312332-3

The Silver Boat

In this heart-wrenching yet heartwarming portrait of a family, the McCarthy sisters struggle to say good-bye to their family's beach house. But when a cache of old letters spurs them to visit Ireland, each woman comes to see her life in a new light.

ISBN 978-0-14-312103-9

AVAILABLE ONLY AS E-BOOKS

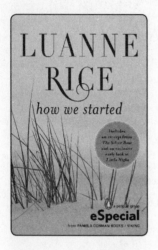

How We Started

In these stories featuring characters from *Little Night* and *The Silver Boat,* Rice delivers two tales of early love and longing. "Paul and Clare" introduces the heroine of *Little Night* as she meets the love of her life. "Miss Martha's Vineyard" is a snapshot of a quirky friendship that has kept Rory McCarthy from *The Silver Boat* afloat even in rough romantic seas.

ISBN 978-1-101-57975-6

Blue Moon

For generations, the Keating family has served the catch at Lobsterville. But when an unthinkable crisis strikes—testing the clan's deepest passions and loyalties—the three Keating sisters must fight to keep their lives together.

ISBN 978-1-101-64083-8

PENGUIN BOOKS

PAMELA DORMAN BOOKS
VIKING